DEATH WATCH

Books by Dale Crotts

The Reckoning
Death Watch
The Ruby Earring

DEATH WATCH

A MACY MERIT NOVEL BY

DALE CROTTS

Jan-Carol
Publishing, Inc
"every story needs a book"

Death Watch
Dale Crotts

Second Edition Published June 2018
RoseHeart Publishing
Imprint of Jan-Carol Publishing, Inc
All rights reserved
Cover Design by CH Creations
Copyright © 2018 by Dale Crotts

ISBN: 978-0-9834885-9-0
Library of Congress Control Number: 2018950575

You may contact the publisher:
Jan-Carol Publishing, Inc
PO Box 701
Johnson City, TN 37605
publisher@jancarolpublishing.com
jancarolpublishing.com

Acknowledgments

I would like to express my sincere thanks to Terry M. Meinecke, Assistant United States Attorney, for his expertise and collaboration regarding military protocol and legal practices. As a former JAG officer, he provided invaluable advice to make the military aspects of the book as accurate as possible. I would also like to acknowledge the many men and women in uniform who daily place themselves in harm's way in order to secure our freedom and way of life. May God strengthen and protect them in their dangerous and honorable stations. And may our nation never forget, or fail to appreciate, the tremendous sacrifices they make for all of us.

CHAPTER 1

SOMEWHERE IN A FOREIGN LAND

The usually quiet midnight air was filled with the sounds of AK-47 rounds buzzing over the heads of the Alpha Team as they made their way back to the beach. While it was apparent their visit to the compound had not gone unnoticed, it was without incident, as the ammunition missed its intended targets. Alpha had acquired the target and was removing it to the beach to board the small raft for the trip back to the sub. The Alpha Team consisted of five members of an elite Navy special ops force, trained in covert operations. For Macy Merit, it was her tenth op, making her an established veteran of the team. Macy was a twenty-five year old Seaman, having served four years and ten months in the Navy. She was recruited for special operations, after she proved her proficiency in weaponry and subterfuge while stationed at Naval Intelligence. As they neared the Zodiac, Macy could not help but think this operation seemed easier than most, a little too easy. She could feel that alarming burn in her gut that told her something was not right. But the mission was clear, they had achieved their objective, and with nothing to prove the contrary, Macy was committed to carrying out her orders. The team deftly loaded their cargo, shoved the Zodiac into the icy waters, and climbed aboard for the trip back to the sub waiting a few hundred yards off the coast. The team leader, Commander

Gordon McCain, or Gordo, as he was commonly called, insisted on radio silence during the operation. Once they were fifty yards from shore, he broke the silence only to check on his team, then ceased communications for the remainder of the trip. All members of the team were accounted for and in perfect shape, each reporting no injury or concern. They sped along quietly until they reached the sub, where two divers were waiting to retrieve the cargo and assist them in boarding the craft. Once on board, the cargo was taken to a room, which was placed under guard, while the Alpha Team dispatched to the briefing room to discuss their next move. Each of them took their place at the conference table, patiently waiting for Gordo to make the first statement.

"Is it just me, or did that seem like the easiest job we've ever done?"

"Well, I'm glad I'm not the only one who thought so," replied Macy.

The rest of the team nodded in agreement as they discussed possible explanations for the light resistance they encountered. Of course, the pre-mission intelligence revealed a rather weak defense system, but surely their soldiers could shoot more accurately than that.

"Now for Phase II of the operation," Gordo continued, pointing to the map spread across the table. "Once we reach point A, we will remove the cargo and proceed to the safe room," he said, dragging his finger down the map to another place marked in red.

"Any questions?" he asked.

"Just one, sir," said Simon, the newest member of the team. "How long will the entire operation last?" Simon was twenty-five years old, and had an extremely high IQ. He was five feet eleven inches tall, with a very muscular build. He had short, dark brown hair, and deep brown eyes. He was the kind of man every mother wished for their daughter, complete with boyish shyness, which only seemed to enhance his charm.

"As long as necessary to achieve our objective, Seaman," Gordo barked.

Seeing no one had any other questions, Gordo said, "Okay. Go get some chow, find a bunk, and rest up for the rest of the mission. We'll reconvene here at 0-four-hundred." He dismissed the team and they left the room heading in the direction of the mess hall. Gordo went in the opposite direction, having stashed some sea rations in his quarters before they left port. The soup of the day was clam chowder, very appropriate for a seafaring mission. There was meatloaf smothered in ketchup, for the meat course, and creamed potatoes, green beans and corn as side dishes. Macy passed on the chowder, opting for some meatloaf and potatoes only. The other guys loaded up on everything, especially Simon. Macy smiled to herself as she remembered her first op and how she wished she had eaten lighter, almost vomiting after running three miles in the jungle. Simon would learn, she decided, just as she did. They sat together at one table since they were the only ones in the mess hall. The crew was either working on their shift, or snoring in their bunks.

"Well, it looks like I've got my feet wet with my first mission," Simon beamed.

"Not so fast," laughed Mark, one of the other members. "The mission's not over yet. A lot can happen in a short time," he smiled, leering with an evil look on his face.

"Come on, guys," Macy sighed. "Lighten up on the rookie. You're gonna scare him to death." She laughed and Simon laughed too, but his was nervous laughter, as if he were afraid their teasing might foretell misfortune. He quickly continued to eat, hoping they would not detect the beads of sweat that suddenly broke out across his brow. They finished their meal and headed for their quarters. With a little luck, they just might catch an hour or two of sleep before their appointed meeting time. Macy purposefully lagged behind the others, so they would be in their cabins with the hatch closed before she reached her quarters. Once she saw the last door shut, Macy turned and knocked on one of the cabin doors. The door opened almost immediately, a strong arm grabbing Macy, pulling her into the cabin. Then the hatch was shut securely behind her.

Gordo leaned down placing his lips securely on hers, as she encircled her arms around his neck. He removed her beret, exposing her shoulder-length red hair, which curled inward at the bottom. The kiss lasted for what seemed like minutes, the embrace lasting much longer. He ran his left hand through her bangs as she stroked the back of his neck. Because he was nearly six feet tall, Macy had to stand on her toes to reach her five feet four inch frame high enough to stroke his short sandy hair, which he kept in the familiar military cut.

"No one saw you, did they?" he asked.

"No," Macy replied. "I waited until everyone was in their quarters with the hatch closed. Don't be so paranoid."

"We could both get into a lot of trouble for this," he said, frowning.

"Only if we get caught," said Macy. "And I have no intention of letting that happen." She smiled. "Besides, we've kept it a secret for nine months now."

"True," said Gordo. "But don't get too cocky. We still need to be careful."

"Okay. Okay." Macy laughed. "Have it your way."

"I think I will," he said, grabbing Macy around the waist, pulling her closer to him. They kissed again, a long passionate kiss, as he led her to the bunk. They continued their embrace as they collapsed on top of the bunk, their bodies writhing in anticipation. Gordo had conveniently kept the fact he was married from Macy, believing all was fair in love and war. Macy believed he was available, and had fallen hard for him. He decided he would wait and see how things played out. If they were still together when it was time to leave the service, he would find a way to break the news to her. Most affairs like these usually ended when one or the other was transferred, so he was not worried about explaining things to Macy at the moment. Gordo lived life on the edge, preferring to have his cake and eat it too.

Their lovemaking session lasted for about an hour, with a couple of breaks in between. Then Macy got up and began to dress. She gave Gordo another long, wet kiss and waited while he peeked out the door. Gordo gave her the 'all clear' sign, and Macy retreated to her cabin, securing the hatch behind her. She was unable to sleep, feeling much like a schoolgirl with her first crush. Although they had been an item for nine months, Macy still felt weak in the knees when she was around him. She really had to fight to keep her emotions in check during operations. She was, however, a professional, and never wore her emotions on her sleeve. Macy was determined to keep her relationship with Gordo a secret, believing she had found the real thing. She was still thinking about him when the time came for the team to assemble in the briefing room. Gordo showed no expression as Macy entered the room.

The rest of the team was already seated at the table. Gordo began the meeting as soon as Macy sat down.

"Okay, team," he began. "The sub is almost in place for us to begin Phase II. We will land here," he said, pointing to a spot on the map, and continued, "and then make our way to the destination point. Remember, there are no opposition forces here, so we should not encounter any hostile fire. Just the same, treat it as if we're not sure so we don't let our guard down. We don't want to get soft," he said, smiling. "Sanders, you will carry the cargo to the destination point. Merit and I will lead, with the rest of you covering the rear," Gordo barked. "Any questions?" he asked, as he fixed his stare on Simon. This time Simon remained quiet, almost shaking his head no. "Good," said Gordo. "Let's go." And with that, they exited the briefing room together and made their way to the main hatch, stopping long enough to retrieve the cargo from one of the cabins.

Once topside, they loaded the cargo on the raft, then climbed aboard and headed in the direction of the shoreline. There was no need to worry about noise, so they opened the throttle on the motor, traveling at top speed. It did not take long to reach the beach, where Sanders unloaded the cargo while the others secured the raft. They began their journey to the place marked on the map. Gordo took the lead because he had been here before and knew exactly how to get to the destination point. Also, he had this thing about power and wanted to lead the group to symbolize his authority over them. They walked for about five hundred meters through some low brush until they arrived outside a small hut. It was approximately twenty feet square with tin sides and roof. There was only one small window on the left side of the building, and a small door in the front. Gordo ordered Sanders to take the cargo inside, while he led the rest of the team to the adjacent building, which was probably three times the size of the tin hut. This building appeared to be in much better shape, with wooden sides and a metal roof. There were several windows in each side of the building, and larger doors in the front and back.

The team entered the building to find several bunks and a latrine at the far end. They stowed their gear next to the bunks and removed their wet suits. Then they donned their fatigues and followed Gordo to the hut.

Once there, Gordo relieved Sanders and motioned for him to go to the other building to change and store his gear. It was now time for the most important part of their mission. The room held two chairs that faced each other, and a table on the right, just inside the door. The cargo had been placed on the chair facing the door, just as instructed. Gordo walked to the table, picked up the pitcher on it, and poured some water into a glass. Then he walked over in front of the chair and tossed the contents of the glass onto the cargo, causing him to awaken with a snort, still groggy from the effects of the tranquilizer.

Gordo began the interrogation by first asking his name.

The man replied, "Ahmed Zarfur."

Gordo informed Ahmed that he was aware of his position within the government, and wanted to know about his country's latest endeavor known as Operation Zebra. Ahmed shook his head, declaring he knew nothing about it. Gordo was not convinced, as he struck Ahmed across the face with the back of his hand. He repeated the same question again, this time with some anger in his voice. Ahmed again declared he had no knowledge of this matter, stating he was merely an attorney for the government and was not privy to such information. Gordo struck him again, harder, grabbing his hair and pulling his head upward to stare directly in his eyes. The rest of the crew observed while Gordo pressed on with the same question, each time escalating the force of his blows when Ahmed professed his lack of knowledge regarding Operation Zebra. The interrogation lasted for hours, until Ahmed was bleeding considerably from the face and ears. He was sobbing, begging Gordo to stop. Gordo turned to Macy and instructed her and Johnson to retrieve the equipment box they had brought along. They retreated to the building, returning with the box. It was long and heavy, requiring each of them to lift one end. They placed the box in front of the table and stepped back to their place of observation.

Gordo opened the box and gathered a pair of jumper cables and a battery from inside. He placed the battery on the floor beside Ahmed and began attaching the cable to the battery. He asked Ahmed what he knew about Operation Zebra, touching the other ends of the cable together to produce a spark. Ahmed pleaded with him to stop, again stating he knew nothing about the military operations of his country. Gordo touched the cable to Ahmed's hand, sending a searing pain all through his arm and into his body. He ordered the men to strip Ahmed's body, leaving him naked and exposed. After Ahmed responded in the same manner as before, Gordo touched the cable to Ahmed's private area, causing him to jerk and scream in pain.

The torture continued for hours, each punishment worse than the last. Ahmed's face was nothing more than a bloody pulp, barely recognizable as the face of a man. His eyes were swollen shut except for tiny slits, from which he tried desperately to see through. His skin was burned in several places from the electric shocks from the battery cables. His tears mixed with blood as they streamed down what was left of his face. Gordo retrieved a syringe from the box and filled it with truth serum. He injected Ahmed and waited for it to take effect, then he posed the question again, and again received the same response. Macy grabbed Gordo by the arm and motioned for them to go outside.

"Why did you do that, Seaman?" he demanded.

"Sir, I believe he is telling the truth," answered Macy. "I believe that is why we did not encounter much resistance, because they knew he could not give us any information. I believe we should let him go back to his family. He appears to be an innocent civilian caught in the middle by his government, probably complying with their requests to protect his family from persecution," said Macy, almost pleadingly.

"Well, I say he's lying," barked Gordo, pulling his arm from her grasp and walking back toward the hut. Macy followed closely behind him, as both entered the hut again. Gordo pulled his forty-five from its holster and placed the end of the barrel against Ahmed's head.

"I'm only going to ask you one more time," Gordo hissed. "Tell me about Operation Zebra!" Ahmed began sobbing uncontrollably, praying in his native language, and continuing to swear he knew nothing. Gordo squeezed the trigger, discharging his firearm. Macy's ears rang from the blast as it echoed through the small tin hut. She could see and smell the smoke as it wafted from the barrel of the gun, as Ahmed's lifeless body slumped forward in the chair.

Chapter 2

Springtime in Washington meant the emergence of cherry blossoms bursting forth in a vibrant sea of pink. The white dogwoods offered a contrasting color to add to the natural canvas Mother Nature painted this same time every year. The air was filled with the sweet songs of the many varieties of birds, returning from their winter homes in the South to once again grace our nation's leaders with their presence. This was truly a time of year that most people looked forward to, because they knew summer was just around the corner.

Wilson Crawford sat behind his desk, his chair facing the window, as he observed the blossoms dancing in the gentle breeze. Two squirrels scampered across the lawn, engaged in what seemed like a game of hide and seek. President Crawford had cleared the oval office of all staff members fifteen minutes earlier to allow himself time to relax and reflect before the cabinet meeting, which was scheduled for nine o'clock, exactly ten minutes from now. He would certainly do a lot of reflecting, but would not be able to relax with the current issues of the country looming like a dark cloud over his first term in office.

President Crawford found it was less than two years before re-election, yet he had not solved the problems of the country that were the big campaign issues of the prior election. Of course he, like all politicians do, assured the citizens that he would find solutions to the problems facing this nation, but so far was unable to deliver on his promises. Now with the election less than two years away, President Crawford was struggling, as he searched for any plausible answers for the nation's ills.

Wilson Crawford was born the son of a United States Senator from Ohio, and was groomed from birth for a life of political success. Will, as he was known by his family and closest friends, attended Duke University, where he majored in political science. He continued on at Duke's law school, graduating in the top five percent of his class, demonstrating his high intellect and capacity to learn. He immediately went to work for one of the more prestigious law firms in New York, while planning his political career.

After two years in New York, Will returned to his home state of Ohio, becoming a partner in a Cincinnati firm. His first venture into the political arena was successful, as he was elected to the Ohio State House of Representatives. He held this position for two consecutive terms, before making a bid for Mayor of Cincinnati. The previous mayor had finished his second term, so there was no incumbent, which gave Crawford an easy path to the mayor's office. Will completed two successful terms as Mayor of Cincinnati before setting his sights on the governor's mansion.

While serving as Mayor of Cincinnati, Will met a beautiful woman by the name of Claire Wilson at one of the fund raising dinners for the Cincinnati Arts Guild. Claire worked for a local realtor, but loved to paint in her spare time. She donated several of her paintings for the art auction, most of which Will bought as a way to impress her, or at least, he hoped so. Will was able to get her address through a mutual friend, and soon came to call on her. After a six month courtship, Will and Claire became engaged to be married. It was another six months before they actually became man and wife.

His first attempt at campaigning for Governor fell short by less than five percent of the vote. Will returned to the law firm to wait for the next election. During the next four years, Ohio was plagued by a poor economy and staggering inflation, prompting the disapproval of the current Governor's handling of the state's affairs. This opened the door for Will, as he easily breezed into the Governor's seat, winning by a landslide over the incumbent. Will was quickly on his way to political stardom, surrounding himself with some of the best financial minds as he worked diligently to solve the economic problems facing Ohio. He was successful, creating many new jobs in his first term, while limiting the previous upward spiral of inflation. This success earned him a second term as Governor of Ohio. During his second campaign, there were already rumors about a potential bid for the Presidency.

Will finished his second term as Governor of Ohio much like his first, establishing an approval rating of sixty-three percent. He had quickly become a strong political figure in his party, and soon began making the circuit of political news programs in order to gain more recognition among voters across the nation. Much of the voting public still remembered his father's successful career as a United States Senator, and was confident Will also possessed the same political savvy. Unfortunately, Claire was killed in an automobile accident on her way to visit her parents in Dayton. Will took her death very hard, and remained heartbroken and bitter for months following the accident. It took his best friend Bob, everything he could muster to convince Will to run for the Presidency. Will had not dated publicly since Claire's death.

The previous two Presidential terms were held by the opposing party, with the President taking credit for the largest creation of new jobs in the country's history, along with the lowest unemployment rate. Having served his two terms, the sitting President eagerly endorsed his Vice-President as his successor. Vice-President Joseph Barry was not the flamboyant speaker the President was. He was often seen as stiff and impersonal, rubbing many Americans the wrong way and causing concern among party members. Still, he was his party's best candidate, and given the past eight years, surely would be able to keep the White House for at least the next four.

Will faced a very tough election against the next best thing to an incumbent, a sitting Vice-President. The economy was still a major issue as companies were moving many jobs overseas in favor of cheaper labor. Another major issue for this election was Social Security, which since Congress had been allowed to tap into the Social Security fund, was in danger of depleting its reserves and being unable to fund the retirement needs of the baby boomers. Although Will had an excellent track record as Governor of Ohio, he had never faced an issue quite like Social Security.

Probably the most important issue at hand, though, was the continuing rise in gas prices fueled by OPEC's ever-increasing price for crude oil. Americans were beginning to voice strong concerns as the price of a gallon of regular unleaded gasoline was currently just under four dollars. This would soon become a political hot button and major discussion for the Presidential debates.

Barry ran his entire election campaign around what the previous administration had achieved, vowing the same would continue as long as the country stayed the course. He promised the good times of the prior eight years would continue, even as more and more jobs were being eliminated. Barry assured the voters that Social Security remained very viable, leaving no need for concern about the fund becoming depleted. He argued this was merely a political maneuver by his opponent to unnecessarily scare elderly voters.

Will decided to take a different approach to his campaign. He hired professionals in the area of economics and industry to provide alternative industry and employment opportunities, offering job training for displaced workers to be able to change careers, rather than insist on protectionism of outdated industries against foreign imports and overseas labor. He also decided to weigh in on Social Security, pronouncing the fund's impending doom unless something was done to replenish the deleted funds that were, as he put it, stolen from the American people.

As the election drew near, Barry continued his stance that all was well and the nation should stay the course. Will provided study after study to prove Barry wrong, insisting all was not good, and senior citizens would be the ones to suffer the most from a Barry administration. Monday, prior to the election, the polls showed each candidate in a dead heat, too close to call an apparent favorite. The country waited in anticipation, as the election results began to stream into the major television networks. In an effort not to influence the voters on the West coast, the networks agreed not to release any exit polling predictions until after all the polls had closed across the country.

Once all the polls closed, the television analysts began predicting states for either candidate based upon their exit polling data. It was one of the closest elections in political history, coming down to a couple of deciding states and their electoral votes. In the end, Wilson Crawford was elected President of the United States by a margin of only eleven electoral votes. Barry had actually won the popular vote, causing many voters to call for the abolishment of the Electoral College in favor of the popular vote. Supporters of the Electoral College argued that without it, candidates would be more able to stuff ballot boxes and rig elections. Eventually, the call for the repeal of the Electoral College subsided as the Crawford administration took control of the nation's business.

Now, less than two years away from re-election, President Crawford found he was in the middle of a quandary of rising interest rates, manufacturing industries continuing to close under the pressure of foreign competition, and a Social Security trust fund that would be insolvent in less than thirty years. To date, he had been unable to provide a viable solution for either the economy or Social Security, which were his main two platform issues in the previous election. Although the unemployment rate was currently below five percent, many Americans believed the economy was in poor condition. Will dropped his six feet two inch frame into his chair, pondering his options as he waited for the cabinet meeting. At the age of fifty-four, the stress of his position was beginning to take its toll. His hair was now mostly gray, having spread from just around his temples when he was first elected to office. It was time for some solutions from his hired professionals, or he would soon be out of a job.

As he neared the conference room, President Crawford set his teeth and furrowed his brow in an attempt to look intimidating to the cabinet members. He was tired of his approval rating continuing to plummet, and wanted viable solutions to make his election promises come true and reassure his re-election. He took his place at the head of the table, continuing not to smile as he said his hellos. He was all business, providing an air of tension you could cut with a knife.

"Gentlemen and ladies," Will began, paused, then continued, "we have less than two years until the next election and we continue to have this Social Security issue staring us in the face, not to mention the majority of the people are convinced the economy is going to hell. I need answers that will pacify the voting public, or we will all be joining the ranks of the unemployed. Now, who wants to fire the first shot?" he asked, as he glanced around the room, searching for some sign from the blank stares looking back at him. Everyone remained silent for what seemed like an eternity before someone eventually spoke.

"Mr. President," a female voice sounded from the right side of the table. "If I may, I would like to point out that with a majority in Congress, we could opt for a small tax increase to shore up the Social Security fund." The voice belonged to Meagan Stanley, the Secretary of the Treasury. She was forty-five, the daughter of wealthy parents, who made their fortune in the oil business. She had always lived a life of privilege, and spoke in favor of tax hikes every opportunity she could. Meagan was slightly overweight and not a very attractive woman, although she considered herself to be one of the most desirable single ladies in Washington. It took a sizable campaign contribution from her parents to persuade President Crawford to appoint her to his cabinet.

"May I remind you, Miss Stanley," Crawford began, "we ran on the promise of no tax increases last election. Doing so now would only make us out to be liars in the eyes of the voters. Besides, everyone knows you don't win elections by raising taxes," he snorted.

"Come on people," he pleaded. "There must be someone who has a positive solution to the mess we're in," he demanded, shouting and pounding his fist on the table, which brought one of the Secret Service agents into the room. The President waved his hand in the direction of the agent to signify all was okay. The agent nodded, glanced around the room briefly, and resumed his post outside the conference room.

"Mr. President, how about the surplus tax revenue from the tobacco transition payment program?" asked Elliot Rankin, the Secretary of State.

"Actually, Elliot, the tax revenue from the tobacco buy-out program was only sufficient to cover the tax relief checks the President awarded to the people last summer," replied White House Chief of Staff Robert (Bob) Gorman. President Crawford and Robert Gorman were college roommates, who quickly became best friends. He could see the potential in Will, and decided to take advantage of the situation by making himself an asset too valuable to ignore. He was constantly pushing Will to excel, providing poignant observations and advice. Naturally, Bob climbed the ladder of success along with Will. Chief of Staff was a perfect fit to enable Will to continue to benefit from the advice and direction of his old colleague. It suited Bob as well, considering he was able to affect much of the nation's business from behind the scenes.

He was somewhat smaller than Will in stature at five feet eight inches tall, but what he lacked in height, he made up for in tenacity. Even when he lost the small finger on his left hand in a skiing accident while in college, he never lost a step. He was like a pit bull when it came to carrying out orders, even the ones he carefully placed as Will's ideas. At fifty-four, he was the same age as Will, but showed little sign of stress, as he managed to maintain his blonde hair with only a few stray gray ones here and there. He thrived under pressure, and made certain he remained in top physical condition so he was ready for any situation.

"Well, we need to generate some extra money from somewhere in order to prop up the Social Security fund," President Crawford continued. "I suggest each of you take a copy of the budget, review it, and we'll discuss possible adjustments that will not be too painful for Congress, but will free up the necessary funds. Now, what are we going to do about OPEC?" he asked.

"Where are we with the alternative fuels program?" asked Elliot, fixing his gaze on Steve Hollister, the Secretary of Energy.

"We have perfected the hydrogen fuel cell as an alternative to petroleum, but have yet to lay the groundwork for a delivery system," answered Steve.

"Where would this leave the major oil companies?" asked Bob.

"Once we have an acceptable delivery system in place, they can either choose to participate as a supplier, or not," said Steve. "Either way, they will not see the same profits they do with petroleum due to the way we will need to regulate the hydrogen fuel cell technology."

Bob began shaking his head and replied, "That won't do. We receive too much support from the oil companies to simply cut them off like that. If we implement the hydrogen fuel program, the oil companies will find a sympathetic candidate from the opposing party to put their money behind. No, we cannot risk alienating them this close to election," he finished, looking up at the President.

"Bob's right," President Crawford said. "We need the support of the oil companies more than we need alternative fuels at this time. Elliot, where do we stand in our relations with the oil-producing countries?"

"As you know, most of the Middle East hates us," replied Elliot. "We have had several positive meetings with Venezuela regarding oil imports, but they insist on maintaining their pricing relative to the spot price on the market. They feel they should be allowed to profit from OPEC's greed as well."

"Are we in any position to pressure any of them from a military perspective, without the risk of all out war?" asked the President, looking at Ron Fields, the Secretary of Defense.

"Given the current climate in the Middle East, I believe any such operation would have very negative ramifications," said Ron. "We are already seen by the majority of the world as the neighborhood bully. Any military intervention would only strengthen the negative image we have in the eyes of the rest of the world."

"Amazing," said President Crawford, shaking his head. "Some of the most intelligent minds in the world are gathered here in this room, and still we have no solutions to our current dilemma. How are we supposed to craft an effective platform for our next campaign if we cannot deliver what we already promised we would do?"

"Perhaps we could offer some sort of subsidy or tax incentive to alleviate the burden of higher fuel costs to the American people," said Meagan. "Of course, this, too, will require further study of the budget to see where we can cut enough to free up sufficient funds for such a plan, especially since we are definitely opposed to any tax increases."

"Okay," said President Crawford, raising his hands.

"Meagan, you and your team work on your idea for subsidies or tax incentives to combat the fuel problem. Steve, you join them in their effort. The rest of you study the budget for a way to finance a rebuilding of the Social Security fund. We'll meet again next week to see where we are. I expect some solutions by then," he finished, rising from his seat and quickly exiting the conference room in the direction of the oval office. Bob followed closely behind him, as the rest of the staff scattered in various directions. The staff had worked with President Crawford long enough to understand when he meant business. This was definitely one of those times.

President Crawford walked past his secretary, requesting she clear the next thirty minutes from his schedule. He entered the oval office with Bob in tow. He closed the door behind him, walked to one of the chairs in front of the desk, and sat down almost simultaneously with the President. Crawford retrieved a cigar from the small humidor on his desk, offering one to Bob. They sat silently as they puffed on their cigars until they were sufficiently lit. It was Bob who broke the silence.

"Mr. President, I believe I have a solution to all of our problems," he said.

"Come on Bob," said Crawford. "How many times have I told you to call me Will when we are alone? We've been friends too long to stand on formalities."

"Maybe in the residence, but not here," he said. "Too much of a risk that someone could hear. And we certainly don't want to give the impression you play favorites amongst your staff."

"Okay. You win," said Crawford. "Now, what's this big idea you have and why did you not speak up in the meeting?"

"I'm still working on the details," said Bob. "Just leave everything to me. And whatever you do, don't make any other decisions based on the others' recommendations, at least not without consulting me first," he said, clenching the cigar between his teeth.

"I'm not sure I like the sound of that, Bob," said Crawford, rubbing his chin.

"Relax," laughed Bob. "Haven't I always come through for you? Besides, desperate times call for desperate measures," he said smiling.

"Look Bob," Crawford said sternly. "I don't want to end up like Nixon with my own personal version of Watergate. Can I have your assurance there will be no illegal activity that can be traced back to me?" he demanded.

"Mr. President, there will be nothing connecting you with any illegal activity," said Bob.

"I promise. Besides, I can keep you completely at arms length from the entire operation."

"As long as I have your word that's good enough for me," said Crawford, taking a rather long draw from his cigar.

After a few minutes of small talk as they enjoyed the rest of their cigars, Bob rose from the chair and headed for the door. He closed the door behind him, leaving the President alone. Crawford still had ten minutes of peace before he would be inundated with the responsibilities of his office. He swiveled his chair around so he could see out the window. Watching the blossoms dance in the sunlight, he could not help but wonder what Bob had in mind as a solution for the problems facing the nation. Surely he could trust his friend not to bring shame to the office of the President of the United States. Still, he was puzzled by all of the secrecy surrounding the matter. Suddenly, his secretary buzzed from outside the office, advising him that his thirty minutes were up and he had appointments waiting to see him. *So much for a little quiet time*, he thought.

CHAPTER 3

PEARL HARBOR NAVAL BASE, HAWAII

These are very serious accusations, Seaman," barked Captain Landreu. "Do you have any evidence to back them up?" Captain Jacob Landreau was the commanding officer over all of the ONI teams stationed at Pearl Harbor. He had served in Vietnam and the first Gulf War, and was nearing retirement. Given the eras in which he served, the Captain still believed women should have limited supporting roles in the military. He felt the fighting should be left to the men, whom he believed to be stronger and better able to serve their country during combat.

Captain Landreau stood six feet two inches tall, having shrunken at least two inches in his older years from when he first enlisted in the Navy. His uniform was always neatly pressed, especially the creases, with old-fashioned spit-shined shoes. He believed in doing things the old way, and was very resistant to the modern computer age; at least until he learned it gave him a tactical advantage. Then he attacked computer learning with the same voracity that earned him the Navy Meritorious Service Medal and the Bronze Star.

Macy bit her lip and said, "Only my word, sir."

"What about witnesses?" asked the Captain. "Were there any other members of your team present when this alleged incident occurred?"

"Yes sir!" replied Macy. "Both Seaman Simon and Seaman Johnson were present at the time of the incident. I believe you will find their account of what happened will corroborate mine."

"Well, you see Seaman, that's the problem," he continued. "Both Seaman Simon and Seaman Johnson reported they were present at the time. But their version of the facts supports Commander McCain's exactly. Now, would you care to amend your previous statement, Seaman? Perhaps you did not have a clear view of the entire area and thought you saw what you say you did. It happens," he said smiling.

"No, sir," Macy quickly answered. "I stand by the facts as detailed in my report."

"I'm sorry to hear that, Seaman, given the seriousness of these accusations without the proper evidence to back them up," Captain Landreau said, shaking his head, staring at Macy over the top of his glasses before he continued. "You realize, Seaman, a move like this can be very detrimental to your career."

"I understand, sir," answered Macy, maintaining eye contact. "But I just cannot file a report filled with lies. It's just not in my nature, sir."

"Okay, Seaman," he sighed. "If that's your final answer, I have no choice but to appoint someone to conduct a 15-6 investigation. So I'll ask you one last time. Are you certain your report contains an accurate description of these events as you witnessed them?"

"Positive, sir," Macy responded without hesitation. The Captain then dismissed Macy, allowing her to return to her duties. He immediately summoned Commander McCain to his office. Gordon glanced at Macy as he walked out of his office and headed to the Captain's office. Macy kept her eyes directly on the paperwork in front of her, not because she felt guilty for reporting Gordon, but because she had been unable to look at him ever since the incident occurred. Even though they were lovers, in Macy's mind, the relationship was over. She felt she would never be able to trust Gordon again after what he did. The Captain informed Gordon of the accusations Macy alleged in her report. Gordon was not thrilled at the news, but maintained his professional military demeanor while in the presence of Captain Landreau. You could almost see the steam boiling from his head as Gordon walked back to his office. Captain Landreau also spoke with Seaman Simon and Seaman Johnson to once again confirm their version of the events that took place on their last operation. Satisfied, he had thoroughly questioned everyone, Landreau summoned Commander Thomas to his office. Commander Thomas was a close personal friend of the Captain, having served alongside him in Vietnam. After they exchanged pleasantries, Landreau got right down to business.

"We have a situation, Mark. One of the Alpha Team members, Seaman Merit, has filed a report accusing Commander McCain of executing a civilian in cold blood while on their last op."

"Seaman Merit... Isn't that one of our female team members?" asked Thomas.

Captain Landreau rolled his eyes and let out a long sigh. "Yes. And you know how I feel about women among our fighting ranks, Mark. I don't need to tell you how damaging something like this can be, not only to the Navy, but to national security."

"Yes, sir. Don't worry, Captain. Based on what you've told me, I doubt the 15-6 investigation will lead to an Article 32."

"See that it doesn't," said Landreau.

Landreau dismissed Commander Thomas, easing back in his chair and rubbing his head, as if he suddenly had a migraine. He hoped what the Commander said about there being no need for an Article 32 hearing would indeed be the case once the outcome of the 15-6 investigation was revealed. He was too close to retirement to become involved in a scandal. Landreau knew from past experience, that even though he followed proper procedure, situations like these usually ended up as a reflection on the commanding officer.

"Seaman, can I see you in my office please?" Gordon asked Macy after he returned from his meeting with Captain Landreau.

"Yes, sir," said Macy, rising from her desk and following him to his office. Gordon closed the door behind them, then turned toward Macy, his face still blood red from the anger welling up inside him.

"What the hell did you tell the Captain?" he demanded, trying to maintain an even tone so no one outside the office would hear.

"I assume from your tone you already know the answer to that," said Macy.

"Why did you do that? Why didn't you back me up?" he asked.

"I'm sorry, Gordon, but I just couldn't keep quiet after what you did out there. You know, as well as I do, that man was innocent and did not deserve to die. We should have let him go after questioning."

"And just how would we explain it when he went public about our abducting him in the middle of the night? I was trying to save the country from some embarrassing press."

"Oh, come on, Gordon," sighed Macy. "You know he probably wouldn't have said anything. And even if he did, no one would believe him. You're just making excuses for your need to satisfy your own blood lust. Admit it! You were angry because you would have to report back with no information and you didn't want to look bad. So you killed an innocent man in cold blood because you were enraged," sneered Macy, eyeing Gordon with contempt.

"Look. I'm in it for the long haul. What's so wrong with wanting to look good in front of my superiors? Maybe you should consider a career change if you don't have the stomach for it," said Gordon, gesturing toward the door.

"Maybe I will," replied Macy, placing her hands on her hips. "Macy, I've always had your back," pleaded Gordon. "Don't you think this one time you could tell the Captain you were confused about what you saw and back me up? I mean, really, I thought we had something good going."

"*Had* is right," Macy quipped. "That's all ancient history now as far as I'm concerned. And I intend to leave the report just the way it is. Is that all, sir?"

"I suppose so," sighed Gordon, as he motioned for her to leave. Macy turned and started toward the door, but he spoke again without looking up from his desk.

"Commander Thomas will begin the 15-6 investigation at 0-eight hundred," he said. Macy left his office and walked back to her desk to resume her work. Gordon remained in his office with the door closed; probably calling the other team members to make sure they were still behind him.

After finishing her work and straightening up some, Macy suddenly had a chilling thought run through her mind. She was afraid if they were sent out on another mission with the investigation hanging over Gordon, her life might be in danger. She had some leave time accrued, and decided this would be a good time to take it and get away from Gordon for a while. Macy walked back to Gordon's office and knocked on the door.

"Enter!" Gordon shouted from within. Macy opened the door and stepped inside.

"Sir, it has come to my attention I have accrued a considerable amount of leave time. With your permission, I would like to take some time off," said Macy.

"What about the investigation?" Gordon asked.

"I can give my statement to Commander Thomas before leaving," answered Macy.

"Okay," said Gordon. "It might be better if we put some distance between us for a little while anyway. Just make sure you leave a contact number in case Commander Thomas needs to get in touch with you," he finished, never looking up from his desk. Macy turned and walked out of his office, closing the door behind her. She returned to her desk and began calling the airline to book a flight to the mainland. Then she gathered her things and left the office.

Macy always parked as far away from the building as possible, believing it was good exercise for her, even though she worked out almost every day. Today was no exception, as she made the long walk from the building to the far end of the parking area. It was a beautiful day, but Macy couldn't help but feel like a dark cloud was looming over her. She felt a little sorry for Gordon, but was resolute in her need for justice. She just hoped this incident wouldn't somehow negatively impact her. Just then, she had that burning inside her stomach that meant all was not right. Even with all of her training, she found her hand trembling as she fumbled for her car keys.

Macy left the parking lot, heading in the direction of her apartment. It was a modest two bedroom loft just ten miles from the base. Several of the other military personnel lived there, including Gordon. She had furnished the apartment in Oriental décor from things she had collected on her travels, trying to give it a feminine touch. That was often difficult for military women, as they often had to appear tougher than their male counterparts in order to garner some respect.

Immediately upon entering her apartment, Macy could tell something was amiss. It was obvious someone had been there going through her things. Whoever it was tried to cover their tracks, but Macy's trained eye could see the results of their efforts. Almost everything was in its place, except for some photos of her and Gordon, along with some jewelry he had given her. She wondered who could have done this and why, and decided to make an inventory list of exactly what was missing.

After combing through her personal effects and jotting down the missing items, Macy grabbed a beer from the fridge and collapsed into an easy chair. She reached for the remote control and turned the television on, searching for the news channel. She took a long pull from her bottle as she watched the news ticker at the bottom of the screen for the latest headlines. Of course, there was no mention of their covert operation, or the death of the attorney. There never was any press about their missions, as they were always top secret. The attorney would simply be reported missing by his family until his body turned up a few months later, apparently the victim of a random mugging.

After she finished her beer, Macy went to the bedroom and began packing for her trip. She had decided to visit her brother, George, in Kentucky for a few days. Once her luggage was ready to go, she picked up the phone and dialed George's number. He answered after two rings, using his professional business voice. He had been a field agent with the FBI for the past few years, having moved up from the Kentucky SBI office in Lexington. He had tried unsuccessfully for the past two years to get Macy to leave the Navy and work with him, but she refused, stating she did not want to become a member of the establishment. They both laughed at that statement, as she sounded like a throwback from the sixties demonstrating against the war.

"Hello," greeted Macy. "How's my favorite brother?"

"I happen to be your only brother," George laughed. "And what do I owe this outpouring of love to?"

"I'm taking some time off and thought I would fly out for a visit," she answered. "Will you be in town the next couple of days?"

"Sure," said George. "I would love to see you. It's been a while."

"I know," she said. "I'm sorry, but I do the best I can." "That's okay, sis," he laughed. "Don't beat yourself up over it. When will you get in?"

"My plane arrives tomorrow afternoon at three o'clock."

"Good. I'll pick you up then."

Macy gave him the flight information and agreed to meet him at baggage claim. Then she hung up and decided to take a long hot bath. After the events of the day, she needed to relax and unwind. After her bath, Macy returned to her bedroom and put on her robe. Then she walked barefoot across the carpeted floor to the kitchen for another beer. The television was still covering the same news stories as she sat down in her easy chair. Macy decided to change the channel, seeking a diversion from reality for a while. She settled on an old episode from the original *Star Trek* series, which she used to watch with George when they were young. Her brother loved to imitate Captain Kirk back then, but she couldn't get him to do any impressions from their childhood since he joined the bureau. Now he was all business, but he still loved her and she knew it.

Macy fell asleep about halfway through the program and did not wake until after dark. She looked at the clock and realized it was ten o'clock. She had been asleep for four hours, which meant she probably wouldn't sleep any more that night. She got up from her chair and went to the kitchen to pour a glass of tea and make a sandwich. She returned to the television to eat while she watched the ten o'clock news.

Once the news was over at ten-thirty, Macy decided to turn the television off and try to lay down for some rest. She was glad she had turned all the lights off when she heard a hard knock on her door. Before she could get her robe back on and make it to the door, she heard a recognizable voice calling her name. It was Gordon and he was obviously drunk. He was saying how sorry he was and asking her to let him in and forgive him. He professed his love for her and how much he needed her.

Macy remained quiet in order to give the impression she wasn't home. After a few minutes of his drunken tirade, Macy heard Gordon walk away from her door and head down the hall to his apartment. Macy could feel the tears streaming down her cheeks, as she stood naked in the dark, her heart breaking, feeling betrayed by the man she loved. Even under the circumstances, it would take her a long time to get over Gordon. She certainly didn't want to speak to him when he was in that condition.

Macy walked to the kitchen and grabbed a beer, hoping it would help calm her nerves. She laughed, as she thought how many times she had persevered through extremely dangerous operations only to be shaken to the depths of her soul by one man. She took a long gulp of beer and shook her head as if to say, "Get a grip." She downed the rest of the beer and headed back to her bedroom. As she lay down on her bed, naked and uncovered, she felt certain it would be a very long night.

Macy awoke to the sound of her clock radio, having ultimately fallen asleep from sheer exhaustion. She walked sleepily into the bathroom for a quick shower, then dressed and grabbed her luggage for the trip to Kentucky. Since she wasn't sure when she would return, Macy decided to call a cab to take her to the airport, rather than leave her car in the long-term parking area.

The cab arrived within minutes and Macy carried her bag to the curb where the driver loaded it in the trunk. As the taxi pulled away from the curb, the driver glanced up at the rear view mirror. He saw a man running toward the cab and asked Macy if she knew him. As Macy turned her head to look out the back, she could see it was Gordon. Macy told the driver she had no idea who it was, and asked if he would please hurry so she would not miss her flight. The cab sped away, leaving Gordon behind to suffer from the choking exhaust fumes and the hangover that resulted from last night's debauchery.

Chapter 4

San Antonio, Texas

Bob Gorman stepped through the doorway of the Lear jet and descended the steps that led from the plane to the tarmac. It was nine-thirty in the evening as darkness cast long shadows from the few lights illuminating the base. Lackland Air Force Base was no longer open for civilian tours, but he had clearance, given his cabinet position and purpose for his visit. Lackland was now a military research facility used for animal and human programs, considered one of the best facilities of this type in the Department of Defense. Bob made sure they knew ahead of time he was acting on behalf of the President of the United States.

Colonel Marcus Wagoner was the only one waiting at the bottom of the steps, extending his hand outward as he approached. "Mr. Gorman, it's a pleasure to meet you," said Colonel Wagoner. The Colonel was six feet and three inches tall, very thin and wiry. He was fifty-five years old, with a head full of gray hair. His uniform was neatly pressed, typical of most career military men. He wore no glasses, but his face was red from either a bad case of Rosacea or many years of alcohol.

"Likewise Colonel," replied Gorman. "I trust everything is in order."

"Certainly, but then I assume you didn't fly all the way out here just to take my word for it," smiled Wagoner. "If you will follow me," he continued, turning toward the base. Wagoner maintained a steady pace, which Bob had no trouble matching, as he was led to a jeep parked just outside the hanger. Colonel Wagoner climbed into the driver's seat while Bob settled in beside him. They sped off toward the southern end of the base to a small building which was somewhat isolated from the larger facilities. The entire base was enclosed by a fence which was ten feet tall with razor wire around the top. The smaller building also had its own fence of equal height and construction providing a ten foot perimeter surrounding the building.

Colonel Wagoner stopped directly in front of a small guard shack located just inside the fence. He climbed out of the jeep and walked up to the fence to speak with the guard. After an exchange of salutes and a brief conversation, Wagoner motioned for Bob to join him. As Bob approached, the guard pressed a button somewhere inside the shack, causing the metal gate to roll open in front of them. Wagoner stepped through the gate with Bob closely in tow. The gate sprang to life again, as the guard pressed the button to close the gate securely behind them.

The building had no windows, and appeared to have no doors either. As they neared what one would assume was the front of the building, Bob could barely make out a small key pad located at the bottom of the wall, concealed by a heavy growth of weeds which made the building appear as if it had been neglected for years. Wagoner stooped over and pressed a sequence of numbers into the key pad, causing a small opening to appear in the building wall. He motioned for Bob to follow, as he walked through. The door sealed tightly behind them, as they followed a dimly lit hallway to an inner door. There Wagoner punched another sequence of numbers into a key pad and the inner door slid open, revealing a much brighter light.

It took a moment for their eyes to adjust to the light, as they looked around the room. Bob noticed several personnel wearing white lab coats busily going about their tasks as if he and the Colonel were not even there. The room exuded an aura of energy from the rapid but deft movements of the lab technicians. Bob suddenly felt somewhat recharged himself, as he observed the skill and pace at which they performed their duties. He noticed several different workstations, each appearing to have its own necessary function in the order of operation.

Wagoner stopped on the small observation platform just inside the door overlooking the lab. He had a smug satisfied look on his face as he turned to Bob and said, "Well, what do you think? Pretty impressive, huh?"

"It appears adequate," he replied, not wanting to show too much enthusiasm. Wagoner grunted, "Humph," as he began descending the stairs to the main level of the lab. Bob followed closely behind as they approached the first work-station.

"This is where it all begins," said Wagoner. "The samples are delivered to that large storage freezer," he continued, pointing to the far left side of the room. "From there, they're brought to this first station for analysis to determine exactly what we're working with. We learned a long time ago never to trust what was written on a vial. Of course, most of what we receive now is not labeled anyway."

"How do you ensure the discretion of your staff?" asked Bob.

"Oh, you mean how we make sure they don't go around telling what they were working on?" said Wagoner. "Well, that's the easy part. We simply use a system of diagrams the technician can compare to the live samples. Once there is a match of the molecular makeup of a sample to a corresponding diagram on the chart, the sample is labeled with the number above the matching diagram. This way no one knows exactly what they're working with, but we will be able to identify the sample by its code number."

"And there's no way to identify it based solely on appearance?" asked Bob.

"No way," said Wagoner. "You must remember we're working with previously undetermined and unidentified samples, at least as far as the science books go. These technicians have never seen the stuff they're working with before they got here. From here the samples are separated and grouped together according to code. Then the ones we aren't working with at that particular time are placed back into storage. We typically work with a maximum of six different sample types at one time, depending on how many and what types of experiments we're performing."

"And who knows the code combinations?" asked Bob. "Only I and Major Harris, who oversees most of the experiments," answered Wagoner, as he stepped away from the second station. "Of course, there's also a set of codes maintained at the Pentagon under dual control in case something happens to the Major and me at the same time." They continued the tour of the lab as Wagoner pointed out how various tests were performed at each station, mainly to determine stability, volatility, and interactions with other substances. Then he led Bob to a door at the far end of the lab.

"Behind this door is where the real fun begins," said Wagoner, as he punched the key pad and opened the door. The room was twice as large as the lab, but not as brightly lit, with only a small number of technicians. You had to pass through a decontamination room in order to enter or exit the lab. Along the left wall were cages of various sizes containing many different species of animals, from mice to monkey. Several of them were connected to machines which monitored their heart rate, respiration, temperature, and brain function. There were four empty examination tables in the middle of the room, complete with wrist and ankle restraints. The right side of the room contained several computers and analytical equipment.

"This is where we conduct our live experiments to determine physical and mental reactions and formulate antidotes for viruses, bacteria, and chemicals, which could be used against us by terrorists or hostile governments with biological or chemical weapons," said Wagoner. "We have studied the effects of dirty bombs being detonated in crowded cities, as well as bacteria and viruses entered into an entire population's drinking water. Of course, we can't anticipate every possible assault, but our intelligence has been able to keep us abreast of most potential threats, enabling us to remain prepared in case anyone should decide to employ one of these deadly weapons against us," he concluded.

"Have the samples we requested arrived yet?" asked Bob.

"Yes. They were delivered this morning," said Wagoner. "We are in the process of verifying their validity and performing our initial tests. From there, we will proceed with the animal testing process. I understand this is something that has already presented in certain animals."

"Yes, there have been some reports of that," replied Bob, trying to avoid the question.

"Well then, we should have no trouble replicating it here," said Wagoner. "Are there any particular species you prefer us use, or should we just proceed with the known carriers?"

"We will supply the test subjects when we are ready to proceed with that phase of the operation," said Bob.

"Very well," replied Wagoner. "You can contact me as soon as you're ready to introduce the live virus into the subject animals."

"Fine," said Bob. "Until then, I recommend you change the entry protocol for this area to allow only yourself, Major Harris, and me entry into this room."

"What about the technicians we will need?" Wagoner asked.

"I will supply the technicians necessary for this operation as well," said Bob. "I assure you, they are highly trained and will maintain the highest level of discreet professionalism. Remember, this is a top secret experiment of vital importance to our national security. The fewer who know about it the better."

"Whatever you say," sighed Wagoner. "You're the boss on this one."

"Make sure you remember that and we will get along just fine, Colonel," smiled Bob, as he turned to leave the room. They walked back through the lab and into the dimly lit corridor. From there, they exited the building and approached the guard shack. Colonel Wagoner and the guard exchanged salutes before the gate began to open again. They proceeded through the gate and back to the jeep, where they both climbed into the vehicle and sped off in the direction they came from. Both remained silent for the entire return trip back to the tarmac. Once they reached the hanger, Wagoner parked the jeep and climbed out. He and Bob exchanged pleasantries, then Bob climbed aboard the Lear jet. In just a few minutes, the jet was airborne again and on its way back to Washington. As soon as they reached cruising altitude, Bob reached for the phone, punching in a sequence of numbers. After a moment, another voice answered at the other end.

"Harry, it's Bob," said Gorman.

"Yes sir," answered Harry. "How'd the inspection go?"

"Everything is in order," answered Bob. "Where are we with the list?"

"I've located six possible candidates," replied Harry. "They are all from the same location, and have no family or close community ties."

"Perfect!" exclaimed Bob. "Where are they located?"

"USP in Marion, Illinois," answered Harry.

"Have you already scheduled the meetings?"

"Yes sir. They begin at eight o'clock tomorrow morning, continuing until completed. It should take no more than forty-five minutes for each one."

"Good," said Bob. "I'll head there tonight. I don't suppose you would happen to know where I can stay tonight."

"I took the liberty of booking you at the Drury Inn," said Harry. "There will be a car and driver waiting at the airport to take you to the hotel."

"Excellent. We'll talk again tomorrow." And with that, Bob ended the call and instructed the pilot to change course and head to Williamson County Regional Airport just outside of Marion. Then he sat back and poured a glass of bourbon. Bob sipped on his drink, as he reviewed a list of questions he had prepared for the interviews. Each person would be asked the same questions. Then he would select the best five based upon their answers.

The flight from Lackland to Marion took approximately two and a half hours, which gave Bob enough time to enjoy a few drinks while he relaxed. It was around one-thirty in the morning when the jet touched down just outside of Marion. He stepped off the plane and walked to the black limousine waiting outside the terminal. The driver simply acknowledged Bob with a nod as he opened the rear door. When he was securely inside, the driver placed Bob's luggage in the trunk, and climbed into the driver's seat. Once inside, neither spoke as the limo headed to the hotel. After the car arrived at the front entrance to the hotel, the driver handed the luggage to the bellman and told Bob he would return in the morning at seven-thirty. Bob thanked him and headed through the revolving door.

The hotel lobby was deserted at this hour, so there was no line to wait in. Bob walked to the counter and seeing no one, rang the bell. A young man appeared from the room behind the counter and asked if he could help him. Bob explained he had a reservation and handed the clerk his license and credit card. The clerk punched a few keys on the computer, and handed him an envelope containing a key card for his room with the room number written on the outside. Making his way to the elevator, he pressed the third floor button upon arrival. When he reached his room, he inserted the key card and turned the handle. He entered, hung his bag in the closet, locked the door, and climbed into bed for the few hours of sleep he would get before starting early in the morning.

At exactly six o'clock, the telephone rang announcing the wake up call Bob had placed with the clerk when he checked in. He proceeded to shower and dress before heading downstairs to the restaurant for breakfast. He'd always believed breakfast was the most important meal of the day. Today, he decided to have scrambled eggs with corned beef hash and toast. Of course, he had to have his morning coffee, regular, as he felt decaf was for the weak. He had just enough time to eat, gather his things, and check out before time to exit the hotel for the day's meetings. He walked outside at exactly seven-thirty, finding the limousine waiting as promised.

He climbed into the limo and directed the driver to proceed to the United States Penitentiary in Marion. It was a short drive, and again there was no small talk between Bob and the driver. The car was reserved for the day, so when he got out in front of the main gate, the driver parked the limo and retrieved a paperback from the seat beside him, beginning to read as a way to pass the time. Bob flashed his identification to the guard, and was immediately allowed to enter.

The USP in Marion was a state of the art maximum security facility designed to house some of the most hardened and dangerous criminals. Many were either on death row or sentenced to life in prison. The death row inmates had temporarily become lifers after the Governor of Illinois placed a moratorium on the death penalty, citing several instances where death row inmates were later found to be not guilty with the use of DNA testing, some narrowly escaping lethal injection. Of course, the moratorium could be lifted at any moment causing the lethal injections to resume.

Bob was escorted to a secure interview room to await the arrival of the first inmate. The warden had been given strict instructions regarding which prisoners to assemble for the interviews. Those who were on death row were preferred, especially ones with no family or close friends, and whose appeals had all been exhausted. He neatly laid out his papers and information sheets on each inmate, which Harry had faxed to the jet last night. He had already studied the profiles during the flight, but decided to look over the first interviewee's information while he waited for him to arrive.

After approximately ten minutes had passed, the door across from Bob creaked open, revealing a prisoner in an orange jumpsuit with wrist and leg shackles. There were two guards behind him, escorting the prisoner as he shuffled along slowly. The shackles rattled with each movement, but were extremely effective in limiting the prisoner's mobility. The guards led him to the chair directly across the table from Bob and eased him into a sitting position. Then they backed away, remaining in the room with their backs against the wall directly behind the prisoner. Bob instructed them to leave, assuring them he had already cleared it with the warden. After exchanging puzzled looks of concern, the guards checked with their supervisor who verified Bob's request. They exited the room, locking the door behind them.

Bob began by asking the prisoner to state his name and where he was from. Then he asked about his crime and how he had carried it out. Lifers usually had no problem recounting the gory details of their crime, often finding it arousing to tell their story. Bob carefully made notes as the prisoner continued. Next, he asked about family members, who they were, were they still living, and had there been any contact within the last two years. Finally, he asked about friends or anyone who might be waiting for them on the outside and whether he received any mail.

He proceeded with the same line of questioning for each of the six inmates until he was satisfied they had all answered his questions as truthfully as he could expect. After the last prisoner was returned to his cell, he requested the logs of incoming mail to see exactly what kind of letters or correspondence these inmates were receiving from the outside. According to the records, none of them received any mail in the past year. He smiled to himself, thoroughly satisfied these were the ideal people he was looking for. He thanked the guards for their cooperation and walked out of the facility to the waiting limousine.

Bob instructed the driver to return to the airport as they sped away from the prison. There was no conversation during this trip either, in keeping with the past pattern. They arrived in front of the terminal and Bob exited the limo without saying a word to the driver. He climbed aboard the Lear jet, settling into a seat before the plane taxied down the runway. In just a few seconds, the jet was airborne again on its way back to Washington. Once the plane reached cruising altitude, he reached for the phone, punched the numbers and waited expectantly for Harry's voice.

"Yes sir," said Harry. "How did it go?"

"Excellent," said Bob. "You know what to do next," he continued in a half whisper, then placed the receiver back into its cradle, ending the call. He poured some bourbon into a glass and sat back in the chair, unbuckling his seatbelt. Everything was coming together nicely, he thought as he closed his eyes for a short nap.

Chapter 5

Lexington, Kentucky

The plane touched down on the runway with a jolt, waking Macy from her slumber. This was the third leg of her trip and she tried to sleep while traveling for hours. She was somewhat rested, but still groggy, as she sat upright in her seat and peered out the window. There were a few wispy white clouds in the sky, as the sun shone brightly, indicating another beautiful sunny day in Kentucky.

As the plane came to a stop at the gate, Macy began retrieving her carry-on bag from the overhead compartment, and waited for the passengers seated in front of her to exit the plane before she could move toward the door. The flight attendant smiled and waved goodbye as Macy passed by her and stepped through the cabin door and onto the ramp. It was a short walk up the ramp and through another door to get inside the terminal. Macy had been in this airport many times, so she knew where she needed to go, heading straight for baggage claim.

As she neared the conveyor that would soon produce the luggage from her flight, Macy spotted George. They greeted each other with a warm hug, as he gave her a peck on the cheek. He was three years older than Macy. He stood six feet tall with wavy red hair he kept neatly trimmed because of its natural curl. He was dressed in a dark business suit, which was the usual attire for a FBI field agent.

"It's great to see you, Macy," said George. "How was your flight?"

"Uneventful. Just the way I like them," smiled Macy. "Good to see you too." She gave him another hug while they waited for the buzzer to announce the unloading of the baggage from the flight. After a couple of minutes, the buzzer sounded and the conveyor began spitting out bags onto the carousel, circling round and round until the passengers removed their bags. Macy recognized her suitcase as it came out of the chute, and grabbed the handle, pulling it from the carousel to the floor beside her.

"Here, I'll take that," said George, as he reached for her luggage.

"Thank you," replied Macy, still tired enough from the trip not to argue over equal rights and who should carry the bag. George left the terminal with Macy right behind him, her carry-on securely around her shoulder. It was a short walk to George's car, as he had been able to procure a close parking space. He placed her suitcase in the trunk, grabbed her carry-on bag, and placed it beside the suitcase, closing the lid. He stepped around to the passenger side and opened the door for Macy. She slid into the seat and he closed the door securely. He walked around to the other side and climbed into the driver's seat. In just a few seconds, they were heading out of the parking garage and away from the airport.

"So, how long will you be able to stay?" asked George.

"I'm not sure," said Macy. "I guess I'll just have to play it by ear."

"That sounds kinda suspicious," he smiled. "What's up?"

"I'll give you the quick and dirty once we get settled. For now just find a restaurant. I'm starving," she said, rubbing her stomach.

George chuckled as he drove East on Highway 60 toward Lexington. Just outside of Lexington, he turned onto New Circle Road. New Circle Road made a loop around the entire city of Lexington, with many restaurants scattered among the various streets it was connected to. George knew of a steakhouse just off New Circle on Harrodsburg Road. He took the exit and turned into the parking lot in front of the restaurant.

"How did you know I was in the mood for steak?" asked Macy.

"I didn't," replied George. "This is where I wanted to go." They both laughed as they climbed out of the car and walked in the front door. The hostess smiled and greeted them as she grabbed a couple of menus. She led them to a table, informed them their server would be Jon, then turned and walked back to her station. It was only a minute before Jon arrived to get their drink order. "I'll have a beer," said Macy.

"Me, too," agreed George.

Macy gave him a suspicious look. As Jon walked away, she said, "Drinking on duty, huh. That's a first."

"For your information, I took the afternoon off to spend with you."

"That's sweet," she smiled. "But you didn't have to do that."

"Well, I don't get to see you often enough," said George. "I wanted to catch up."

Jon arrived with their beers and proceeded to tell them about the daily specials. Macy ordered filet mignon, medium well. George ordered the same only medium rare. Jon retreated to the kitchen to place their order, and returned in just a few seconds with a nice garden salad and warm bread for each of them. He turned to check on the other tables he was waiting on, while George and Macy removed their utensils from the red cloth napkins placed carefully at their right side.

"Okay," said George. "Now that we're eating, tell me what's been going on."

"Not much," answered Macy. "Just the usual stuff."

"Come on, Macy," he pressed. "I know you better than that. I can tell when something's bothering you. Now fess up."

"Okay. Okay," she sighed, and proceeded to tell him about the last mission and what Gordon did to the attorney.

She was careful not to reveal too much information since she was still a Naval officer, but she was able to paint him a good picture of what happened. She stopped her story briefly when Jon returned to check on them, then continued as soon as he left. After she finished, George sat silent for a few minutes trying to digest both his steak and what Macy had just told him. He shifted in his seat, leaned forward, and looked Macy directly in the eyes.

"You're in big trouble, sis," he said, shaking his head. "What do you mean?" she asked.

"You should know by now those guys are going to stick together," he began. "They will end up turning this thing into something negative against you, if you're lucky. Then again, they may just wait until an opportune moment to take you out," he finished, making a slashing motion across his throat with the index finger of his right hand.

"That's what I was afraid of," she said. "That's why I decided to put a little distance between me and Gordon for a while."

"Macy, this seems like an excellent opportunity to tell them to shove it and join the ranks of the FBI," George urged.

"That would be like trading the devil for the witch," she sighed. "I joined the Navy at first to rebel, but once I signed up for special ops, I thought I would be able to actually make a difference in the lives of people, changing them for the better. Now I realize this group is just as corrupt as the rest of the government."

"Easy, sis," said George, holding up his hands. "We're not all bad guys."

"I know, George. It's just that I hoped it would be different," she said.

"So what are you going to do?"

"Nothing for now. I met Commander Thomas at the airport before I left to come out here. He took my statement and assured me he would look into the matter thoroughly and give it the attention it deserves, whatever that means."

"That means he will report whatever he is told to report," sneered George.

"You're probably right," agreed Macy. "But for now all I can do is wait."

"I'm going to take some more time off to keep an eye on you."

Macy laughed. "My brother, the big protector. I am quite capable of taking care of myself."

"I know, but just the same I would feel better if I hung out with you while you're here. Besides, I've got a bunch of days saved up since I have no life."

"Fine with me. Just don't say I didn't warn you. I'm afraid I will bore you to death," she giggled.

They finished their meal, paid the check, and left the restaurant. Macy had already planned on staying with George since he lived alone and had plenty of room. They left the city and headed out of town to the country. George bought a house two years ago that was just too good of a deal to pass up. The house was a foreclosure a friend told him about. He was able to buy it for less than half of the appraised value. Normally, most single bachelors lived in apartments or condos, but George decided he wanted to invest in real estate, just in case he found Mrs. Right one day.

The house was situated on ten acres used by the prior owner as a small horse farm. It was an eighteen hundred square foot brick ranch with three bedrooms and two baths. A small pasture and barn overlooked a pond. George worked in his spare time refurbishing the barn as a recreational building, complete with a pool table and wet bar. He left the fencing up to add to the charm, but instead of horses, he had worked out a deal with one of the local farmers to keep the pasture mowed by giving him the hay to mow it. It was a good arrangement that kept the property looking neat, and satisfied the farmer's need for feed as well. George kept one of the bedrooms furnished as a guest room. The other he converted into an office where he kept his computer.

George pulled the car into the garage and turned off the motor. He grabbed Macy's bags from the trunk and led her inside to the guest room. He laid her bags on the queen bed and advised her he would give her some time to settle in while he checked his email. He told her to call him if she needed anything, but to otherwise make herself at home. Macy unpacked her bags, hanging some clothes in the closet while placing others in the dresser. After she finished, she lay down on the bed for a short nap.

George suddenly sprang from his chair and ran to the guest room. He threw open the door to find Macy sitting upright on the bed clutching a pillow. She was soaked with sweat and crying. He sat down on the bed and put his arms around her to comfort her. He could feel her heart racing as he held her.

"You're okay," he said. "You just had a bad dream." She sobbed softly against his shoulder as he rocked her back and forth. "Do you have these dreams often?"

"Only since the last operation," she sniffled. "Would you like to tell me about it?"

"It's always the same," she began, choking back her tears. "Gordon and I are in bed making love when, all of a sudden; he jumps up with a knife and begins stabbing me all over my body. I'm trying to fight him off as the blade continues to thrust into my chest. That's usually when I wake up," she sobbed.

"You happened to leave the part about you and Gordon being intimate out of the story you told me earlier," said George.

"I felt embarrassed discussing my sex life with my own brother," she said. "Besides, after he went crazy in the field like that, I broke off the relationship."

"That's probably for the best anyway," said George. "You can get into a lot of trouble for having an affair with your commanding officer."

"Yeah, pretty dumb of me, huh?" she sniffed.

"Let's just say it wasn't one of your more thought out ideas," George said smiling, which brought a smile to Macy's face as her tears began to subside.

"Why don't you take a nice long hot bath to help you relax? Then maybe we'll go take in a movie if you feel up to it."

Macy nodded her approval as George loosened his grip to allow her to get up from the bed. He walked out of the room, closing the door behind him. Macy walked into the bathroom and filled the tub with hot water. Then she undressed, removing her blouse and jeans to reveal a matching pair of red panties and bra, which she purchased from Victoria's Secret. Although she was in a profession where most would consider her a tomboy, Macy was very much a feminine woman, and preferred to dress so when she could. Her petite body was well suited for intimate apparel, and she filled every stitch in all the right places.

Once she was completely naked, Macy slid into the tub, allowing the warm water to cover her body. She laid her head back against the edge of the tub and closed her eyes as the warmth from the water cascaded over her in waves of heated pleasure. For the moment, she had forgotten about her problems with Gordon, succumbing to the euphoric sensations caressing her body. She soon found herself floating on an ethereal plane as she relaxed deeper, basking in the comfort of the warm water that encircled her body like a blanket on a cold winter day.

After a few minutes of relaxation, Macy opened her eyes and began to bathe her body with the rich lavender soap she had brought with her. Then she submerged herself into the warm water to rinse away the suds. When the water began to lose its warmth, she climbed out of the tub and began drying her body with one of the plush guest towels George had hanging on the wall.

Macy walked back into the bedroom and retrieved a lavender bra from the dresser, carefully placing it around her back while fastening the clasp in the front between her breasts. Since she forgot to pack the matching pair of lavender panties, Macy decided to wear a pair of jeans with nothing underneath. Occasionally, she preferred to dress this way because it gave her a feeling of freedom, much the same as walking around naked, yet her body was covered. She slid her feet into a pair of leather sandals, sprayed a little perfume on her neck, and walked out of the guest room to find her brother.

George was sitting on the sofa in the living room, scanning the newspaper to see what movies were playing. He looked up as Macy walked in, and began running down the list of films now showing at the multiplex. None of them sounded particularly interesting to Macy, so she asked if he would like to stay home and play cards instead, especially since she was still a little tired from her trip. George was okay with that idea, so he went to get the cards while Macy walked to the kitchen to make some popcorn.

Together, they sat and ate popcorn and drank sodas while playing cards. Their favorite game was Contract Rummy, which they had played since one of her brother's friends from high school introduced the game to them. After the first game, George looked at his watch. It was eleven o'clock and he asked Macy if she wanted to retire for the evening. She was afraid of having another nightmare, though, so they decided to play another game. A typical game of Contract Rummy lasted at least forty-five minutes, but sometimes would go on for an hour.

When they completed the second game, it was almost midnight. George had always required more sleep then Macy, so he headed to bed. Of course, he told her to make herself at home and stay up as long as she wanted. She felt tired enough now, though, to hopefully be able to sleep without the nightmares. They said goodnight and retired to their respective beds for the night.

Macy opened her eyes to discover the entire room was illuminated from the sunshine streaming through the window. She looked at her watch to see what time it was. To her surprise, it was already ten o'clock. She had really crashed last night, she thought, as she climbed out of bed and walked to the bathroom. She wrapped a robe around her body and opened the door to the guest room. Immediately, she was hit by the aroma of freshly brewed coffee and bacon. She smiled, thinking how sweet it was of George to fix breakfast.

When she walked into the kitchen, George motioned for her to sit down across from him while he got up to pour her some coffee. He had prepared scrambled eggs, bacon, hash browns, and toast. Macy had a little of everything, feeling extremely hungry since she had not eaten since their late lunch yesterday. George had already eaten, and was sipping his coffee while he scanned through the morning paper.

"Well, what would you like to do today?" he asked, looking up from his paper.

"I'm not sure..." Macy started to answer, but was interrupted by her cell phone ringing from the guest room. She jumped up from the table and ran to the bedroom to retrieve the phone from her purse.

"Hello."

"Seaman Merit," said the voice on the other end. "This is Commander Thomas. We met yesterday at the airport."

"Why yes, Commander," said Macy. "What can I do for you?"

"I need you to report back to the base at once," he continued. "Something was brought to my attention yesterday during my investigation that we need to discuss. I'm sorry to interrupt your leave, but I wouldn't call if it was not important."

"What exactly came up that we need to discuss?" asked Macy.

"I'd rather we talk about it in person, if you don't mind," replied Commander Thomas.

"Yes sir," she said. "I'll be there as soon as I can." She ended the call and looked up at George. "That was Commander Thomas. They want me to return to the base immediately," she said, looking confused.

"What do you think they want?" asked George.

"He said something came up during his investigation that he wishes to discuss in person with me," answered Macy.

"Any idea what it could be?"

"I don't know," she said. "But I certainly intend to find out."

Chapter 6

Washington, DC

The Lear jet landed at Ronald Reagan National Airport at six o'clock that evening returning from Marion, Illinois. Bob Gorman had spent most of the flight pouring over the prisoner profiles and answers to the interview questions. There was no doubt this was an excellent selection of candidates for his operation, but now came the difficult task of narrowing down the group of six to the five best candidates. The sixth one would remain on the short list as a potential backup should one of the top five not live up to expectations.

Candidate number one was a black male, forty years old, and on death row for the rape and murder of three college co-eds at Illinois University. He was a custodian at the university, which provided him with access to the dorms. Each victim was attacked on a Wednesday night, which the prisoner said was his bowling night. However, no one could corroborate his alibi, while further DNA tests placed him at the scene. It took the jury only two hours of deliberation to convict him of all three murders and sentence him to die by lethal injection.

According to his response during the interview process, he had no close family, as he was raised in and out of foster homes until he was sixteen, at which time he went out on his own. He had no idea who his parents were, much less whether they were still living. Gorman checked the prison records and determined he had not received any outside mail in over four years, with the last items merely magazines. There were no records of him either making or receiving phone calls within the last two years. His last telephone contact was with his attorney shortly before his last unsuccessful appeal. Candidate number one was a go.

Candidate number two was a Caucasian male, twenty-nine years old, serving a life sentence for killing his girlfriend's eighteen month old infant. According to the trial transcript, the girlfriend left him alone with her child to baby-sit while she was at work. Unable to stop the child from crying, the prisoner shook the infant until it stopped crying. When he went to check on it later, he noticed the child was not breathing. He dialed 911 and remained on the phone until the paramedics arrived, but they were unable to revive the infant. The jury felt the death was not planned, the defendant definitely showed remorse, and therefore did not give him the death penalty. The girlfriend ceased all contact with the prisoner after the incident. He had received no phone calls in the last two years, but was receiving mail from a pen pal in Mississippi. Bob would have Harry check this one further to determine if indeed the pen pal was real and what the likelihood would be that an interruption in contact would raise suspicion from the Mississippi resident.

Candidate number three was a Caucasian female, twenty-three years old, sentenced to life in prison for the murder of her husband and his lover. According to the court record, she came home early one afternoon from work to find her husband in bed with another woman, who just happened to be their next door neighbor and the defendant's best friend. Consumed by rage and embarrassment at catching them in the act, the defendant walked to the garage, grabbed her husband's shotgun, and returned to the master bedroom where they were still engaged in their lascivious act. Apparently, they were having too good of a time to even notice the wife had come home. The first shot struck the woman in her back as she was positioned upright above the husband. As she fell on top of him, he rolled her body off the bed and shouted at his wife just as she pulled the trigger again, hitting him squarely in the chest. Both victims died at the scene. The jury deliberated a long time before finally returning a guilty verdict. Many felt she was justified, but the prosecutor maintained that even in a case like this, the wife had no right to dispense justice on her own terms.

The couple had no children of their own, and since they were both orphans from early infancy, there was no immediate family on either side. They grew up in the same group home, dating secretly in high school. According to prison records, she received no mail or phone calls for the past two years. Candidate three was a go.

Candidate number four was a black female, fifty years old, who had been in prison for twenty years awaiting death by lethal injection for the murder of her daughter, who was fourteen at the time the crime was committed. The trial transcript revealed the defendant came home early from a church meeting one Saturday morning to find her boyfriend in bed with her daughter. Because she loved the man so much, she believed his story about the girl coming on to him and always dressing sexy around the house whenever he was there. She believed her daughter was trying to steal her man, so she grabbed a kitchen knife and stabbed her daughter ten times in the chest. Then she cleaned herself up and went out to dinner with her boyfriend while her daughter bled to death on the living room floor. The jury came back with a conviction and death sentence after only one hour of deliberation.

The boyfriend died three years after her incarceration from an apparent drug overdose. She was an only child whose parents had been dead for ten years. The prison had no record of her receiving any mail or telephone calls since her final appeal ten years ago. Bob placed a large red check by her name, as candidate number four was a go.

Candidate number five was a Caucasian male, thirty-five years old, recently sentenced to life in prison for the murder of a police officer. According to the trial transcript, the defendant was in the process of robbing a convenience store when an off-duty police officer pulled his weapon and ordered the defendant to lay down his weapon. The defendant panicked and shot the police officer once in the chest. The officer died on route to the hospital. The jury sentenced the defendant to life in prison without the possibility of parole.

Based on the personal information in his file, this candidate seemed to have dropped into the system from thin air. There was little background information on him. The prison records showed he had been in several altercations with guards, and was constantly being placed in solitary confinement. He stated he had no family or friends during the interview, and seemed to be a genuine sociopath. The only telephone calls he made from prison were to an 800 number which turned out to be a phone sex operation. Apparently he was able to keep the payments current on his credit card from the money he earned in prison, which he used to fund his telephonic sexual activity. He almost seemed too good to be true for this operation, but without any negative data, candidate number five was a go.

The final candidate, candidate number six, was a black male, forty years old, serving a life sentence for the beating death of a security guard. The inmate broke into a warehouse to steal some electronic equipment, when he was surprised by the security guard on duty. The guard was armed with only a stun gun, so the inmate was able to overpower him. He grabbed a metal pipe lying on the floor and beat the guard about the head and upper body. The guard, who was sixty-one years old, died a week later from the injuries.

According to his file, the prisoner was divorced and had not spoken to his ex-wife in over five years. He received no mail or phone calls in the last two years. He was a loner in prison, staying away from others when in the exercise yard. He was a huge man at six feet five inches tall and weighing three hundred pounds. He will make the team completely diverse, thought Bob, as he smiled at the profile in front of him. Candidate number six was a go.

Bob exited the jet and walked to the limousine waiting for him just off the tarmac. As he climbed in, he noticed Harry was seated in the back as well. Harry Durbin was forty-two, mostly bald, except for some brown hair around the sides and back of his head. He was only five feet six inches tall, probably hired by Bob to have someone to look down at. He graduated from Harvard Law School, but always wanted to work in Washington in the political arena. One of his law professors who knew Bob well, placed a call to him, helping Harry initially get his foot in the door. After a grueling interview, Bob was convinced Harry had what it took to be a power broker some day, and would be the perfect person to groom in his own image.

Harry proved to be quite resourceful, and had already established many valuable contacts all over the country. Gorman could count on Harry to carry out whatever he ordered while maintaining a professional level of discretion. He also provided Bob with many of the ideas he took credit for as his own, but he never seemed to mind. He admired Bob and the way he handled himself professionally. In fact, Harry would probably walk through fire for him if he asked him to.

Bob had marked the top five candidates' files with a red check and handed the files to Harry, who compared the notes to his own. It appeared Harry had selected four of the same five, based solely on the background information they had without the benefit of the personal interview data. He had included candidate number two instead of number five, since there was little background information on candidate five.

"Looks like we're pretty much in agreement," said Bob as he looked at Harry.

"All but one," said Harry. "I didn't have a good feeling about candidate five, given the limited amount of information we could find on him. I take it the interview provided more insight into the psyche of this mystery candidate?"

"Yes, after speaking with him, I'm satisfied he's right for the team. Besides, I wasn't sure about number two's connection to the pen pal in Mississippi. I want you to check it out thoroughly just in case we need number two as a backup."

"I'll get on it right away," declared Harry. "Do you need me to look at any of the others, or are we good to go with them?"

"I believe we have all we need on these," said Bob. "Is everything in place?"

"Everything is ready and waiting on Colonel Wagoner's go ahead."

"How soon can we have them in place once we hear from Wagoner?"

"Within twenty-four hours."

"Good," said Bob. "Just be ready to go when I give the order."

"Yes sir," Harry answered.

"I have another assignment for you, Harry. But it will have to wait until we get back to the office. I'll give you the details then."

"No problem."

They rode the rest of the way in silence until they reached the White House. Bob's office was located in the West Wing of the White House where most of the President's close staff was located. Of course, Harry had an office just outside of Bob's so he could handle the affairs of the White House Chief of Staff.

They made their way through the building finally reaching Bob's office. Once inside, Harry closed the door behind them while Bob made his way to the desk. He sat down as Harry settled into one of the wing backed chairs across from him. He reached into his briefcase and retrieved a file with bold red lettering which read 'Confidential.' He handed the file to Harry and began his instructions.

"Harry, I'm concerned about the Vice President lately. I have heard on several occasions that he's involved in some sort of scheme to unseat the President and take over the White House in the next election. You know he and President Crawford rarely see eye to eye on the issues. In fact, they were primary opponents in the last election. President Crawford selected him as the running mate in order to take advantage of his strong following in the South. Between the two of them, they made a rather formidable ticket, but now I'm not so sure he can be trusted," sighed Bob.

"What do you want me to do?" asked Harry.

"I will be receiving information regarding secret military testing operations from Colonel Wagoner," he said. "I want you to make sure you find the link between them and the Vice President." Bob smiled. "Do you understand?"

"Perfectly," answered Harry, smiling back at Bob. He rose from his seat and headed back to his office to start laying the groundwork for the assignment Bob had just given him.

Vice President David Sims was a former Senator from Georgia. He had served three consecutive terms before announcing his candidacy for President of the United States. Although most of the country was unfamiliar with him, he was very popular among the southern states. As he began campaigning and appearing on the political news programs, his popularity, especially among young voters, grew exponentially. He ran second in the Iowa caucus, but by the time the primary was held in the South, he was very close to Crawford. When the convention began, it was clear Crawford would get the nomination, but Sims had made several good arguments that made voters question Crawford on some of the issues. Crawford's campaign manager knew it would be a much tougher road to the White House unless they could get the endorsement of Sims. And the only way to do that was to add him to the ticket as the Vice Presidential candidate.

David Sims was forty-nine years old, the son of hosiery mill workers. He was an only child, and grew up in an atmosphere of honesty and hard work. The Sims family attended church regularly, and were of the Southern Baptist faith. His parents made sure he went to college because they wanted more for him than they had. David worked hard during college, holding down two jobs to help pay for tuition. He graduated near the top of his class at Emory University, where he majored in political science. Sims went on to law school at the University of North Carolina, and after graduation, joined a prestigious law firm in Atlanta. It was not long before the political bug bit David and he began his political career in the state legislature.

His no-nonsense style and straight forward speaking earned him the nickname "The Truth," which he used in his campaigns. People found him to be genuine and honest and believed what he said. Every promise he ever made during his campaigns for Senate, he delivered. He believed in being a man of his word. None of his colleagues to date ever questioned his integrity. And yet, now Bob Gorman was alluding to corruption and conspiracy by the man known by many as "The Truth."

Harry began placing calls to test the waters regarding the Vice President and his agenda lately. Where had he been traveling? Who did he meet with? Had he been to any military bases, and if so, which ones? Harry also placed a call to the cleaning crew, as the CIA were sometimes affectionately called, to order the Vice President's office be wired per authorization of the President and the Attorney General. Even if the bugs never revealed any incriminating evidence, the mere fact they were in place gave some credence to Bob's allegations in the eyes of the CIA.

While Harry was running his little covert operation, Bob had a meeting with the President. Actually, they were playing pool in the billiard room, as President Crawford tried to unwind from another hectic day. Ever since he had been elected to the office of President of the United States, he felt as if everyone wanted a piece of him. It was as if he was supposed to solve all of the world's problems without help from anyone. Now he knew how Superman must have felt, only Crawford did not possess any supernatural powers. "Boy, what a day!" began Crawford.

"Anything I can help with, Mr. President?" asked Bob. "Only if you can single-handedly bring peace to the Middle East," sighed Crawford. "The fighting between Syria and Israel resumed today, causing the death toll to rise more in one day than it has since the fighting began. The United Nations is looking to us to step in and initiate peace talks. It's funny how they didn't support us against Iraq, but now want us to play policeman to the world," laughed the President.

"Well that comes with the territory, Mr. President."

"Any suggestions on how we should handle it, Bob?"

"I'd stay out of it for now. Wasn't Israel simply defending its border by retaliating against an air strike launched by Syria without provocation?" he asked. "I mean, surely they should have the right to defend themselves."

"I agree," said Crawford. "And that's exactly what I told the UN, but they insist on the United States becoming involved in the peace process. I told them that as soon as Israel is ready to sit down to peace talks, we will be glad to assist them in any way we can."

"Sounds to me like you've got it covered, Mr. President. Eight ball in the corner pocket," Bob continued, as he sank the shot and won his second straight match against Crawford. "Mr. President, I don't believe your mind is on the game today."

"I'm sorry, Bob," he said, tossing his cue stick onto the table. "Do you have any good news for me regarding your plan to solve all the nation's ills and make me a hero?"

"Patience, Mr. President," chuckled Bob. "Saving the nation takes time and a lot of hard work."

"Well it couldn't happen soon enough for me," said Crawford. "How about some dinner Bob?" he asked, motioning toward the dining room.

Chapter 7

Pearl Harbor, Hawaii

Macy caught the first flight out the following day from Lexington and made the long journey back to Hawaii for her meeting with Commander Thomas. She had given him no set day and time because she wanted to be able to rest and refresh so she would be alert, just in case the meeting evolved into an interrogation. Macy was unable to rest during the trip, and was extremely anxious to get off the plane once it landed at the airport. She hurried with her carry-on and exited the plane as quickly as possible.

Macy retrieved her luggage from baggage claims and walked outside to the taxi area, hopped in a cab, directing the driver to take her to her apartment. The cab drivers were very familiar with the location of Macy's apartment complex since many of the military personnel lived there and usually took taxis to and from the airport when traveling.

It did not take long for the taxi to reach Macy's apartment complex, as the driver turned into the parking lot and pulled alongside the curb in front of her building. He removed her suitcase from the trunk and placed it on the curb while Macy rummaged through her purse for money to pay the taxi fare and a nice tip for the driver. He climbed back into the cab and sped off in the direction of the airport while Macy made her way to her apartment. It was mid-afternoon, Hawaii time, so she felt certain Gordon would still be on the base. This would give her time to get in and get settled, and hopefully, he wouldn't know she was back in town.

Macy collected her mail from the central mailbox station outside her group of apartments, and made her way to the door. She searched intently for the tiny thread she had placed in the door to make sure it was still in place, indicating no one had been in her apartment while she was gone. She let out a sigh of relief as she saw it was exactly how she had left it. She entered her apartment, securely locking the door behind her. She carried her luggage to the bedroom and left it lying on the floor, deciding there was plenty of time to unpack later. Macy was vibrating from too little sleep and too much anxiety, so she walked to the bathroom and began running water for a bath.

As the tub filled with warm water, Macy added some bath oil to help soothe and replenish her skin. She began to undress in the bedroom, as the water continued to pour into the tub. She had worn a pair of jeans and a knit blouse on her return trip, knowing she was not heading straight for the base and did not need to dress in uniform. Macy preferred to travel in civilian clothes as much as possible, especially since there were so many people who were not very fond of the military these days.

Macy pulled the knit blouse over her head, tossing it to the floor. Unsnapping the clasp in the front of her bra, she exposed her creamy slightly upturned breasts, sighing from the relief at freeing them from the pressure of being restricted for hours. Macy stepped out of her sandals, and slipped out of her jeans, now clothed only in the black thong that matched her bra. She grabbed the thong along the side straps and slid it down her legs, leaving it lying in the floor as she stepped out of it and walked back to the bathroom.

By the time Macy returned to the tub, the water had reached a sufficient level to suit her needs, so she turned the tap causing the water to cease flowing. She eased into the tub, feeling the warmth caress her body. The bath oil felt silky against her skin, and she could feel her soft flesh regenerating to its tight and supple form. She didn't realize how tired she was until she eased back in the tub, resting her head against the end. She felt her muscles begin to unwind beneath the shroud of warm milky water.

Macy closed her eyes, completely relaxed as she stretched out in the tub. As the water began to cool, she drained some of the old water out, running fresh hot water to keep the temperature at a perfect level. She didn't want to finish her bath so soon; as she was feeling the most relaxed she had felt for a while.

Eventually, Macy climbed out of the tub, pulling the plug to allow the water to drain away. She grabbed the plush soft towel she had placed beside the tub and began to dry her body thoroughly. Then she hung the towel across the gold metal bar against the bathroom wall and walked back in the bedroom. Although the bath oil had done an excellent job softening her body, Macy decided she needed some moisturizing lotion to add the finishing touch.

She reached for the bottle she kept on the night stand and lay down on her bed, squeezing some of the lotion into her hand. She worked the lotion between her hands to warm it some before beginning to coat her body. Macy began at her feet and worked her way up. After a few minutes her body relaxed and she crashed from the release of pressure that had built up over the past few days. Macy needed the rest, as she slept for hours before being abruptly awakened by the sound of someone beating on her door.

Macy stood up from the bed and grabbed her robe, pulling it around her body as she walked to the door. She peered through the peephole to find Gordon standing outside, apparently just arriving from the base since he was still in uniform. He beat on her door again and called her name, but Macy did not respond. She still had no desire to talk to him. Eventually he gave up, assuming she was probably still out of town, and walked down the hall to his apartment.

Macy walked to the kitchen and grabbed a beer from the fridge. Then she opened the freezer and removed a frozen lasagna dinner, placing it in the microwave to heat. She sipped her beer as the frozen dinner turned round and round inside the microwave for several minutes until it beeped, signaling it was ready. Macy removed the dinner and opened the plastic cover to allow the steam inside to escape, as it billowed up in front of her. She let it cool for a few minutes before taking a bite.

As she ate, Macy thought to herself, this is how single people live. While she and Gordon were together, they had cooked real meals together, experimenting with new recipes. They had also gone out of town several times to restaurants where they felt certain they would not be recognized. Now she was reduced to a beer and a microwave meal since cooking and going out were not much fun alone.

Macy scooped up her carton of lasagna, grabbed her beer, and headed to the easy chair in front of the television. She flipped through the channels trying to find something interesting to watch. After going through the entire selection twice, Macy finally settled on an old Perry Mason movie. She had always loved courtroom dramas, but suddenly found she was nervous at the prospect of becoming entangled in her own personal trial. "It's just an interview," she kept telling herself, refusing to believe it would amount to anything more serious than that.

Suddenly the telephone rang, startling Macy as she jumped in her seat. She did not recognize the number displayed on her caller I.D., so she decided to answer it.

"Hello," she said into the receiver.

"Seaman Merit, this is Commander Thomas," said the voice at the other end of the line. "I trust you had a good flight."

"It was fine, sir," answered Macy, trying to remain on guard.

"I was hoping you would be available tomorrow so we could meet again," he said. "As I explained before, there are a few details we need to discuss so I can clear up this investigation. I'm sure we all want to put this behind us as quickly as possible."

"Certainly sir," said Macy. "How about eleven hundred tomorrow?"

"That sounds fine," answered Thomas. "We will meet in Captain Landreau's office."

And with that, he ended the call. Macy placed the receiver back into its cradle and turned her attention back to the movie, but had trouble focusing after Commander Thomas' call. She wondered why they were meeting in the Captain's office instead of one of the conference rooms, but maybe she was just being paranoid.

Macy finished her meal and decided to read for a little while before going to bed. She was tired of television and hoped she would be able to immerse herself in a good book to ease her anxiety over tomorrow's meeting with Commander Thomas. She began reading the first chapter of the new book she bought at the airport during her layover on her trip back to Hawaii, but she was unable to concentrate as she kept mulling over her statement in her mind. She could not help but wonder what else Commander Thomas needed to discuss with her. After all, he had her statement. Surely by now he had talked with Gordon, as well as Simon and Johnson. Why was he not ready to make a determination regarding the 15-6 investigation based on the information at hand? Macy wondered what more she could possibly add to the investigation.

Macy decided she could 'what if' all night, but realized she needed sleep in order to be ready for tomorrow. Perhaps she was worrying about nothing, and Commander Thomas was simply ready to announce his findings to all of the parties involved. Yes, that had to be it, she decided. That's why he wants to meet in Captain Landreau's office. Feeling as if she had resolved the conflict in her mind, she retired to her bedroom for the night. It was just a matter of minutes before she was sound asleep.

Macy was on top of Gordon as their bodies writhed together as one. It was the best feeling she had in a long time as he held her closer to him, his breath warm upon her neck. Suddenly, he rolled her over, settling on top of her in one smooth motion. Pinning her arms above her head, he reached behind his back and pulled a knife from somewhere in the sheets. He stabbed her once in the chest, and repeatedly plunged the knife forward into her body as she began to scream.

Macy sat straight up in bed, her entire body soaked with sweat. Her heart was pounding so hard it felt as if it would jump out of her chest. It was the same nightmare she had at George's, causing her to scream out in the night. Trembling with fear, she tried to clear the cobwebs from her brain. She examined her body as if expecting to find wounds from the knife Gordon was wielding in her dream. Her breathing began to slow as she realized there were no cuts on her body. It had, in fact, all been a dream. She looked at the clock. It was four-thirty in the morning.

Not eager to return to her nightmare, Macy got up and walked to the kitchen to make a cup of tea, rubbing her hand through her red tousled hair. She was still shaking as she filled the kettle with water, spilling some as she placed it on the stove. She paced around the room until the kettle began to whistle, announcing the water had reached the boiling point. Macy removed the kettle from the stove and poured the hot water over the tea bag she had placed in her mug. Then she returned the kettle to the stove and began dipping the tea bag up and down into the steaming cup.

Once the tea was ready, she poured some sugar into the cup, stirring it gently to mix it in thoroughly. She grabbed the mug in both of her hands, lifting it from the counter to feel the warmth from within. Macy walked slowly to the easy chair, stopping to take a sip along the way. Then she settled into the chair and turned on the television. She needed some sound to comfort her and make her feel as if she were not alone.

After watching a thirty minute infomercial while finishing her tea, Macy decided she might as well take a shower and get dressed. There was no need to lie back down now that she was fully awake. Besides, she did not want the nightmare to return. She took off her robe and tossed it on the bed as she passed through the bedroom on her way to the shower. She turned the water on hot and stepped inside, letting the warmth caress her body. The steam rose around her, clearing her head of the cobwebs she awoke with earlier. Macy lingered longer than usual, as she enjoyed the liquid heat cascading over her shoulders and down her body.

Stepping out of the shower, she dried her body with the towel she'd placed on the rack the night before. She walked to her bedroom and opened her dresser, carefully selecting what she would wear underneath her uniform. She decided on a pair of pink French-cut panties and matching bra. She delicately slid into the panties, pulling them up to her waist. Pulling the bra around her, she fastened it in the front. She grabbed her pink garter belt from her lingerie drawer and stepped into it, also bringing it up to her waist. She slid black stockings over her smooth shapely legs, attaching them to the straps on the garter belt. Since the uniform she would wear today was slacks, the color of her hose did not matter.

Macy pulled on her robe, deciding to wait until later to put on her uniform. After all, the meeting was not until eleven, and she was still technically on leave. She walked from the bedroom to the kitchen and retrieved a box of cereal from the cupboard, pouring some into a bowl she had placed on the counter. After placing the cereal back inside the cupboard, Macy went to the fridge and took out the carton of milk, pouring some over the cereal. She grabbed a small glass out of the cabinet and poured orange juice into it and sat down at the bar to eat.

She was finally getting her nerves to settle down as she ate her breakfast. She began to think about the meeting with Commander Thomas and immediately consoled herself with the belief he was merely going to declare his findings and be on his way. Suddenly, Macy felt her stomach burn as if something were not right. She began to get nervous again, as she contemplated several different scenarios of how the meeting could possibly go. She just sighed, shook her head, and told herself to get it together.

Macy decided to call George for some moral support. She dialed his number and waited expectantly while it rang two times before he picked up.

"Hello," said George, rather sleepily into the phone. "I'm sorry, George," said Macy, suddenly realizing the time zone difference. "Go back to sleep."

"I'm already awake now," he yawned. "Is something wrong?"

"No. Not really," said Macy. "I just wanted to call you before my meeting with Commander Thomas today."

"What time is the meeting?"

"Eleven," said Macy sheepishly, knowing she could have waited before calling George. "I know it's probably nothing," she continued, "but I've got that feeling in my gut I usually get when something's not quite right."

"And just how accurate is your gut?" he asked, although he already knew the answer to his question. She had predicted many things which came true when they were children based solely on her gut feelings. She even had that feeling before they were told about their parents' death.

"Well, lately it's been dead on," she sighed.

"Just relax, Macy," he encouraged. "Worst case scenario is you can always resign your commission and come home."

"If I don't end up in the brig."

"Look, you've done nothing wrong," assured George. "Don't worry."

"Thanks, George," said Macy. "I guess I just needed to hear that from you. You always know how to make me feel better. Now, go back to sleep." She laughed as she hung up the phone yet her conversation with George seemed to have no effect on the burning in her stomach. Either way, eleven o'clock was fast approaching, and it would all be over shortly thereafter, or possibly just the beginning, depending on the outcome.

Macy removed her robe and laid it on the bed then carefully retrieved her uniform from the closet, handling it delicately in order to maintain its neatly pressed appearance. She slid it on over her undergarments and fastened the buttons before going to the bathroom to apply a soft hint of makeup and brush her teeth and hair. Now she was ready to go.

As she walked from the bathroom into the bedroom, the phone began to ring. She recognized the number on her caller ID as Captain Landreau's office. Macy picked up the receiver, realizing she was on the speaker.

"Hello," said Macy.

"Seaman Merit, this is Commander Thomas," he said. "I know we scheduled our meeting for eleven hundred this morning, but something has come up. Would it be possible for you to come now to the Captain's office for our meeting?"

"Certainly sir," replied Macy, almost choking on her words.

"Very good," said Thomas. "I will see you shortly."

Thomas ended the call, leaving Macy staring into space for what seemed an eternity as her moment of truth had suddenly been moved up. Her guts were really burning now, as Commander Thomas' phone call had caught her completely off guard. She blinked hard to break herself out of the trance, knowing she needed to focus and calm her nerves before the meeting. She would have to rehearse her answers in the car as she drove to the base. The only problem was she did not know what the questions would be. Macy let out a long sigh, grabbed her purse, and headed for the door.

CHAPTER 8

WASHINGTON, DC

Bob exhaled a long sigh as he looked over the dossiers Harry had provided on the lab technicians from Annapolis. The list read like a 'Who's Who' of lab rats, each with their own set of accomplishments and accolades. But it was not the good points he was interested in. Instead, he was searching for the character flaws in each candidate. It was necessary to determine not only how proficient they were in their jobs, but how far they were willing to go in following an order from a superior, and how loyal they would be to their leader. These were qualities not everyone possessed, but Bob considered them to be of utmost importance if the operation was going to succeed. It was absolutely crucial that he select the right people for the task, given the high level of security surrounding this. None of the work performed in the lab could be discussed, not even among themselves, let alone with someone from the outside. Even a small leak within the team could undermine the entire operation, bringing down the President and the current administration in the process.

Bob made two stacks, one made up of culls considered to be either too noble or too renegade to trust as members of the team. The other stack contained potential candidates that would need to be carefully questioned before a team could be selected from among them. When he was finished with his initial review, he had twenty possible candidates from over one hundred Harry had originally submitted. That was the easy part. Now he had to begin the arduous task of interviewing each of the twenty candidates in order to select the best ten for the operation. He lifted the receiver from its cradle and punched some numbers on the phone, and began speaking. "Harry, I need you to make the necessary arrangements for the interviews. I have the final candidate files ready," and with that, he hung up and leaned back in his chair. It was only a matter of seconds before there was a light knock on the door and Harry entered, flashing a smile at Bob, who kept his same expressionless face as he handed the stack of files to Harry. Harry's smile melted into a solemn countenance as he took the files and walked out of the office, closing the door behind him.

Bob spent the next hour reviewing the President's schedule, making any necessary telephone calls to arrange the most efficient use of the President's time. He had just finished when Harry buzzed to let him know the interviews were scheduled for the day after tomorrow. The meetings would take place at a small motel just outside of Baltimore where Harry had already booked a room under an assumed name. Bob's face broke into a smile of relief as he felt another cog being put into place in his operation machine. Now he had just over one day to prepare the questions he would use to interrogate the candidates. He left strict orders with Harry not to be disturbed for the rest of the day as he began to formulate his plans for the interviews.

PEARL HARBOR, HAWAII

Macy knocked firmly on Captain Landreau's door, and waited for the familiar "Enter" from within. She opened the door to see Captain Landreau seated in his usual position and Commander Thomas standing to the Captain's right, facing the door. Macy closed the door behind her and came to attention in front of the Captain's desk.

"At ease, Seaman," said Landreau, paused a moment and continued, "please take a seat."

Macy sat down in one of the chairs facing the Captain. She noticed neither Captain Landreau nor Commander Thomas exhibited any facial expression, which was typical for military operations, lest a soldier should tip his hand to the enemy. Based on her observations, Macy concluded she must be the enemy at this skirmish, which did not bode well for her situation.

"Seaman Merit," Commander Thomas began, "I have read your report regarding the alleged incident involving Commander McCain and an unidentified foreign national. I must say, these are very serious accusations given the lack of evidence to support your statement. Are you prepared to offer any additional evidence at this time that will substantiate your claim?"

"No sir," replied Macy. "All I have is my word."

"Seaman, do you recognize this?" asked Landreau, holding up a necklace Gordon had given Macy for her birthday. "It looks like a necklace someone gave me for my last birthday," said Macy. "But mine seems to be missing somehow."

"That's because Commander McCain took the liberty of removing it from your apartment the last time he was there," said Landreau, "along with these." He held up a couple of pictures of Gordon and Macy together.

"I don't understand, sir," said Macy.

"Then let me spell it out for you," said Commander Thomas, as he placed his hands on the corner of the Captain's desk and leaned closer toward Macy. "You and Commander McCain were having an affair when he decided to break it off. That's when you decided to file this report against him in retaliation. Isn't that true, Seaman?"

Macy hesitated for a second. "No, sir. I mean, yes, we were having an affair, but he didn't break it off. I did after he killed that foreign national."

"Come on, Seaman," said Thomas. "Your fellow team members all agreed with Commander McCain's version of what happened, right down to the little meeting you two had on the sub just after you picked up the foreign national."

"That's impossible," said Macy. "I waited until the others were in their cabins before I went to Commander..." and then her voice trailed off, as she realized she was admitting to what the others had already testified to.

"So you admit that what the others said about you meeting with Commander McCain on the sub was true?" asked Commander Thomas as he pressed on.

Macy knew she was caught as she responded with a simple, "Yes sir."

"I must say, I'm terribly disappointed in your behavior, Seaman," said Landreau.

"I'm sorry," replied Macy. "But my statement about the operation and Commander McCain is true. I stake my reputation and honor on it."

"Well, in light of the fact you disobeyed military protocol and lied about it," said Commander Thomas, "your honor and reputation are of little value."

"The Alpha Team was the best special ops group I have had in a while," said Landreau, shaking his head. "It's a disgrace to have it destroyed by a scandal like this."

"Seaman Merit, I'm sure you understand the policy the Navy has regarding personal involvement between commanding officers and their subordinates," said Thomas.

"Yes sir," replied Macy.

"In order to spare the Navy from further embarrassment in this matter, Captain Landreau and I have reached an understanding as to how to handle this situation," continued Thomas. "You may resign your commission immediately and forfeit all military benefits and you will be spared from court martial proceedings. We believe this is more than fair, considering the seriousness of the charges that could be levied against you, Seaman."

"Court martial? I don't understand. I didn't think having an affair with my superior was grounds for court martial."

"That in and of itself is not, but possession of stolen merchandise, breaking and entering, and burglary are," said Thomas, holding up the necklace McCain had taken from her apartment.

"But that's mine. That was a gift."

"Wrong, Seaman Merit. This belongs to Commander McCain's wife, and she will testify to that if it becomes necessary. There are at least two other witnesses that will testify to your bragging about breaking into their home and stealing the necklace. Now, I believe it is best for all parties concerned, especially you, that you resign your commission and put this behind you."

"Wife," gasped Macy. "I didn't..."

"Oh, you didn't know Commander McCain was married?" Thomas smiled. Macy lowered her head for a moment then looked back up at Thomas.

"What about Commander McCain?" Macy asked.

"We will deal with him similarly regarding the matter between the two of you," said Thomas. "Of course, the allegations about Commander Mc-Cain killing the foreign national are unsubstantiated, and therefore will be dropped."

"But sir, I know what I saw," insisted Macy.

"Even if it were true, Seaman," Commander Thomas continued, "your behavior with Commander McCain has made it impossible for a panel of peers to objectively rely on any testimony you give in this matter. With the statements of the other team members, there is no way we could ever prove Commander McCain is guilty of killing this person in cold blood." Thomas let out a sigh.

"So he just gets a free pass?" said Macy, an expression of disgust washing over her face.

"I assure you, Seaman, we will deal with Commander McCain," said Thomas sternly. "If I were you, I'd be more concerned about myself and be glad to get out of this situation as lightly as you have."

"I'll have Ensign Waters prepare your discharge papers. They should be ready by twelve hundred hours which will give you time to clean out your station. You can sign them today, but of course, you know it will take several weeks to process your discharge. I understand you have quite a bit of leave available. I am comfortable granting you the remainder of your leave time accumulated so you won't need to report back here. That will be all, Seaman."

"Aye, aye sir," said Macy, as she stood, turned on her heels, and walked steadily out of the office. Once she was outside with the door closed behind her, she almost collapsed in a heap. She grabbed hold of the nearest desk to steady herself, her head still spinning from Commander Thomas' statements floating around her brain. As she made her way to her desk and began to carefully place her personal items in a cardboard box, she suddenly realized it was all over. She didn't have to wrestle with the decision of whether to retire her commission as George had suggested. The decision had been made for her, yet there was no feeling of relief. All Macy wanted to do was sit down and cry, but she could not show her emotions in front of the staff. She would make her exit just as strongly as the day she first walked in. No one would be able to question her intestinal fortitude in the face of adversity. After all, she had faced tougher enemies in her time. Maybe, she thought bitterly, this is just the thing she needed to motivate her to finally strike out on her own to help others, as she professed was her calling for several years now. "Always look for the positive," she told herself, as she placed the last item in the box.

Macy carried the box to her car, and returned to Ensign Water's station to sign her discharge papers. She would soon be a civilian again, unfettered by the Navy's chain of command. She reasoned this moment must be akin to a prisoner's release ... on one hand, the relief of a weight being lifted from one's shoulders, while on the other hand, the anxiety over the uncertainty of what to do next. Much like a baby's first steps, it was time for her to walk on her own into the world of ordinary citizenship. Macy walked to her car almost robotic, barely acknowledging the half-hearted nods from passing team members as she continued on her way, shrouded by a fog of unreality. She did not even remember getting into her vehicle and driving off the base. It was not until she had driven a mile before she suddenly snapped to attention, almost flipping her car as she slammed on the brakes and turned sharply to the side of the road. The motorists behind her blasted their horns in expression of their disapproval of her sudden movement, then sped on past her. Macy dropped her head to her chest, sobbing uncontrollably, as she relived the meeting in Captain Landreau's office, the embarrassment of the situation, and the piercing character assassination by Commander Thomas. She was overwhelmed by a feeling of worthlessness as she digested the fact she had been summarily dismissed from the Navy and what she thought would be her career. She shuddered as she felt the cold blanket of loneliness spread over her, enveloping her in a sea of despair. She took a few moments to wipe the tears from her eyes and get composed enough to pull back onto the highway and head to her apartment.

Once inside her apartment, Macy broke down again, tears streaming down her cheeks, as she dropped the cardboard box on the kitchen floor. She sat down in the middle of the floor and buried her face in her hands, sobbing the word 'why' over and over, as her body shook with grief. Her entire world had come crashing down in just a week's time, from losing her boyfriend, to her career, and finally to her dignity. Macy cried for what seemed like hours until she felt she had no tears left inside her. She stood up and walked to the refrigerator to get a beer, then deciding she needed something stronger, reached for the bottle of bourbon she kept in the pantry. She unscrewed the cap and poured some in a glass, quickly downing the amber liquid, as she filled the glass again. She made her way to the couch where she turned on the television and continued to drown her sorrow. Macy was not the type to get drunk on a regular basis, but under the circumstances, she felt intoxication was the only thing that would ease her pain at the moment. She continued to drink until she passed out. At least this way, she would be able to escape her grief while she slept off the effects of the bourbon.

The next morning, Macy could barely open her eyes as she awoke with a terrible hangover, causing her head to ache as if it would explode. Her mouth was dry as cotton as she felt the rhythm of her heart pulsing through her brain producing a searing pain with every beat. She decided to have a little hair of the dog, and she remembered why she drank the day before. It was not long until she was crying again and drinking straight from the bottle. Finishing the bourbon, she desperately scrounged around in the pantry until she found two bottles of vodka. By now, the alcohol had dulled her taste, so she needed no mixer, as she poured the alcohol down her throat in hopes of washing away the pain of yesterday's memory. Soon she was out again, this time for several hours. She had enough alcohol in her apartment to continue this cycle for at least three more days. As she drained the first bottle of vodka, Macy wondered exactly how many days it would take before she could muster up the courage to even look in the mirror, then decided that could wait, as she unscrewed the cap on the second bottle.

CHAPTER 9

BALTIMORE, MARYLAND

Bob Gorman had just finished interviewing the final candidate for the ten lab technicians he needed for his operation. By now he was an expert at interviews, and therefore was able to narrow his choices as he went through the process. Now that he had concluded the last interview, he had his list of ten. He grabbed his cell phone and punched in the number to his office.

"Harry, I've got the list and am on my way back to Washington."

"Great," said Harry. "Everything is ready on this end."

"What about the payroll situation?"

"That is set up as well."

"Good work. I'll see you soon," he said, ending the call. He placed the files in his briefcase and left the hotel room. He took a car to the airport and was soon flying on the private jet back to Washington.

As soon as he entered the office, Harry appeared, taking the list Bob handed him and disappearing back into his office. Bob closed his door and sat down behind his desk, rubbing his face in his hands. When he looked up, he had a self-satisfied smile on his face. "Everything is falling into place," he said to himself, as he reached into his bottom desk drawer and pulled out a bottle of scotch and a glass. He poured a congratulatory shot and lit a victory cigar, propping his feet up on the desk as he leaned back in his chair. After a few minutes, there was a soft knock on the door and Harry stepped quickly inside. He handed the list back to Bob and informed him that everything was set. Then he retreated back to his office, leaving Bob alone to pat himself on the back.

He picked up the phone and dialed the number to Colonel Wagoner's private line at Lackland. "Colonel, this is Bob Gorman. I've assembled my team and am ready to begin phase one of the operation. Is everything I ordered there?"

"Everything is here and in order, Mr. Gorman," said Wagoner.

"Excellent," he replied, smiling. "My team and I will arrive the day after tomorrow to begin the animal tests. Did you change the entry protocol as I instructed?"

"Yes, Mr. Gorman. Only you, I, and Major Harris have access to the experimental area of the lab."

"Well done, Colonel. We'll see you when we land," said Bob, and then hung up the phone. He poured another scotch and took a few puffs from the cigar, unable to contain the smile that flashed across his face.

Pearl Harbor, Hawaii

George arrived at Macy's apartment and knocked on the door. He waited a couple of seconds then loudly pounded on the door. There was no sound coming from inside so he took one step back and kicked the door in. He ran into the apartment frantically calling her name as he began searching from room to room. He shuddered from the sudden chill that ran up his spine when he entered the bathroom. His sister was lying on the floor in a pool of vomit. He quickly checked for a pulse and made sure she was breathing. He let out a sigh of relief once he determined she was still alive. He had tried to call her for the last couple of days to see how her meeting with Commander Thomas went, but he became worried when he was unable to reach her and decided to fly to Hawaii and check on her in person. He was glad he did when he saw the shape she was in. Another few days like this and she very well could have died.

George lifted her from the floor and helped her to the shower, where he proceeded to run cold water all over her to sober her up. Macy screamed as the cold water shocked her senses. She struggled with her brother in an attempt to get free and flee the cold water, but she was in no shape to put up much of a fight as he firmly held her under the icy torrent. When he was satisfied she was awake enough, he turned off the water and handed her a towel to dry off with. Then he left her alone so she could dress while he went to the kitchen to make some strong coffee.

Macy looked at George through red, puffy eyes as she entered the kitchen. He thought she looked like someone who had the flu for a week. He could tell she was hurting from the days of self-abuse, but was not about to let her see his sympathy. He pointed to a chair for her to sit in and shoved a cup of black coffee in front of her, instructing her to drink. She looked up at him again with those sad eyes, but he sternly pointed to the coffee and told her again to drink it. She took the cup with both hands and lifted it to her lips, sipping it first to make sure it was not too hot. She grimaced at the first taste, which assured he'd made it strong enough. Realizing she was going to have to drink it all, even if he had to pour it down her throat, she gave in and began taking larger sips.

George remained silent until she was well into her second cup. "I take it your meeting with Commander Thomas did not go well." Macy shook her head no as she took another sip. George decided to press on. "Well, tell me about it."

"Do I have to?" she asked pitifully.

"Look Macy, I'm not here to bust your chops," he said. "I'm your brother and I'm concerned about you. Frankly, I was scared to death when I found you in the bathroom."

"I'm sorry," said Macy, touching his arm. "I didn't mean to scare you like that."

"I love you, Macy. I know it sounds like a cliché, but it will help to talk about it."

"I love you, too," Macy said, smiling up at George.

"Thank you for coming." Then Macy proceeded to tell him everything about the meeting with Commander Thomas and Captain Landreau. She told him how betrayed she felt by Gordon, and how she hit bottom when she realized she had lost everything.

George remained expressionless as he listened attentively to Macy's recount of the entire conversation. Then he assured her she had not lost everything, but still had him and he would always be there for her. She put her arms around him and hugged him tight, as if she were afraid to let go. He held her until she released her grip and sat back in her chair.

"What do I do now?" asked Macy. "Where do I go from here?"

"Why don't you move in with me for a while until you figure out your next move?" asked George. "I have plenty of room, and quite frankly, I'd welcome the company."

"Thanks, George. That's so sweet of you," said Macy, as she leaned over and kissed him on the cheek. She finished her coffee and stood up from the chair, having to catch her balance by leaning against the table as her head began spinning like a top. George grabbed her arm to help steady her until the dizziness passed. He helped her to the bedroom so she could lie down while he packed her clothes. Once he had packed her essentials, he went to the apartment manager to inform them she was leaving and they could do whatever they wanted with the furniture. He paid them for the cost to repair the door, plus extra to dispose of the furniture and an additional month's rent for their trouble. He and Macy took a cab to the airport to catch the next flight back to the states. They had to wait an hour before the next flight to Los Angeles, so she rested her head on George's shoulder while he read a newspaper. Once they were airborne, Macy continued to drink coffee as she tried to clear the cobwebs from her head. George bought her a sandwich at LAX while they waited for their connecting flight. It was the first thing besides alcohol she had put in her stomach in the last few days. By the time they were on the last leg of their journey back to Lexington, she was starting to feel more like her old self.

Once they made it back to George's house, Macy took a hot bath and went straight to bed. She needed some quality sleep after her ordeal, and besides, she had plenty of time to decide what to do with her life. George was relieved to have her back in Kentucky where he could keep an eye on her, at least until she was over her depression. He decided to call his supervisor and request a few days off since he did not want to leave her alone. He retired for the night as well.

Macy felt a strong hand grip her shoulder and the warmth of a man's breath on her neck as she felt soft, wet kisses across her shoulders. She turned as Gordon pulled her on top of him, firmly planting his lips on hers. She dug her nails into his flesh as she writhed on top of him, matching his movements in perfect rhythm. She was panting for breath as she felt wave after wave of passion explode within her body. She relaxed her grip on his strong shoulders as he grabbed her sides, deftly turning her body over until he was on top of her. She could feel his passion and strength as he continued to pleasure her body. Suddenly, he paused for a moment as if catching his breath. He reached behind him with his right hand as he held her by the throat with his left. She saw the reflection of the moon glimmer against the blade of the knife as he thrust it down in one quick motion, burying it deep into her chest. She tried to scream, but could only hear a gurgling noise coming from her mouth as the blood pooled in her throat. He removed the knife and plunged it into her again and again, stabbing her repeatedly as she tried to struggle helplessly against his strength. As her body began to weaken from the loss of blood, she could feel the tears streaming down her cheeks while she tried desperately for one last breath; just enough wind to alert anyone within earshot of her need for help. In moments, she felt him pull her up into a sitting position as she let out a blood curdling scream.

Macy opened her eyes expecting to see blood everywhere, and realized it was not Gordon who held her, but George. Every nerve in her body was shaking as he rocked her gently, his arms wrapped tightly around her sweat-soaked skin. He kept telling her over and over that it was just a nightmare and she was okay. It took a few minutes for her to come to the realization it had indeed been a dream, especially since it all seemed so real. She began to describe the dream in detail to George, but was soon overcome with emotion as she began crying again. She was shaking and snubbing just like a child, as he continued to hold her in his arms. He tried once to let go long enough to go to the kitchen and heat a glass of milk for her, but she grabbed him so tightly he was sure he would have a bruise the next morning. After a little coaxing, he lay down beside her and gently stroked her hair until she fell asleep, completely physically and emotionally drained from the entire ordeal. She would repeat the dream twice more in the night, but both times George was able to awaken her before they became as bad as the first. After that, he was glad he had stayed with her during the night. At least she was able to get some rest.

Macy awoke the next morning to find she was alone.

Her body ached all over as if she had the flu, but she knew she did not have a fever. She could smell the aroma of freshly brewed coffee coming from the kitchen as she rolled over. Sitting on the edge of the bed, she could feel her heartbeat pulsing in her head. Obviously, she was still suffering the after-effects of the last few days of alcohol consumption. She waited for a few minutes to compose herself before standing and shakily making her way to the bathroom. Wrapping a robe around her body, she stumbled to the kitchen, where George sat reading the newspaper. When he saw her, he got up quickly to help her into a chair, and poured her a cup of hot coffee. She held the warm cup carefully in her hands, sipping slowly, breathing the steam into her nostrils to help clear her head.

"How do you feel?" asked George.

"I've felt better," replied Macy, trying hard to offer a half-hearted smile.

"You had a pretty rough night."

"I vaguely remember you waking me from a nightmare. But my head is still so foggy, I'm not sure what's real and what's not."

"It's the depression," said George. "Just give it some time."

"Well, it appears I will have plenty of that on hand," said Macy, again trying to smile.

"I know this is hard for you, Macy. But it's not the end of the world."

"I know you're right. But it sure feels like it."

"I took some time off. I thought we could kick back and spend some time together. No pressure, just take it easy while you get back on your feet."

"Thanks, George," she said. "I can really use someone to talk to."

"I think we should just hang out around here today. You look like you could use another day just to lie around and rest."

"Thanks, I'm still a little shaky from the whole ordeal."

George poured her another cup of coffee, then returned to his newspaper while she sat in silence. Macy smiled a faint smile as she thought about how lucky she was to have a brother like George. She glanced in his direction, but he was deeply immersed in the sports section. She finished her coffee and stood up from the table. He folded the paper and looked up at her as if to say "What can I do now?" She touched him on the shoulder as she walked over to the couch and sat down. He followed her into the living room, settling into the recliner.

"Can I get you anything?" he asked.

"No," she answered. "I just want to sit here for a while."

She stared out the window across the field as the grass swayed back and forth in the breeze. The slow pace of country living was an inviting change from the hectic world of Naval Intelligence. Finally, she felt her muscles relax and the tension begin to slowly melt away. Although it had only been a few days since her meeting with Commander Thomas, she felt strangely at ease, as if a lot of time had passed since then. Inside, she was still heartbroken, but outwardly, she was no longer crying. She realized life still held many more adventures for her, but it would be a long journey back from the inner depths of her pain. For now she was sober, which she told herself was the first step of many on the road to recovery. She looked at George and smiled as he winked at her, offering a reassuring nod that displayed his confidence in her.

"You will be back," Macy told herself. "You must."

CHAPTER 10

SAN ANTONIO, TEXAS

B ob Gorman and his team of ten technicians landed on the tarmac at Lackland right on schedule. Colonel Wagoner sent a personnel truck to transport them to the lab. As they rode from the tarmac toward the isolated building, Bob addressed the team.

"Okay team, this is it," he said. "Remember what we discussed before. This will be your home for the duration of this project. We have no set completion date, so I can't tell you how long you will be here. This is a top secret mission of vital importance to national security. You are not to discuss what you see or do with each other, or anyone on the outside. You were specifically chosen for this project because you possess the professional training necessary, and because each of you has little or no outside family members with which to communicate with or distract you from your work. Colonel Wagoner has prepared a separate barracks where you will sleep. You will take your meals in the mess hall at different times from the other base personnel. When I am not here, you will take your orders from Colonel Wagoner or Major Harris. Are there any questions?" he asked.

All ten participants remained silent, their stoic expressions displaying their full understanding of his instructions. Each one had been a former member of at least one official government project requiring absolute confidentiality and security. They recognized the importance of maintaining secrecy in these matters, and had no intention of betraying the trust their government had placed in them.

Once they reached the compound, Bob entered the key code combination and led his team into the building. Colonel Wagoner was waiting for them inside the lab.

"Mr. Gorman, I trust you had a good flight," said Wagoner.

"Fine," replied Bob. "Is everything ready?"

"As you requested," said Wagoner. "Follow me."

He proceeded to the testing lab with Bob and his team in tow. Once inside, Bob noticed the lab had been thoroughly cleaned and all prior animals had been removed. The animal cages held several of the test animals for his team to use in their operation. The examination tables were also cleaned and ready for that phase of the operation. He could not contain a half smile as he looked around the room. Since the team was eager to get started, he asked Colonel Wagoner to show the team where the vials were held so they could begin their work. Colonel Wagoner led them to the storage area and identified the vials reserved for their use. Two of the members retrieved the first batch of vials while four others began removing some of the test subjects from the cages that lined the left wall. Bob informed them he would leave them to their work and left the room with Colonel Wagoner.

Bob left the base and instructed the driver to take him to the Drury Inn. He had decided to stay one night and spend tomorrow with the lab team before heading back to Washington. He wanted to make sure everything was running smoothly before he turned it over to them completely. He checked in with Harry who informed him everything was okay at the office, and then he phoned the President just to check in and make sure he was not needed.

"Mr. President, this is Bob," he said, after President Crawford came on the line.

"Where are you?" asked Crawford.

"I thought I would spend a little time in Cleveland checking on some polling data," he answered, not wanting the President to know where he actually was.

"When will you be back?" asked Crawford.

"I planned on flying back tomorrow unless you need me before then."

"No that's fine," said Crawford. "Everything here is running smoothly." He wished Bob a good evening and ended the call.

The car arrived at the hotel just as the call ended. Bob retrieved his bags and headed to the lobby to check in. Once in his room, he decided to take a short nap before dinner. He stretched out on the bed and was soon sound asleep.

After he awoke from his nap, he picked up his cell phone and punched in a sequence of numbers. After a couple of rings, a female voice answered. He had appointed Maxine West as team leader for this operation. He had worked with her before on one other occasion and was pleased to see her file in the stack of candidates Harry had given him. Max was very good at what she did and he knew from past experience that she could be trusted.

"How are things going, Max?" asked Bob.

"Right on schedule, sir," replied Max. Bob could picture her short spiked dark hair and dark-framed glasses as she spoke. She was not one for a lot of makeup, but he thought she could actually look good if she tried. He had never seen her without a lab coat on, so was not sure what her body looked like. One thing he was sure of though, was that her five foot, six inch frame was very thin. Her wrists, ankles, and neck gave that away.

"Is there anything you need?" asked Bob.

"No sir. Everything seems to be in order," she replied. "Good," said Bob. "I'll see you in the morning."

He decided he would order room service instead of taking the trouble to leave the hotel. He ate dinner and watched television until ten o'clock, and retired for the evening.

The next morning, he rode back to the base. He entered the lab to find the technicians already hard at work. He immediately made his way over to Max for an update.

"When did you get started this morning?" he asked.

"Oh, hello sir," said Max, as she turned around. "We got underway at six o'clock."

"When did you leave last night?"

"Seven," she replied. "We plan on finishing at six today and working twelve hour shifts each day until the operation is completed. Is that okay?"

"That's fine," said Bob. "As long as you get in twelve hours each day, we should be able to complete the project on schedule. How about bringing me up to speed on your results so far."

"Well, we've isolated the virus and have injected these ten subjects," said Max, pointing to the cage on the right side of the lab, which was kept isolated from the rest of the cages. Then she continued, "Now, we will monitor this group to see if the virus will work as it's supposed to before we begin working on the vaccine."

"Excellent. Keep up the good work," he said, patting Max on the shoulder.

She looked down at his hand as if to say, *Don't touch me*, then looked up at Bob and feigned a half-hearted smile. He recognized the look on her face, and quickly removed his hand. *Probably a lesbian*, he thought as he turned and walked out of the lab. He said goodbye to Major Harris who was on duty now, then headed out the building to his waiting car. He rode across the base to the airfield and climbed on board the private jet. In a couple of minutes, the jet was airborne and on its way back to Washington.

MARION, ILLINOIS

"Southern Belles, what's your pleasure," said the sexy female voice on the phone.

"Scarlet, please," he answered.

"Just a minute," said the lady with a cute southern drawl.

Soon another voice came on the line. "This is Scarlet, honey. What can I do for you today?"

"It's Rhett," he answered, "246793, sports section, page 5, coach, place, week."

"Hello Rhett," she replied without the accent. "What's the word?"

"Nothing so far," he said. "I've heard a few rumors about the warden, but nothing I can hang my hat on. Anything new on your end?"

"Try hooking up with an inmate named Bobby Watson," she said. "We got a tip yesterday about him and the warden involved in something."

"Okay, will do."

"How's everything else going there?"

"Fine," he said. "Just a barrel of fun."

"Frank's been climbing the walls since you got in there," she said.

"Well, tell Frank to keep his shirt on," he said, laughing. "We've worked too long and too hard on this one to get sloppy by rushing."

"I'll try to slip something in his coffee to help him relax."

"Did you guys get anything on that guard I told you about last time?"

"Yeah, as a matter-of-fact, we did," she answered. "It seems our guard had a run in with the law himself when he was a juvenile. The record was sealed so he hid it when he applied for the job. You may be able to turn him for the right price."

"Great, I'll keep that in mind."

"Make sure you check in on regular schedule."

"Haven't I always?" he asked.

"Just the same, I don't want to be left here worrying, only to see your face on the evening news."

"Listen, you worry about Frank," he said. "I'll take care of me."

"I'm serious," she said. "They don't call us caretakers for nothing."

"Okay, okay, take it easy," he said. "I'll call you at the usual time."

"You better," she said.

"Bye, bye, Scarlet," he said.

"Please be careful, Rhett," she said as she hung up. Rhett placed the receiver of the pay phone back onto the cradle. He paused for a moment reflecting on what Scarlet said about Frank. There were many times himself when he wished this was over. Deep cover work sometimes had a way of messing up your head if you stayed under for too long at a time. Rhett turned and nodded to the guard that he was finished. The guard walked over and escorted him out of the visitor area where the pay phone was located. Then he was led back to his cell. He usually checked in with Scarlet once a week, unless there was something urgent he needed to call her about before then. Of course, Rhett wasn't his real name. Vince Vrama had been an undercover agent for the Organized Crime Bureau for ten years. Currently, he was posing as an inmate in the U.S. Penitentiary in Marion, Illinois, investigating a report that the warden and some of the inmates were involved in an illegal drug operation that was supplied by the Carillo crime family from Chicago. According to informants, cocaine was being brought into the prison where inmates would cut it and bag it for resale on the outside. The inmates were given some of the drugs for their help and the warden was paid a cut of the proceeds from the Carillos for arranging the manufacturing facilities and personnel inside the prison. Vince came to the prison as a convicted cop killer two months ago, but so far had been unable to gain the confidence of the warden or any of the inmates he believed was part of the drug operation. Hopefully, the tip Scarlet just gave him would pan out.

The OCB established a call center under the disguise of a phone sex line. The agent called in with a code number which was always the same. The first two numbers represented the agent number. The next three numbers represented lines on the newspaper page. The last number was the position of the word on the line. The agent could tell which section and page from the paper, and then read off the words that corresponded to the locations based on the code number. The caretaker, as the person at the call center was called, compared the words to that day's local newspaper to verify it was their agent calling in. Anyone from the outside would simply think the agent was calling a phone sex line. Deep undercover operations like this were extremely dangerous, which was why only the best agents were chosen for these missions. He especially had to play it cool when the gentleman from Washington interviewed him last week so he wouldn't blow his cover.

Vince was successful in gaining the confidence of one of the guards, but apparently he had no knowledge of the cocaine operation. Vince had hinted about wanting to score some coke, but the guard merely told him he could arrange a meeting with one of the inmates who supplied the others in his cell block. The guard never mentioned a name, so maybe this guy was Bobby Watson, the one Scarlet told him about. Either way, his next move would be to get the guard to point out Bobby Watson to him so he could make his own introduction. It would soon be lights out, though, so Vince would have to wait until tomorrow. He settled in his bunk, closed his eyes, and drifted off to sleep.

Chapter 11

San Antonio, Texas

Max was watching over the shoulder of one of the other technicians when her cell phone rang. "Any progress Max?" asked Bob.

"Yes sir," said Max. "We've successfully introduced the virus into the live animals and all perished within forty-eight hours. We are just beginning to inject the next group. Then we will place them in with a control group to see if the virus spreads from the infected ones to the others."

"It sure seems like a complicated process," he commented.

"It is, sir," answered Max. "Especially if we do it right. We must be certain the virus can be spread among the test animals first before we can begin work on a vaccine. After that will come the hardest part of trying to mutate the virus without destroying all of the test subjects."

"Well don't worry about that. We can supply you with all of the animals you need. Just let me know if there is anything you need. You know how to reach me." And with that, Bob ended the call. Max went back to observing the technician seated in front of her, carefully taking notes on the clipboard she was holding. Two technicians were busy spraying down the cages where the first group of animals died, making sure there were no remnants of the virus left in them. These cages would sit idle for two weeks just to make sure no live virus remained in them.

Meanwhile, the next group of subjects were injected with the live virus and placed inside a large cage containing fifty non-infected subjects. Max made note of the size and colorations of the healthy subjects for comparison should they become infected. Now, it was a matter of time as they observed this group to see if the virus would spread to the non-infected ones, and at what rate it would spread. The team left the lab, careful to follow decontamination procedures, then headed to the mess hall for dinner.

WASHINGTON, DC

Harry popped his head into Bob's office to inform him he had been summoned by the President. Bob grunted his frustration as he stood up and walked out of his office. He made his way to the oval office and was greeted by President Crawford's personal secretary. Once inside the room, he slumped heavily into one of the chairs across from Crawford, letting out a sigh to indicate he was much too busy for such interruptions.

"You should hear some of these recommendations, Bob," said Crawford. "I feel like I am working with a bunch of idiots. Every suggestion is almost certain political suicide. Yet if I do nothing, we will lose anyway. Tell me you've made progress on this idea you are working on."

"It is coming along nicely, Mr. President," Bob told him, crossing his arms. "But you must be patient. Something like this takes time to develop. I told you not to implement anything until I'm finished with my project."

"I know, Bob and I trust you," Crawford said, as he stood up and paced around the room. "It's just all of this pressure to do something and I don't even know what you're planning. If I just had something to share with the press, maybe they would cut me some slack."

"Relax, Mr. President," Bob responded then continued rather smugly. "You know as well as I do, the press never lets the President rest, even if he gave them all the answers. Besides, if what I have in mind works, there will be no need to tell the press anything. The results will be self-evident."

"Can't you at least tell me some of the details?" asked Crawford.

"Believe me, Mr. President," said Bob. "You don't want to get bogged down with any of the details. You have much more pressing items on your agenda."

"I suppose you're right," said Crawford. "I just feel like a kid waiting for Christmas."

"Well I assure you, Mr. President," said Bob with a smile. "If all goes as planned, you will have a very Merry Christmas." Then he patted Crawford on the back and walked out of the oval office. He wanted to call Max immediately and push her to speed up the project, but by the time he reached his office, he had reassured himself that in order for this to work, he must let the professionals do their job the best way they knew how. It was a waiting game now, but he must not let himself become as impatient as the President.

LEXINGTON, KENTUCKY

Macy sipped on her morning coffee while George read the paper. She had been able to get through the last two days without crying, but still was not her normal self. A wound to the ego such as the one she suffered would take a long time to heal. Her brother had been so patient with her the past couple of days, but it was now time to move on.

"What do you think I should do with the rest of my life, George?" she asked.

He folded the newspaper over in front of him and peered up at her over the top of his reading glasses. "It doesn't matter what I think. You have to decide what's best for you."

"Well, I sure have done a bang-up job of that so far, haven't I?" said Macy with a sigh.

"We all make mistakes, Macy," he insisted. "It's how we choose to deal with the mistakes and go on with our life that determines our character."

"That's deep," said Macy with a laugh. "Did you just read that in the paper?"

"No. I think I saw it in a movie once," he replied, laughing with her. "Seriously, Mace, you don't have to figure all of this out now."

"I know. But I feel if I don't do something soon, I may never get out of this rut."

"Why don't you try something just to get you out of the house and keep you busy?" asked George. "You don't have to do it the rest of your life, but you can stay busy while you figure out what it is you want to do."

"What did you have in mind?" asked Macy.

"I don't know yet, but I can ask around and see what's available."

"Thanks, George," she said, smiling at him. "I would appreciate that." She took another sip of coffee while her brother went back to reading the paper.

After a few minutes, he looked up at Macy. "Here's something," he said. "The University wants to offer self-defense classes and is looking for someone to be the instructor. With your training, you would be perfect."

"Let me see that," she said, grabbing the paper from him. Her beautiful brown eyes moved back and forth as she read the classified ad. She looked up at George with a big smile on her face. He had not seen her smile like that since they left Hawaii.

"This would be perfect to keep me busy until I figure out what I want to do."

"Why don't you go ahead and call them?" asked George, tossing the phone at her. Macy punched in the telephone number listed in the ad and waited patiently for someone to answer. After a couple of rings, a lady answered and Macy inquired about the position. She wrote down some information and hung up.

"Well?" asked George.

"I have an interview today at eleven," she answered. "That doesn't give you a lot of time to get ready," he said, as he looked at his watch.

"I know," said Macy, as she jumped out of her chair and quickly walked to her room. She took a quick shower and dressed, asking George if she could borrow his car. He offered to drive her and wait while she had her interview.

They arrived at the University ten minutes before eleven. Macy asked George to wish her luck as she got out of the car and walked into the building. He brought along the rest of the newspaper to finish while he waited. After about thirty minutes, the passenger door opened and Macy hopped in, a big smile on her face.

"I got the job!" she said with an excited giggle.

"That's great!" he exclaimed, relieved to see his sister happy again. She told him the class started the next Monday evening and would meet three nights a week from seven until nine. They decided to celebrate with Japanese food for lunch. George drove to one of those restaurants where they prepare the food in front of you and put on a little show while they cook. After lunch they went to a local car dealership to buy a vehicle for Macy. He'd sold the one she had in Hawaii for her to one of those used car lots, now she needed transportation to her new job. Since she had plenty of money, she decided on a black Cadillac Escalade, fully loaded with all of the bells and whistles. She followed George back to his house with the windows down and the radio blasting, her red hair blowing in the wind, as she sang with the radio. This was a huge step in her road to recovery.

WASHINGTON, DC

The intercom buzzed on Bob's desk, interrupting him from the memo he was reading.

"Yes Harry, what is it?" he asked.

"It's a lady named Max," said Harry. "She said it is important she speak with you."

"Thank you, Harry," said Bob. Grabbing the receiver, he barked into the phone, "Damn it, Max, I told you never to call me here on the land line."

"I'm sorry, sir, but I accidentally left the cell phone in my quarters and your private number is stored in the phone. Colonel Wagoner was kind enough to dial your number for me from his phone."

"Are you alone?" he asked.

"Yes. Colonel Wagoner left me here and told me to take all the time I needed."

"So what's so important that it couldn't wait?"

"We successfully completed the virus transfer test from the infected animals to the healthy ones," she informed him. "We have also developed a successful vaccine we've tested several times now, all with success. We are now in the process of mutating the virus and should be ready for the other test subjects in a matter of days. I thought you should know so you could handle the necessary arrangements."

"This is very good news," he said. "I will begin the necessary steps to deliver the new test subjects to you. Will next week give you sufficient time to complete your current experiments?"

"Yes sir," she answered. "That will give us plenty of time. We will be ready to proceed once the new test subjects arrive."

"Excellent. I will personally come down for a visit once the subjects are delivered. I am very interested to review your work to date." Bob placed the receiver back onto its cradle and sat back in his chair placing his hands behind his head. He had a huge smile on his face as he contemplated the recent news from the lab. He quickly punched the intercom and summoned Harry to his office. He heard a soft knock on the door before Harry opened it and stepped inside.

"Harry, we need to begin preparations to transport the human test subjects to the lab," said Bob. "Is all of the necessary paperwork in order?"

"Yes sir," answered Harry. "We have the transfer documents and the press release prepared. When do we need to begin?"

"Now," answered Bob. "We need to have the subjects in the lab by next week."

"Not a problem, sir," said Harry. "I'll get right on it." And with that, Harry left Bob's office to begin his assignment. Bob retrieved the scotch from his bottom desk drawer and poured a glass. Then he held it up to his face and said, "Here's to you, Bob," as he brought the glass to his lips and drained the contents. He poured another one and drank it just as quickly. He got up and walked out of his office, informing Harry he was leaving for the day. The news Max delivered was certainly sufficient to call it a good day's work, thought Bob, as he made his way home.

Chapter 12

Marion, Illinois

Vince was awakened by the sound of his cell door opening. A guard he did not recognize entered and demanded he get up and get dressed, tossing a pair of sweat pants and a t-shirt on the cot. Vince quickly dressed and was led out of the cell and through the security doors past the guard station. He followed the guard to a service elevator which they took to the lower garage level. When they reached the garage, they exited the elevator and walked to a van. Vince was ordered to get in as the guard took his place in the passenger seat. There were four other passengers, all inmates, seated inside. The van headed out of the compound and to the airport, driving out onto the tarmac beside a waiting jet. The inmates were ordered out of the van and onto the plane. Soon they were airborne as each of the inmates exchanged questioning looks.

Finally Vince spoke up. "Where are we going?" he asked. The guard remained silent as if he had not heard Vince.

"Excuse me," Vince said louder. "I asked where we're going."

The guard slowly stood up from his seat and walked over in front of Vince. He drew back his hand and punched Vince in the mouth. "Does that answer your question?" he asked Vince, then turned and walked back to his seat. Since his hands were restrained, Vince was unable to wipe away the blood that trickled from the corner of his mouth and down his chin. Instead, he spat out a small pool of blood that had collected at the bottom of his mouth, as he kept his gaze steadily on the guard.

They flew for what seemed like hours until the plane began descending and touched down. The shades on the windows were closed so Vince was unable to see any landmarks from the plane. As they stepped off the jet, it was obvious to Vince they were at some kind of military base, but he had no idea which one it was or where they were. They were ordered into a waiting truck and driven to a barracks. There they were kept under posted guard and close supervision. Food was brought into the barracks instead of the inmates being led to the mess hall. There was no contact with the outside world allowed. Vince knew that if he did not check in at the appointed time, his superiors would assume he was in trouble and would begin searching for him. They would begin at the prison, but he suspected that would be where the trail would run cold. He had been on several undercover operations before, but was never cut off from the outside like this. A chill ran up his spine as he realized he was in the predicament that all undercover agents feared. Total isolation with the possibility he could be killed before anyone knew about it. He could feel the sweat under his arms roll down his sides, as he tried to control his outward expression. He did not want the others to sense his fear. After all, he was supposed to be a sociopath cop killer.

Meanwhile, the prison issued a press release announcing the escape of the five prisoners while being transported to another facility because of overcrowding. Their faces were displayed on every news program and in all of the papers. Scarlet saw Vince's picture with the others in the paper and immediately phoned her supervisor. They decided to wait until time for his next check-in before sending a team to investigate. He was scheduled to call the next evening between seven and nine o'clock. Scarlet waited on pins and needles until nine o'clock passed without a phone call from Vince.

She immediately informed her supervisor and he dispatched a team to Illinois. Of course the warden stuck by his story of the prison break and the trail immediately went cold. Their agent was in the wind with no backup and no way of contacting him. All they could do was wait.

San Antonio, Texas

It had been three days since Vince and the other inmates had been brought to wherever they were. Three days of no communication with the outside world. Each of them had been injected with some kind of drug and had been unconscious for the first twenty-four hours after they arrived. With only each other to talk to, there were wild speculations about what was going on. One of them wondered if they were going to get new trials due to some new kind of DNA evidence. Another thought they were going to be executed by the warden because of some dark mysterious secret that one of them stumbled upon. Whatever the case, they were all beginning to get cabin fever, especially Vince who was sure by now the cavalry was not coming.

Suddenly, the door opened and in walked two guards carrying automatic weapons. They took the forty-one year old black male and the twenty-three year old white female, leaving the others in their barracks. The two inmates were taken to the lab where they were each placed on an examination table and strapped down. They were hooked up to an intravenous solution of saline. One of the technicians administered a syringe of liquid into the IV tube of each inmate. Each inmate was hooked up to heart, respiratory and pulse monitors with readings being charted every fifteen minutes. After two days, the inmates began to show signs of illness which included fever, muscle aches, and severe nausea. The other black male inmate was taken to the lab, but was given no injections of any kind. He was housed in the same area as the infected prisoners. After two days, he began to show the same symptoms as the two infected inmates. The lab technicians, working in their sterile suits, collected blood samples and analyzed them in hopes of developing a vaccine. After one week the first black male who was infected died. The white female lasted two additional days before succumbing to the virus. Max thought perhaps it was because she was younger and in better overall physical condition than the first inmate.

Max and the team finally came up with a vaccine they needed to test, so the black female inmate was brought to the lab. This left Vince alone in the barracks and wondering why the others had not returned and what had happened to them. The fourth inmate was injected with the vaccine then housed in the lab with the last infected black male patient. He died four days later, but there were still no signs of the disease in the black female. Needing further evidence that the vaccine worked, she was injected with a sample of the live virus. There were no symptoms of illness after one week of observation. Apparently the vaccine worked, so Max decided to call Bob with the news. The phone rang just once before he answered.

"Yes," he said.

"This is Max," she said. "I just wanted to inform you that we have isolated an effective vaccine for our experimental virus."

"Excellent," he replied. "Are you sure it is effective."

"Yes sir. We have one test subject left, but I feel confident in our results."

"Listen Max, I want you to just expose the last one to the virus then dispose of him with the others. We will send down another test batch for you to confirm your findings."

"But sir, don't you want us to use this last candidate as a test subject also?"

"No," he returned emphatically, "he may already be contaminated somehow. I want you using an entirely separate group for the last phase of your testing."

"Very well," she agreed, "We will expose him to some of the sick animals to see how quickly it spreads from animal to human." Max ended the call and summoned for the last inmate to be brought to the lab. Vince was led to the lab where he was housed with several of the animals recently infected with the virus. He was given water the infected subjects drank from to ensure he was fully exposed. The animals died within forty-eight hours, but Vince showed no signs of disease. Max decided to inject the virus directly into his bloodstream. They strapped Vince down to one of the examination tables and administered the virus directly then waited for it to take effect. After a week of monitoring his vital signs, Vince showed no symptoms of the disease, so Max called Bob again.

"Yes," said Bob.

"It's Max again," she said. "The last inmate from this first group did not become infected even through direct injection. His body must have built up an internal immunity to the virus, possibly when he was exposed to the animals. What should we do with him?"

"Hold him in a separate barracks until you finish with the second group," he ordered. "If he's still alive and well after you've confirmed your vaccine with the other group, kill him and incinerate his body with the others."

"I understand, sir," she acknowledged, as she ended the call. Vince was immediately taken back to the barracks by two of the guards. On the way, he noticed another group of inmates being placed into the barracks just in front of his. He recognized a couple of them as inmates from the prison in Marion. Vince wondered what they were testing for, since he had been housed with a flock of chickens for days and had to drink from the same water source. He did not feel sick, so perhaps it was some kind of behavioral experiment. Maybe they were testing the effects of close contact with animals on inmate social and psychological function. If that were the case, then he should be rejoined by the others soon. Yet days passed and he was still all alone in the barracks. They fed him well while he was there, but without any human contact, he was beginning to go stir crazy. He began to mark an X on the wall for each day with a rock he found in his shoe. It had been almost three weeks before they came for him again.

Two guards led him back to the lab where he was housed with two inmates he did not recognize. Both of them shook constantly from the high fever ravaging their bodies. As the disease progressed, they complained of the pain in their joints and were unable to keep any food on their stomachs, vomiting until there was nothing left except yellow-green bile produced from their almost constant heaving. Vince could not help but feel a little uneasy, but definitely was not coming down with the same symptoms. After a couple of days with them, one of the inmates motioned for Vince to come to his bedside. He grabbed Vince by the hand.

"Get out if you can," he said in a dry raspy voice. "What do you mean?" asked Vince.

"Did you not see the birds?" he asked, indicating the chickens in the cages.

"Yeah, what about them?"

"Avian Influenza," he said, coughing and wheezing. "What?"

"Bird flu," said the inmate. "Haven't you heard of it?"

"I think maybe I read something about it once, but I'm not sure," said Vince.

"It's bad stuff," said the inmate. "But if it don't kill you, these goons probably will."

"Who?" Vince asked. "What are you talking about?"

"In case you haven't noticed, this is a military base," he answered. "That means the government is involved, which can only mean bad news," he said, coughing again. Then he dropped Vince's hand as he slipped into a coma. Vince stared in disbelief for a few minutes, trying to process what the inmate told him. He was a government employee after all. All he had to do was tell them who he was and surely they would let him go. Suddenly, Vince got that terrible ache in the pit of his stomach as if he had been sucker punched. He had seen too many covert government operations to know that equipment, money and human life were all expendable when it came to obtaining what the government wanted as a suitable outcome. If they were planning something with this virus, they definitely would not want to leave any survivors to tell about it. He needed a plan, and quickly, because once these two inmates were dead, there would be no need to keep him around.

Vince had carefully noted the number of technicians in the lab at any given time. Usually they left only two members during the evening meal time while the rest of them went to the mess hall for dinner. Typically, this was the time for simple monitoring when no injections or procedures were performed. He also made note of their decontamination process, as each one spent exactly the same amount of time in the chamber before leaving the lab. Vince reasoned it must be on some sort of timer that released the exact amount of chemical necessary to render any viral remains non-viable. He decided this would be the best time if he were going to be able to attempt an escape.

Vince waited patiently for evening, pretending to be asleep. Although he was strapped to one of the examination tables, the technician had left his right wrist a little loose. He had successfully been able to work on it enough to pop his thumb out of joint and pull his hand from the restraint. He worked at the other wrist restraint, making sure to place his right hand at his side whenever any of the technicians looked his way. This turned out to be his lucky day as all but one of the technicians left the lab for dinner. Maybe because the other two were so close to death, they believed one man could watch them while the others left. Vince waited until he was sure enough time had passed for the rest of the team to be in the mess hall eating before making his move.

Vince made like he was convulsing and began moving his head from side to side and yelling incoherently. When the technician came over to the examination table, Vince grabbed him around the neck and choked him until he passed out. Then he removed the ankle straps and took the viral suit from the technician and put it on. Vince made his way to the decontamination chamber, then a thought occurred to him. Once he removed the suit on the other side, the people outside would know he was not one of theirs. He decided to proceed through the chamber without activating the decontamination procedure. This set off an alarm indicating there was a contamination breach.

Vince used this to his advantage by yelling for everyone in the adjoining lab to evacuate immediately. He hurriedly left the building and headed to the barracks, as if he was going to get the others. Once there, he removed the suit and stepped out of the barracks into the darkness. There was enough panic and activity around the lab he was able to make his way in the dark to a jeep parked outside the mess hall. The keys were in the ignition, so he started the jeep and sped away in the direction he thought was the main gate. However, after going a few hundred yards, he could tell he was headed deeper into the compound. He turned the jeep around and headed in the opposite direction. After a few seconds, he came upon the main gate which was manned by two armed guards. He didn't slow down as he crashed the gate, ducking his head to avoid the bullets flying by.

Vince pushed the gas pedal to the floor, trying to put as much distance between him and the base as he could. He knew it wouldn't take long for them to realize what happened and come after him. The military was known for being able to move quickly, and time was critical if he was going to be able to pull off the escape. How he wished he had a full team of his people here to back him up, but that was the down side of undercover work. You're typically alone and outnumbered. He was driving on what appeared to be a main road, and wondered if he should take a side road to avoid being noticed, but since he didn't yet know where he was, he didn't want to run the risk of ending up on a dead end road with a dozen military vehicles blocking him in. He decided it best to stick to the main roads for now until he could determine exactly where he was and which way to go. He kept looking over his shoulder for the onslaught of pursuers he knew would soon be hot on his trail. He could feel his heart almost beating out of his chest as his adrenaline was pumping at a peak level. He reached his right hand to his face and wiped the sweat from around his eyes, as he surveyed the countryside for any place to pull off and hide. He had no idea where he was, or where he needed to go. But at least for now, he was still alive.

Chapter 13

Washington, DC

The call came in at exactly seven-thirty in the evening. "Yes," answered Bob Gorman.

"This is Max, sir. We've got a problem." Max proceeded to tell Bob about Vince's escape. He berated her for leaving only one member of the team in the lab, and told her he would take care of it as he slammed the cell phone shut. He punched in a series of numbers and waited for the man at the other end to answer.

"Yes," said the man's voice.

"We've got a runner," replied Bob. "It's number five."

"How long ago?"

"Thirty minutes," he answered. "Dead or alive?"

"We have what we need," he said, then answered. "Dead."

"I understand," said the man, ending the call.

Bob quickly got up from his chair and called for Harry. He barked some instructions and headed out the door for the airport and the private jet to take him to San Antonio.

SAN ANTONIO, TEXAS

Vince pulled open the glove box and searched through the contents as he drove along. He found a forty-five caliber handgun with one extra clip. There were also some miscellaneous papers, but nothing of value. He cursed himself for not searching the lab technician for money before he made his escape. He knew it would not take long for the authorities to search out a government Jeep, so he needed to find alternate transportation. And that would require money, which he did not have. As he passed a convenience store, Vince suddenly had an idea. He turned the Jeep around sharply and sped into the store parking lot. He climbed out of the jeep, stuffing the gun into the front of his sweat pants and pulling his t-shirt over it. He walked into the store and approached the counter.

"Excuse me," said Vince. "Can you tell me exactly where we are?"

"Don't you know where you are?" asked the clerk, eyeing Vince suspiciously.

"Well, of course I do, generally," replied Vince with a chuckle. "I meant this particular community. Does it have a name?"

"No sir," said the clerk. "We're considered part of San Antonio."

So that's where I am, he thought. San Antonio, Texas. Vince thanked the clerk and walked toward the drink cooler in the back while the clerk waited on the only other customer in the store. Vince grabbed a soda and headed back toward the front of the store. By the time he reached the counter, he was the only customer left in the place. He quickly pulled the gun and pointed it in the direction of the clerk, demanding he empty the contents of the cash register into a sack. He asked the clerk for the keys to his car parked out back, grabbed a local road map, and hit the clerk in the back of the head just hard enough to knock him out for a couple of hours, taking the kid's cell phone from his belt. He stopped in front of the store security camera and mouthed the words 'help me,' before running out of the store. Vince pulled the Jeep around to the back of the store trying to conceal it as best he could. He climbed into the clerk's old Chevy, which was half-rust and half-primer, and sped out of the parking lot.

Vince headed South on Highway 16 away from San Antonio while he tried desperately to formulate a plan. He tried to remain calm as he was trained to do, but since he had never been in a situation quite like this, he found it difficult to focus. Vince picked up the clerk's cell phone and punched in a number.

"Southern Belles," answered the lady. "What's your pleasure?"

"Scarlet, please," said Vince.

After a few seconds, she answered, "This is Scarlet. What can I do for you?"

"Scarlet, it's Rhett," said Vince. "246793, code seven. Do you read? Code seven." Then the phone went silent. Suddenly, he heard the sound of a helicopter overhead. As he peered up through the windshield, he heard the sound of automatic weapon fire, as a barrage of bullets began to shower the vehicle. He quickly turned down a rural road and stopped the car at the side of the road. He ran into the woods to the right of the road, trying to get out of sight of the chopper. They searched the area with their lights, but were unable to see anything through the thick growth of trees. Four bodies repelled from the helicopter on ropes to the ground below and entered the woods in pursuit of Vince. His heart was pounding as he ran between the trees, almost tripping a couple of times on the undergrowth. Remembering his training, he knew they assumed he would continue to run, so he quickly scaled a tree, climbing all the way to the top so the branches would conceal him from below. He tried to control his breathing so he would not give away his location, while he listened for his pursuers on the ground. They were very good at stealth, but Vince was still able to tell when they passed by. He waited until he heard the helicopter pass over the woods on its way to pick up the men before climbing down the tree. He assumed they must have made it all the way through the woods to the other side, and finding nothing called for transport. Vince remembered passing by a farm house on the way down the road, and decided to make his way back through the woods to the farm and see if he could find a place to lay low and plan his next move.

Vince emerged from the woods on what appeared to be the back side of the farm. There was very little moon tonight, and he could barely make out the shape of two long buildings directly in front of him. He carefully made his way up to the first one and peered through the door. It was full of chickens from one end to the other. He had heard about poultry houses but had never actually seen one until now. He could tell there would not be enough room to conceal him in one of these. He walked quietly toward the farm house. He saw what appeared to be a barn to his left and decided to check it out. As he got closer, he could tell it was an older structure which was used only for storing hay. This would work perfect for now, he thought, as he climbed into the loft. He was just about to make a place to lie down for a nap when he heard voices outside. He looked out of the loft in time to see four dark figures approaching the barn from the woods. One was holding something with a light as he pointed in the direction of the barn. They must be tracking me somehow, thought Vince, but how? He quickly climbed out of the loft and ran out of the barn toward the farm house. He could tell from the sound behind him that his pursuers had picked up their pace. Vince reached a pickup truck parked in front of the house. He jumped in and pulled down the sun visor and luckily, a set of keys fell in his lap. He turned the ignition and sped off toward the road with the sound of automatic weapons interrupting the still night air.

Vince knew he had little time before they caught up to him again, especially if they were able to somehow pinpoint his location. He remembered seeing a road sign indicating an airport when he left the base, and drove back in that direction as fast as he could. When he reached the airport, he parked in the loading zone and ran inside the terminal. He quickly made his way to the security check point, where the alarm went off as soon as he stepped through it. He watched carefully as the guard passed a wand around his body. It beeped when the wand was over his right shoulder. He acted like he had forgotten about a metal plate that had been inserted from an old injury. The guard asked for his medical paper that he was supposed to carry with him to confirm that and Vince said he left it in the car. The guard was already eyeing him suspiciously because he was wearing only sweat pants, a t-shirt, and sneakers. Vince told the guard his flight did not leave for another hour so he had time to go back to the car and retrieve the paper. Vince left security and walked to the nearest restroom. Once inside he ripped the metal towel holder from the wall and struck the mirror three times before it cracked. Carefully retrieving a shard of glass, he began cutting into his right shoulder. He tried to keep his mind off the pain as he dug around in his flesh. Just under the skin, he found a small micro-chip similar to the one the Bureau installed when he became an agent. They must have replaced the FBI chip with one of their own the first day at the base when he was unconscious. He grabbed some paper towels and stuffed them under his shirt to keep the blood from showing through and walked out of the restroom. He passed by a man on one of the pay phones and carefully dropped the chip into his open briefcase sitting on the floor. He walked out of the airport and climbed into the truck, which fortunately had not yet been towed, and sped away. He glanced in the rearview mirror as he turned the corner just in time to see four men in black jumpsuits enter the airport. That should buy him enough time to get away and regroup, especially since they could no longer track him now.

Vince headed East on Highway 10 out of town and drove for a while before pulling off at a motel for the night. He parked in the rear so no one would see the truck. He was glad he had stuffed the money and gun in his sweats before running into the woods, as he paid for the room with cash. Exhausted, he lay down and tried to rest, his head spinning from the day's events. He tried to think of what he had become involved in as he remembered what the inmate told him about the bird flu.

Apparently, they were being used for some sort of scientific experiment. He reached into his sock and pulled out a vial he had retrieved from the lab before he escaped. It was in a group he saw one of the technicians use to inject the inmate that did not get sick, and assumed this was the vaccine. However, he could not explain why he did not get sick given his prolonged exposure to the virus. Perhaps he was one of those lucky few who sometimes come in contact with a disease, but instead of contracting it, they simply become a carrier. Vince remembered how blood from these people had been used to develop vaccines and serums in the past. Maybe when this was all over, they could use his blood to stop whatever virus this was. That is, if he was able to live through this entire ordeal. After an hour of wrestling with all of the questions, Vince decided he needed some rest if he were going to be able to think clearly the next day. He used a technique he learned in training to empty his mind of thoughts, similar to self-hypnosis, and before long he was asleep.

Quantico, Virginia

Upon hearing the term code seven from Vince, Scarlet immediately pressed the red button on her console, which alerted the agency they had a man in trouble. Code seven was used when an agent's cover was blown and he or she needed extraction immediately. Unfortunately for Vince, the call dropped before she was able to pinpoint his location. It took only ten seconds for Vince's supervisor, Frank Pickard, to appear beside Scarlet.

"Fill me in, Agent Phipps," barked Pickard.

"I received a code seven from Agent Vrama, but the call was cut off before I could secure his location. I'm sorry, sir," she said, dropping her head.

"Don't be sorry," he replied. "Just find my agent."

"I wish we could, sir," she said. "But the tracking chip we placed in agent Vrama was recently removed. We have no way of locating him."

"Damn!" he exclaimed. "Phipps, I haven't lost an agent yet and I don't intend to start. Get the Director on the phone. We have work to do."

"Yes sir," she said, as she began punching numbers on her phone.

Frank headed back to his office for a map of Illinois. He was hoping Vince was not too far from the prison, but without the tracking chip, there was no way to determine exactly where he was. He returned to the operations center.

"Agent Phipps, send a team to Marion to search the penitentiary," he said. "And interrogate the warden. I want to know everything he knows about this."

"Right away, sir," she said as her fingers flew on the keyboard in front of her.

"If he calls in again, I want a trace on the phone," said Frank. "He may be using a cell phone that has a GPS chip in it. Either way, we've got to find him soon."

"Sir, I have the Director on the phone," said Phipps.

"I'll take it in my office," said Frank as he walked back to his office.

She transferred the call, and continued her other tasks Pickard had assigned. She established the necessary links to trace any calls coming in to their center, and also had technicians ready the systems for GPS location, should Agent Vrama be using a cell phone. The team was on their way to Illinois, but it would take a couple of hours to get there. Phipps knew the more time that elapsed after an agent went missing, the less likelihood there was for a positive outcome.

Frank picked up the receiver and said, "Mr. Director, we have a situation. I need to see you ASAP. We have a field agent missing, and need cooperation from the other various government agencies to help locate him. Yes sir, I can be there in ten minutes. Thank you sir," he said, then hung up. He grabbed his jacket and adjusted his tie. The Director was a stickler for a neat appearance and Frank did not want to disappoint him, especially when he needed a favor. He made one last trip to the operations center before heading to the Director's office.

"Where are we, Phipps?" he asked.

"The team is on their way and we have everything in place to trace the call, should Agent Vrama contact us again," she answered.

"You mean when he contacts us again," he said. "Think positive, Phipps."

"Yes sir."

"I'll be with the Director for the next few minutes if you need me," he said, then turned and walked out. It was always a little intimidating for him to speak to the Director, especially in person. This was partly due to the fact they worked together as field agents several years ago, and the Director was promoted above Frank because he played a better political game with the power brokers than he did. He always believed he was a better agent than the Director, so it was difficult sometimes to follow orders, especially when he knew it may not be the best course of action. Then again, Frank thought, maybe it is better this way. The Director needs to be someone who can play the political game and he was definitely not one for politics. He continued on his way up to the mezzanine level to the Director's office, intent on getting his agent back.

CHAPTER 14

SAN ANTONIO, TEXAS

Bob Gorman stepped off the plane and walked hurriedly to the car waiting for him. He rode to a nearby hotel and checked into the room Harry had reserved for him. He would visit the lab later, but for now there was a more pressing matter. After a few minutes, there was a knock on the door. He peered through the peep hole, and opened the door. He closed the door after his visitor and locked it securely. "Okay, fill me in," he said.

"The subject has not been neutralized yet," said the man. "What? Why not?" demanded Bob.

"Somehow, he was able to figure out we were tracking him, so he removed the micro-chip and planted it on someone in the airport. By the time we got there, he was long gone. According to his chart, he never became sick after being exposed for a prolonged period, so we're not looking for a sick man."

"No, we're looking for a potential carrier," said Bob. "Damn it! We've got to find him before he spreads this thing enough that the CDC finds out about it."

"There's one more complication, sir," said the man. "The technicians removed this from him when they planted our micro-chip," he said, holding up another micro-chip. "Unfortunately, they dismissed it at first. Then, during his escape, he called a toll-free number from a cell phone that we were able to trace to Quantico. We were able to disrupt the call quickly, but don't know how much information he was able to give them."

"So our runner is a federal agent," said Bob. "I don't have to tell you how much further this complicates matters. Find this man, and dispose of him ASAP!" The man left the room and Bob secured the locks again, then grabbed his cell phone and placed a call. When the voice answered on the other end, he said, "Charlie, this is Bob. Listen, you have an agent working undercover at the penitentiary in Marion. As of this minute, he is a rogue agent and considered armed and dangerous. This is a matter of national security, Charlie. Do I make myself clear?" After a couple of seconds, he spoke into the phone again. "Good. I knew I could count on you, Charlie. The President is grateful for your loyalty." He ended the call and left the hotel on his way to the base. As soon as he arrived, Bob pulled Max to the side and asked for an assessment. Apparently they had developed the virus, isolated a vaccine, and finished testing the second group of subjects. He instructed her to pack everything up and close the operation down. They could manufacture the necessary amounts of both the virus and the vaccine at their lab in Washington. He did not want any information leaked because of all the excitement that went on at the lab today. She nodded her head in agreement and assembled the team for further instructions. Bob left the lab and rode back to the airport, where he boarded the jet and flew back to Washington.

QUANTICO, VIRGINIA

Frank Pickard knocked on the door and waited patiently for a response. "Enter," said a voice from inside and Pickard stepped through the door.

"Frank, I understand you have a missing agent," he said. "Yes sir, Director," replied Frank. "Agent Vrama was working undercover inside the penitentiary in Marion when something happened and now he's on the run and in trouble."

"What happened?"

"We're not sure," said Frank. "We lost contact with him."

"I know this is hard, Frank," said the Director. "But as of this moment, consider Agent Vrama a casualty and move on."

"But sir," said Frank, "I've never left an agent in the field."

"Well, there's a first time for everything. Look, I don't mean to sound cold-hearted, but we have other concerns. Besides, if this agent is as valuable as you claim, he'll probably figure a way out of this without our help."

"Damn it, Charlie!" said Frank. "What's going on here?"

"Honestly, Frank, I don't know," said Charlie. "But I do know this. The order is coming from much higher than me so we're in the same boat on this one. I'm sorry, Frank but my hands are tied."

"What if he calls in again?" asked Frank.

"This agency is to have no further communication with Agent Vrama," he answered. "From now on, we have no knowledge of an agent Vrama working for OCB." Frank slammed his fist on the Director's desk and stormed out of his office.

When he returned to the operations room, Phipps asked, "Well, what's our next move?"

"Nothing," said Frank. "We move on. Officially, this is a dead issue. Unofficially, if you get any information at all on Vince, bring it to me personally and don't share it with anyone else. Do you understand?"

"Perfectly," she answered.

Frank turned and headed to his office. He was still steaming over his conversation with the Director. Vince must have fallen into something big to get this kind of reaction, he thought. Frank rubbed his forehead for a minute, then reached for his rolodex. He flipped through it until he found a particular entry, and picked up the phone. After a couple of rings, a man's voice came through the receiver.

"George, its Frank up in Quantico," said Frank.

George Merit and Frank trained together at the academy. When they graduated, they worked together for several years before Frank went to OCB and George went to the FBI field office in Kentucky. They had stayed in touch over the years, but like all long distance friendships, the calls and visits became fewer and fewer.

"Why Frank, it's been a while. To what do I owe this call?" asked George.

"I need a favor, George, and quite frankly you're the first person I thought of."

"I'm flattered, I think," he said. "How can I help?"

"I know sometimes you come in contact with people in the field who, for lack of better words, know how to get things done. Am I right?"

"Maybe," said George. "Now tell me exactly what's going on?"

Frank proceeded to explain the situation with Vince and how he had been instructed to leave it alone. He almost choked up one time as he described the value of Vince to their department, and how he had never before left a man alone in the field. George agreed that it sounded like a difficult situation, but at this point they had no idea who was calling the shots. After Frank finished laying out his dilemma, George informed him there was someone he knew who just might be able to help. He assured Frank he would talk to this person and see if they would be willing to help. Then he reminded his friend that even if he could get this person to help, the odds of them finding Vince alive were slim. Frank understood, but still felt the need to see this through. He said he would see what he could do, and then ended the call.

Frank got up and walked out of his office, heading to the parking garage. At times like this, he liked to visit the local batting cages and work off the extra adrenaline. He let Agent Phipps know he was leaving, instructing her to call him if anything developed.

SOMEWHERE IN TEXAS

Vince emptied the contents of the sack onto the motel bed and counted the bills. There was a little over fifteen hundred bucks from his convenience store heist. He knew it would be just a matter of time before the truck was reported stolen and every cop in the state would have the vehicle description on their dash. He left the motel and headed east on Interstate 10, realizing, that even though there was a greater chance of meeting state police cruisers, he could make better time this way. After driving for a few hours, he decided it was time to get rid of the truck. He pulled off the interstate at a small town and found a shady-looking used car lot. He paid one thousand bucks for a piece of junk that looked like it could not even make it out of the parking lot. The owner assured him it was in good running order, but because of its outward appearance he was never able to sell it. Vince told him he would take the title with him, and stuffed it in the glove box. When he cranked the engine, the car seemed to actually run smoothly. He headed back toward the Interstate, exhaling a sigh of relief now that the police would not be looking for the vehicle he was driving.

After he pulled back onto I-10, Vince punched in the number for Quantico and waited patiently for the girl to answer.

"Southern Belles," she said as usual. "What's your pleasure?"

"Scarlet, please," he said.

After a few seconds, Phipps answered. "This is Scarlet."

"Scarlet, this is Rhett," he said, and before he could get out the code number, Scarlet interrupted him. "I'm sorry sir, but I don't know a Rhett," she said. "Please don't call here again." And with that, she ended the call. Vince had heard about agents being disavowed, but this was the first time he actually witnessed it. The fact that it was he who had been disavowed sent a shudder up his spine. He wiped the sweat that popped out from his brow and began to think of what his next move should be. He had five hundred dollars left from the convenience store which should last for a while. Since he was now disconnected from the agency, there was nothing there for him. The most important matter now at hand was who the people were who were running the experiments and what they planned to do with the bird flu virus. He felt he had to get word to someone who could investigate this and stop it before there was a widespread epidemic. He began to think of the different government agencies he knew of, running down the list in his mind. Suddenly, he almost ran off the road as one name seemed to jump off the list in his mind. It was the Centers for Disease Control, or CDC as it was commonly known. Certainly they would be interested in this little covert operation. Now all he had to do was get the contact information for the CDC and hope someone there would seriously listen to him.

Vince remembered the CDC was located in Atlanta, so he called information for the phone number. The operator offered to connect him directly and soon a lady answered, "Centers for Disease Control and Prevention, how may I direct your call?"

"I need to speak to the Director, please," said Vince. "Your name, sir?" she asked.

"This is Charles Norton, Director of the Organized Crime Bureau," he replied.

"One moment please," she said, placing him on hold. Soon another voice answered. "Charlie, how are you doing? It's been a while."

"Sir, this is Vince Vrama. I'm an agent with OCB. Please don't hang up," said Vince.

"And just why did you pose as Director Norton, son?"

"I thought I would have a better chance of you taking my call," said Vince. "I have some information that is a matter of national security."

"Then why didn't you call your supervisor?" asked the Director.

"Because I was in the middle of a deep undercover operation at a prison in Illinois when my cover was blown and now I can't contact my caretaker. Please listen. There is a strain of bird flu that has been developed in a secret lab in San Antonio at the military base there. I don't know who or what they're planning to do with it, but I do know they used prisoners as guinea pigs for their experiments. They've developed a strain of the virus that can be spread from human-to-human and it is highly contagious and deadly," said Vince.

"And just how did you get away?" asked the Director. "For some reason, I'm immune to the virus," he told him. "But the other prisoners were not so lucky."

"If what you're telling me is true, we could be on the verge of an epidemic, or even a pandemic," said the Director. "Do you believe they were terrorists?"

"If they were, they were American terrorists," said Vince. "Oh, by the way, I was able to take a sample vial of the vaccine with me."

"I would like to get my hands on that for testing," said the Director. "Is there some place we can meet?"

"I am in Texas now, but can be in Atlanta in a couple of days," he offered.

"There's a small motel just off Interstate 85 north of the city called The Colonial Inn. Let's plan on meeting there at nine o'clock in the evening on Monday. I'm going to North Carolina for the weekend, but plan to come back Sunday night. Call me Monday morning and let me know what room you are in," said the Director. "Do you have enough money on you for the room?"

"Yes. I will call you first thing Monday," said Vince, and ended the call. He continued on his journey, now mapping out a route to Atlanta. He decided to drive straight through to the motel and stay there until Monday, stopping only to eat, relieve himself, and buy some clothes at a Wal-Mart to replace the sweats he was wearing. He passed several highway patrol cars heading in the opposite direction as he continued down the Interstate. Each time he saw one, his stomach caved in and he stared into the rear view mirror until they were out of sight, fearing he would see one slam on breaks and dart across the median after him. By the time he got to Georgia, he was a nervous wreck. At least he didn't have to worry about falling asleep while driving, since he had enough adrenaline coursing through him for an entire professional football team.

He found the motel with little effort and checked into room eight under the name Charles Norton. He decided to try one more time to call the caretaker. This time he was placed on hold for several minutes before Scarlet came on the line.

"Rhett, just listen," she said. "We're tracking the source of your call so we can send a team to extract you. Just stay where you are and we will come to you." Then the Director walked into the operations room, causing Phipps to change her tone.

"I'm sorry, but I can't talk to you," she said, and hung up on Vince.

The Director walked over to agent Phipps and asked, "Was that Agent Vrama on the phone?"

"No sir," said Phipps. "It was a bill collector," she said, looking embarrassed. The Director gave her a suspicious look, and walked away. Phipps immediately got back on the phone to make sure they were able to pinpoint agent Vrama's location. The technicians told her they had the location on the grid and could email her the coordinates. Once she had the location,

Phipps dispatched a team to the location in hopes they would find Agent Vrama still alive and be able to safely extract him without incident. It would take a few hours for the team to get there, so all Phipps could do now was to wait and monitor the phones.

Vince was unable to say anything to Scarlet since she did all the talking then cut him off. Based on her actions, he could only assume he was still disavowed, but they were trying to covertly pinpoint his location and extract him. That could only mean one thing; Frank must be operating on his own without the Director's approval. Of course it was not the first time Frank had maneuvered around an order from the Director when he believed what was truly the right thing to do was in direct conflict with that order. Still, Vince could not help but feel all alone. He curled up tightly in a ball, his mind racing, until eventually sheer exhaustion consumed him and he was fast asleep.

CHAPTER 15

WASHINGTON, DC

Bob Gorman was working late when the White House operator rang his extension. "Mr. Gorman, the Director of the CDC is asking for the President," she said. "Should I tell him the President is at Camp David?"

"No, Helen," said Bob. "Transfer the call to me, please." After a few seconds, Helen successfully routed the call to Bob's extension.

"This is Bob Gorman, White House Chief of Staff. How may I help you?"

"Mr. Gorman, this is Jack Jordan, Director of the CDC. It's imperative that I speak with the President immediately. It's a matter of national security."

"Well Jack, the President is unavailable now, but I assure you I can get a message to him for you," said Bob.

"I'm not sure if I should discuss this with anyone except the President," said Jack.

"Relax, Jack," said Bob. "I assure you the President and I discuss all matters of national security, along with the head of Homeland Security. Anything that needs immediate attention can be discussed with me." Jack told Bob about the phone call he had received from Vince and his concerns over a possible epidemic or pandemic of the Avian Influenza virus.

"This is a serious matter," said Bob. "That is, if it is true."

"I believe it to be in our best interest to assume it is, until we can confirm it," said Jack.

"You're right," he agreed. "When are you supposed to meet this agent?"

"Monday evening at nine o'clock at the Colonial Inn just off Interstate 85 north of Atlanta."

"Where are you now?"

"I'm on my way to North Carolina," answered Jack. "We have a house at Holden Beach where my wife and I often meet for the weekend since we work in different cities."

"Does anyone else know about this?" asked Bob. "Just you and I so far."

"Good. Let's keep it that way for now. I'll brief the President and get back in touch with you. For now, go ahead and plan on keeping your meeting with Agent Vrama. Where can I reach you this weekend?" he asked. Jack gave him the phone number and address to the beach house, and after Bob reassured him he would speak immediately to the President, ended the call. This was indeed a stroke of luck, thought Bob as he began to place a call. After a couple of rings, a man answered.

"It's me," he said. "I have another assignment for you." Bob continued with instructions as the man listened silently.

"And I want you at the meeting Monday evening to take care of it, once and for all. He should be registered under the name Charles Norton." Bob ended the call and sat back in his chair, releasing a huge sigh of relief, as if he had dodged a bullet. Thank goodness he was there to intercept the call. If the President had been there, it would have ruined everything he had been working on. Now there were just a couple of loose ends to tie up before continuing with the operation.

HOLDEN BEACH, NORTH CAROLINA

Jack Jordan arrived at the beach house around nine o'clock Friday evening. He and his wife Vanessa bought the house ten years ago after Vanessa was elected to the United States Senate. Jack was born and raised in North

Carolina, where he vacationed at Holden Beach every summer with his family. Jack was working at the CDC when he met Vanessa at a fund raiser for her Georgia state legislature election bid fourteen years ago. After one term in the state legislature, Vanessa was elected to the Senate, and was now in the middle of her second term. During this time, Jack was appointed the Director of the CDC and neither of them wanted to give up their professions. It was Jack's idea to purchase a beach house at Holden Beach where they could meet most weekends when Vanessa was in Washington. Of course, when Congress was not in session, they stayed at their home in Buckhead.

Jack remembered the first time he came to Holden Beach many years ago. At that time there was nothing but houses and one old independent grocery store. The bridge connecting the island to the mainland was a single-lane bridge that turned to let tall ships pass along the inter-coastal waterway. Today, there was a new concrete bridge that had two lanes and was high enough for ships to pass under. There were several shops and stores, including a couple of the larger chain outfits. Holden Beach tried to maintain its small family atmosphere by prohibiting tall hotels and resorts, but the number of houses was several times that of when Jack was a young boy. Even with the added rentals, Holden Beach was still less crowded than many of the more popular beaches, especially those along the grand strand. Jack's house was on the far end of Ocean Boulevard in a gated community. It was very quiet and peaceful there, a perfect getaway for Jack and Vanessa.

Jack poured some scotch into a glass and stepped out on the deck into the warm ocean breeze. He never heard the cat-like footsteps approaching as the roar of the ocean sufficiently covered any audible sound. Jack's head snapped violently to the left, as his left hand fell toward the deck, dropping the glass of scotch and sending shards of glass in every direction.

LEXINGTON, KENTUCKY

George Merit returned home to find Macy preparing dinner. "I thought you had class tonight."

"No. It was only for six weeks," replied Macy. "Last week was the last one."

"Well, that's perfect timing," he said. "That is if you still want to do that helping people thing you've talked about so much."

"What are you talking about?"

George filled Macy in on the missing agent and how his friend desperately wanted to locate him before he fell into the wrong hands. Ever since George and Macy's parents died and left them financially independent, Macy felt she should use her resources for good, and often spoke about helping people who were in need or had suffered injustice at the hands of the system. As she listened to George, she realized this may be her chance to make her prior idea a reality.

"It sounds interesting," said Macy. "But there doesn't seem to be a lot to go on. Where do I start?"

"You didn't think this kind of thing would be easy did you?" asked George, adding a slight chuckle and, handing Macy a piece of paper. "It just so happens you're in luck. One of Frank's agents was able to keep him on the phone long enough to get a location. It's some motel outside of Atlanta."

Macy took the paper from George and handed him the oven mitt she was holding. "Looks like you're on your own for dinner. I've got a date in Atlanta." And with that she headed to her bedroom to change and pack a few clothes before leaving.

Macy checked her watch as she headed out the door. It was a little after seven, and she figured she should arrive in Atlanta around one in the morning if she drove straight through. Her heart was beating fast as adrenaline rushed through her veins from the excitement. She felt like she was on another military operation, only this time she was the one calling the shots. She took a deep breath as she reminded herself of the need to remain focused and alert to her surroundings. Although this seemed like it might be a fairly easy objective, Macy knew anything could happen in a matter of minutes. There was no excuse for letting your guard down, and usually no second chance. Macy ran down the mental checklist in her head as she sped toward Atlanta.

It was five minutes after one when Macy pulled into the parking lot at the Colonial Inn. She parked between two other cars so as not to draw attention. She carefully made her way to the front desk and rang the bell. A young man appeared from the room behind the counter, the sound of a television audible when he opened the door.

"What room is he in?" asked Macy, shoving a picture of Agent Vrama in front of him.

"Never seen him before," he said, not even looking at the picture.

"Take a closer look," said Macy, placing a fifty dollar bill beside the picture.

"You a cop?" he asked. "'Cause I don't want any trouble."

"Relax," she said as she flashed a smile. "I'm just an old friend."

"Room eight," he said. "And don't leave a mess."

Macy nodded and walked out of the office. As she searched the doors for the number eight, she looked around to make sure no one else was in the vicinity. When she reached the room, she knocked gently on the door and waited. Vince asked who it was and she told him she was sent by Frank, causing him to open the door and quickly motion her in. He glanced around outside to make sure she was not followed, then locked the door.

"Agent Vrama, I'm Macy Merit," she said, extending her hand. Vince shook her hand, looking rather inquisitively since he did not recognize the name as one of their agents. Macy proceeded to explain who she was and how she was there to help. He told her what little he knew about the operation. She noticed he seemed to be sweating a lot, and asked if he was feeling well. He told her it must be all of the excitement from the past few days, and assured her he was fine. Realizing if she found him so easily, it wouldn't take long for others to locate his whereabouts, she suggested they leave immediately. She opened the door and peered out before stepping outside and leading him to her vehicle. As soon as she slid into the driver's seat, Vince suddenly exclaimed he had forgotten something. She told him to wait in the car and she would go back to retrieve it. He told her where to look and she reentered the motel room. She walked to the bathroom and flipped the wall switch, but the light did not come on. She reached up and pulled open the light fixture where she found a motel wash cloth stuffed where the bulb should be. Macy grabbed the cloth and carefully opened it, revealing a small vial containing some kind of liquid. She reasoned it must be important for him to take the trouble to hide it. She looked around the room one more time before closing the door and walking toward the car. Suddenly, she felt a sharp pain as she fell to the ground. She looked up to see someone standing over her.

"Civilian life has made you soft," the man said. "Don't get in my way again, or next time I will kill you." Then he struck her in the head with the butt of a gun. The grip on her arms felt familiar but there was no mistaking the voice. As she slipped into unconsciousness, Macy uttered the name, "Gordon."

Gordon took the key the clerk gave him and inserted it into the lock on room eight. He turned the knob slowly hoping to avoid detection. Vince hunched down in Macy's vehicle, peering up occasionally to see what was going on. After a few minutes of searching the room, Gordon was convinced Agent Vrama had left the motel. He motioned with his right hand and two others dressed in black joined him inside the van parked at the far end of the motel. They sped off toward the interstate as Macy lay unconscious on the ground.

She slowly opened her eyes, but when she moved to get up, a searing pain shot through her head. She closed her eyes and reached her hand around to the back of her head, wincing as she touched the large goose egg that appeared where she had been hit. She could see blood when she pulled her hand back in front of her face. Vince stood over her, cautioning her to remain still and not move. She was too stubborn to follow orders, though, and instead placed her hands on the ground to brace with while she slowly tried to get up on her knees. After a few minutes, she was able to stand, her head still throbbing from the blow. Agent Vrama took her by the arm and led her back to the car, easing her into the passenger seat and laying her head back. He climbed into the driver's seat and sped off toward the interstate. She cursed under her breath for making such a rookie mistake as to not thoroughly assess the surroundings before getting caught out in the open like that. She carelessly assumed no one else knew about Agent Vrama's location in time to be there that quickly. Now she had a horrible headache as a reminder of her error in judgment.

After a few minutes, her head began to clear, but she was still in a lot of pain. She reached in her purse and retrieved a couple of aspirin, popped them in her mouth, and began chewing and swallowing. She hoped they would start to ease some of the pain, but realized she probably had a concussion. As she sat there, she thought about Gordon and wondered how he was involved in all of this. She thought about what he said and decided next time they met there would be a little payback.

By the time she was feeling well enough to concentrate, she had no idea where they were going. Agent Vrama had not spoken to her since they left the motel. By now, Gordon's trail was cold and she had no idea where they had gone or what their next move would be. At least for now she had the advantage of knowing where Agent Vrama was. The key would be keeping him alive long enough to get to the bottom of whatever was going on in San Antonio.

"Where are we headed?" she asked.

"Well, you said you were from Kentucky, so I thought we might go to your place and lay low for a while," he said, looking over at her and smiling.

She phoned George to let him know what happened and tell him that Gordon was somehow involved. George begged her not to drive back in her condition, but she assured him that Agent Vrama was driving. She had traveled farther than this in worse shape, and besides, she needed to stay awake anyway in case she did have a concussion. He told her to call if she needed any help, and after promising him she would for the third time, she ended the call.

When they arrived back at George's house, he was waiting for them. He helped Vince lead her into the house, then poured her some coffee and handed her an ice pack for her head. Her head was still hurting, so she took two more aspirin. Macy expressed her concern to her brother over Gordon's involvement, and suggested he try to find any information as to Gordon's whereabouts through government channels. She pulled out the vial she had removed from the motel bathroom and asked Agent Vrama what it was. He explained it was a vial of vaccine he had taken from the lab before he left. He suggested they each inject themselves with it so he would not transfer the virus to them. She told George to look for a syringe in her old field kit she used for interrogating suspects. He retrieved a syringe and carefully drew out the amount per Agent Vrama's instructions based upon his observations at the lab. He injected Macy first, and proceeded to inject himself. Based upon the measurements given him, there was only enough in the vial for two injections. Agent Vrama assured George he was fine and must be one of those select few immune to this virus.

George left for the office to search for information about Gordon. Meanwhile Macy decided to take a hot bath to help ease her aching body while Agent Vrama lay down on George's bed for some rest. Her head was so messed up before she didn't realize her knees were also scratched and bruised. She slid into the warm water and lay back against the edge of the tub, being careful to put the weight of her head on the side that was not bruised. She winced in pain as the water touched the opened skin on her knees. Blood from her cuts mixed with the water, turning it a pinkish red color. Macy bathed as best she could since the soreness and stiffness in her body was beginning to intensify. After her bath, she searched through George's cabinets until she found some peroxide and antibiotic ointment. She cleansed the cuts with the peroxide, allowing it to boil for a few minutes, then smeared on some ointment and bandaged her knees. She wrapped a robe around her and hobbled to the kitchen to get another ice pack from the freezer. She placed it against the bruise in the back of her head, squeezing her eyes shut tightly as the pain shot through her skull.

Macy walked to the living room and turned on the television to see if there was any national news regarding the incident outside Atlanta. She knew with Gordon involved it probably would never be known by the public, but she was curious anyway. She flipped through the channels until she reached the news channel. After a few minutes, she suddenly opened her eyes and realized she had fallen asleep. The ice pack had fallen on the floor beside the couch and her head was throbbing. She took some more aspirin and turned off the television. She figured it was probably okay if she lay down for some sleep now, so she made her way to the bedroom. She kept thinking about how Gordon had gotten the best of her again, and wondered if she would ever have the opportunity for payback. She had always heard the old saying 'what goes around comes around,' but knew that was not always the case. Still, her thirst for justice kept telling her that one day she would even the score. As she lay there, seething over her most recent error in judgment, she finally succumbed to the lack of sleep and physical punishment.

Chapter 16

Holden Beach, North Carolina

Detective Josh Price arrived at the Jordan residence at exactly eight o'clock Saturday morning. There were already two marked patrol cars parked in the driveway when he pulled his car to a stop along the curb in front of the house. The call came in as a suspected suicide, so there was no need for lights or sirens. Detective Price climbed out of his unmarked police cruiser and made his way to the front door. The uniform officers had already placed crime scene tape in front of the door, so he lifted one line of the tape and stepped across the threshold.

"Detective Price, I'm Sergeant Lewis," said the officer. "He's on the back deck. Looks like he died from a self-inflicted gunshot wound to the temple. We haven't touched a thing. The gun's still in his hand."

"I understand the wife found him and called it in," said Price. "Where is she?" The officer pointed toward the dining room and Price headed off in that direction. He stopped in front of Vanessa Jordan and expressed his sympathy for her loss. Then he began to ask her some questions. "When was the last time you spoke to your husband?"

"Yesterday morning," she answered. "I called him between meetings."

"And how did he sound to you, Senator Jordan?" "He sounded like he always does," she replied.

"I mean, did he sound depressed or sad, anything out of the ordinary?"

"No. Like I said, he sounded fine," she said.

"Tell me about your last conversation with your husband, Mrs. Jordan," he said. "What did you talk about?"

"Not much really," she offered. "I only had five minutes before my next meeting, so the conversation was very brief."

"Well, if you can tell me what you remember I would appreciate it."

"Let's see," she said. "I asked how his morning was going so far and he said it was going fine. I asked if we were meeting at the beach house this morning and he said yes. Then he told me he loved me, and couldn't wait until Saturday." Senator Jordan became choked up after that, and had to wipe some tears from her eyes with a tissue. Composing herself, she looked up at Detective Price with a puzzled look while she waited for the next question.

"I understand you were the first person to discover your husband's body," he pressed on.

"Yes, I came in like I normally do on Saturday and called out to Jack, but there was no answer. I walked toward the back door and I saw him. I ran out immediately, but I could tell he was not breathing. That's when I called 911," she said, again wiping tears from her eyes. The 911 call came in around seven o'clock, which matched with her story.

"Did you touch anything outside or inside the house after that?"

"No sir," she said. "After I called the police, I came in here and sat down to wait for them. I couldn't stand to look at him again like that," she said, dabbing at her eyes. "Besides, I was a lawyer before I was a politician, Detective," she said. "I'm very much aware of the importance of preserving evidence at a crime scene."

"I'm sorry, Mrs. Jordan," he said. "I hate to ask this, but is there any reason you know of that would cause your husband to take his own life?"

"None," she said, a spark suddenly igniting in her eyes. "Jack did not do this to himself. He had to have been murdered, Detective and you should be out there hunting down his killer." She stared directly into Josh's blue eyes, before continuing, "Instead of here interrogating me."

"Do you know anyone who would want to kill your husband?"

"Not really," she said, becoming calm again. "Of course, you realize, as a politician I have many enemies, but none I believe would do something like this."

"Here's my card, Senator," said Josh, handing her his business card. "If you can think of anything that may help us in the investigation, please call me anytime. I'm truly sorry for your loss, ma'am." He stood up and walked away.

After he finished talking to Senator Jordan, Josh walked out onto the deck to view the scene. Jack Jordan was slumped over in the deck chair with his left hand hanging down just above the broken glass. His right hand was also hanging down and still held the .38 caliber revolver that appeared to be the weapon that killed him. The forensic team had not yet arrived, but from all appearances it was a routine suicide. Price had seen his share of them over the years. He'd worked homicide in Philadelphia, with a lot of them looking exactly like this one. A severely depressed man all alone pours himself a drink then eats a bullet. That was one reason he moved to the small community of Holden Beach. He wanted to get away from all of the dirt, crime, and death of the big city. And yet, here he stood in the middle of an apparent suicide, reminding him of a former life he would never be able to escape.

Price paced all around the scene looking for anything of importance, but kept coming back to the victim. There was no other physical evidence anywhere. No signs of forced entry. No footsteps in the sand from the beach; nothing at all to suggest foul play. He viewed the body from every angle, but found nothing to suggest it was murder. If it was suicide, though, why was his gut telling him something different? Maybe it was too much caffeine, he thought, shrugging his shoulders. He walked back into the house just as the coroner and forensic team arrived.

"He's all yours boys," said Price, thrusting his thumb over his shoulder in the direction of the victim. The forensic team passed by and immediately began snapping pictures and collecting evidence. The coroner knelt beside the body and thrust a thermometer into the liver to check the body temperature. He walked back into the house and told Price he placed the time of death somewhere between nine and eleven o'clock the previous evening. He went on to tell Price he would notify him as soon as the autopsy was complete, but he would be very surprised if the evidence suggested anything other than suicide. The coroner returned to the body to finish his work while Price walked out of the house and back to his vehicle. He sped off in the direction of the station to start his report on the incident, leaving the uniform officers to baby-sit the forensic team and secure the area when they were finished.

Vanessa was obviously still in a state of shock, but assured the officer she was fine to drive. She left the house and drove down to Myrtle Beach to spend the night at one of the resort hotels. She needed to get away from the scene and try to calm her nerves.

As Detective Price was filling out the incident report, something kept gnawing at him, telling him there was something he was missing. He felt Vanessa Jordan seemed a little too calm, considering she was the one who found the body. He picked up the phone and called the coroner.

"Hey, it's Price," he said. "Do me a favor and run a gun-powder residue test on the victim. I know it looks like a suicide, but humor me." He hung up the phone and went back to work on the report. After a few minutes, Price let out a big sigh, pushed his chair back from the desk, and stood up. He grabbed his jacket and headed out the door. Once in his car, he radioed Sergeant Lewis and asked if Mrs. Jordan was still there. Lewis told him she had left, and gave him the information for the hotel she was staying in. He crossed the bridge to leave the island and headed down Highway 17 toward Myrtle Beach. He parked in front of the Sand Beach Resort and entered the lobby. He walked up to one of the clerks, flashed his badge, and asked for the Senator's room number. Then he made his way to the elevator and up to Vanessa's room. He knocked gently on the door and waited patiently for her to answer.

"Detective, how may I help you?" she asked, when she opened the door.

"I'm sorry to bother you again, Senator," said Price. "I just had a couple of questions."

Vanessa invited him in and they sat down in the main living area.

"You said you were unable to reach your husband on the phone last night."

"Yes, I tried several times, but there was no answer."

"You also said you didn't believe he would commit suicide. Why?"

"Jack and I had a good relationship," she answered. "As far as I know, he was not depressed. In fact, he was looking forward to this weekend together."

"But that was his gun?" asked Price.

"Yes, he kept it at the beach house in case of burglars."

"And there were no problems with your marriage?"

"Definitely not," she said. "We were very happy together."

"Were you aware of any problems at work?" asked Price.

"No, but he rarely discussed his job," she answered. "He was mostly interested in what I did. He found politics fascinating."

"So you had no knowledge of missing funds from the CDC budget?" he asked.

"No, and I don't believe Jack would do that," she said. "We certainly did not need the money."

"Well, according to the note, he had embezzled a rather large sum of money," he insisted. "Did your husband like to gamble?"

"Not that I'm aware of," said Vanessa. "Of course, we were together mainly on weekends, so I can't speak for his daily routine in Atlanta."

"Thank you for your time, Mrs. Jordan," said Price. He excused himself and walked out of the room. He climbed back into his car and headed for Holden Beach. He was eager to see the lab report about the gunpowder, but without any other corroborating evidence, the coroner would probably still rule it a suicide. Still, there was something about the scene that didn't feel right to him, but he could not put his finger on what it was.

He arrived back at the station and sat down just as his phone rang. It was the coroner.

"There was no gunpowder residue on the victim's hand," he said. "However, we just learned there was a shower last night, so the rain could have washed away the powder, depending on exactly how hard it rained where he was at. We can't be sure; since the victim was already dry by the time we examined him. Based on the note and the rest of the evidence, I believe it to be a suicide. I'll have the official report to you first thing in the morning, but I thought you would want to know as soon as possible."

Price thanked him for his personal attention to this case, and the speed at which he completed his examination. His instincts continued to suggest there was more to this than a simple suicide, but without any more evidence he would have to accept the coroner's report. He phoned Vanessa at the resort and informed her of the findings. He told her she would be able to claim her husband's body sometime tomorrow afternoon once the coroner officially released it. He again thanked her for her cooperation and expressed his sympathy for her loss. Vanessa expressed her gratitude for his help, but was adamant that her husband did not commit suicide regardless of what the coroner said. She asked him if she could have her own private investigation conducted. He told her she could, but advised against it because he did not want to see her taken advantage of by some private investigator looking to make a quick buck. She assured him she would be very thorough in selecting an investigator, and even asked if he could recommend someone. Unfortunately, since he had not worked with any of the private investigators in the area, he could not give her a positive recommendation for any of them. She thanked him anyway and ended the call. She immediately called her assistant to update her on the coroner's report. They both agreed the Senator should hold a press conference to address her husband's death and squash any rumors before they begin. Her assistant made all of the necessary arrangements for the press conference to be held in one of the meeting rooms at the resort in Myrtle Beach the next morning at ten o'clock. Afterward, she should be able to claim her husband's body and have it flown to Atlanta for burial. Vanessa called the funeral home in Atlanta to make the tentative arrangements. Of course, since Vanessa was a United States Senator, there would be a long list of dignitaries who would want to come and pay their respects, but she would leave that up to her aide.

Once she was finished with business for the day, Vanessa decided to undress and get comfortable. It had been an exhausting day and she was feeling the effects. She removed her slacks and blouse, revealing a matching pair of panties and bra, both black trimmed in lace. Even at fifty, Vanessa still had a slender sexy figure, and liked to dress that way. She filled the

Jacuzzi with hot water and submerged her body in the warmth. The pulsating jets eased her tired muscles and helped her relax. After about fifteen minutes, she turned off the jets and climbed out of the tub. She dried her five foot five inch body and wrapped a robe around her, tying it at the waist. The top opened enough to reveal the cleavage from her size forty breasts, which she recently had lifted so they looked like those of a girl in her twenties. She was a beautiful woman, and very vain too. She liked the way her body looked, and did not mind showing it off either.

Vanessa walked over to the bed and sat down, grabbing her cell phone from her purse. She dialed a number, and after a couple of rings, heard an answer on the other end.

"Hello," she said. "How was your day?" She paused to listen before continuing. "I just finished my bath. I suppose you heard about Jack. It's just awful. I was extremely shocked when I walked in on him like that." She listened some more then said, "That's sweet of you, but I'm okay. Thank you for the offer, though. I may have to take you up on that later. You don't have to come. Lord knows there will be plenty of others there. Just send someone in your place." She listened once again for a minute or two before saying, "Now you behave yourself." She giggled like a school girl, said her goodbyes and ended the call.

She walked to the mini bar and grabbed a small bottle of vodka. She unscrewed the cap and downed it quickly. She had another bottle, and realized she needed more than just the single serving bottles. She dialed the hotel concierge and asked they deliver a bottle of vodka to her suite. There was a knock at her door within ten minutes, and when she opened the door, the concierge handed her the bottle. She smiled, letting her towel open a little, and enjoyed it when he looked down at her breasts. Senator Jordan was comfortable ordering anything in this resort, for they were the best at being discreet. Besides, her family owned a majority interest in the resort, so she could have them fired if they betrayed her.

Vanessa grabbed one of the glasses from the wet bar and poured it full of vodka. She was too tired to sleep, so she decided to turn on the television. She flipped through the channels, but all of the news stories were about her husband's death. She decided she needed a diversion, so she found the comedy channel. She was actually able to laugh, even under the circumstances, as she continued drinking vodka. Before long she was feeling no pain as she flipped through the channels again. She took another long drink, this time straight from the bottle. The combination of alcohol and the stress of the day's events made her feel suddenly warm and sleepy at the same time. In a few minutes, the alcohol eventually took over and she fell sound asleep.

CHAPTER 17

LEXINGTON, KENTUCKY

Macy awoke the next morning still sore from her encounter with Gordon. She needed more information, and decided to go straight to the source. She scheduled a meeting with Landreau, who reluctantly agreed to see her, and hopped a plane to Hawaii. She was hoping he would be able to tell her of Gordon's whereabouts, or at least where to begin to look. Once the plane landed, she wasted no time in renting a car and driving straight to the base. As she entered the Naval Intelligence center, she looked around to see if she could determine who her replacement was, but there was no one at her old desk. Landreau stepped out of his office to greet Macy, acting as if they were two old friends. Once inside his office with the door shut, however, his demeanor changed.

"I know why you're here," he said. "But I'm afraid I can't help you."

"I haven't even asked a question," said Macy.

"Word travels quickly in our world," said Landreau. "You're here to ask if I know where Gordon McCain is, right?"

"Yes, but how...?" said Macy, but Landreau cut her off. "Like I said, word travels quickly," he said. "The fact of the matter is I have no idea where McCain is. All I can tell you is he was asked to resign his commission also and the last I heard, he had gone into business for himself as a mercenary."

"That would explain a lot," said Macy. "Any idea where he set up shop?"

"I'm sorry," said Landreau. "I don't know. If you'll give me your number, though, I will contact you if I should hear anything."

"Thank you," she said, writing her cell number on a post-it note. She left his office and drove back to the airport, eager to leave Hawaii. Ever since she stepped off the plane, she felt dirty, like she needed another shower. She never thought she would admit it, but she was actually looking forward to getting back to Kentucky.

After Macy left his office, Landreau picked up the phone and punched in some numbers. When the voice at the other end answered, he said, "She was just here asking about you. I told her I didn't know anything. Now we're even. Don't call me again." He hung up and sat back in his chair, rubbing his temples.

As she waited at the airport for her flight to board, Macy's cell phone rang.

"Macy, it's George," he said. "Where are you?"

"I'm in Hawaii. I thought I would see if Landreau could tell me where Gordon might be."

"Any luck?" he asked.

"No. If he knows anything, he's not saying," she said, then sighed. "I guess I flew all the way out here for nothing."

"Don't beat yourself up, Mace," he said. "That's all part of the job."

"I guess you're right," she said. "So what's up?" "Is Agent Vrama with you?"

"No, why?"

"Because he's not here, Mace," said George. "I'm concerned about him coming into contact with people and spreading the virus." Just then the door opened and in walked Agent Vrama. "Never mind, Mace. He just walked in." George ended the call and looked up at Vince. "Where were you?"

"I decided to take a short walk to clear my head," said Vince.

"You look terrible," said George. "Are you feeling okay?"

"I'm fine, just a little tired." He walked past George to the sofa and collapsed in a heap on the cushions, quickly falling asleep. He decided to leave Vince alone for a while so he could get some rest.

* * *

After a couple of minutes, the announcement came that Macy's flight was boarding, and she made her way to the gate. Soon she was on her way back home with no leads on Gordon's whereabouts and a dead end case. She felt saddened about what happened at the motel. She was so close, if she had only followed procedure. Her sadness quickly changed to anger as she remembered the words Gordon said into her ear right before he struck her. She vowed she would find Gordon, no matter what it took, and settle the score.

QUANTICO, VIRGINIA

A tear rolled down Agent Phipps' cheek as she watched the convenience store tape, replaying the part where Vince looked straight into the camera and mouthed the words 'Help Me.' Frank had spent the morning stomping and slamming doors after he heard the news about Agent Vrama. He was one of the best agents they had at the OCB and he was having a hard time believing he was dead, especially since the field team found only traces of blood outside the motel room and no sign of Agent Vrama. He questioned what it was that Vince had become involved in, but when he tried to speak to the director about it, the subject was strictly off limits. No one was talking, which enraged him even more. If they could only have made it to him in time, maybe he would be safely at Quantico. He had never lost an agent before and this was especially hard for him, not to mention the months of undercover work Vince had logged was all now worthless. They were no closer to busting the Carillo drug manufacturing operation than when they started.

After spending the morning venting over their loss, Frank began formulating a fake dossier for the next agent to replace Vince. They would have to place this person carefully in prison, but give them a much different scenario for two reasons. First, so as not to closely resemble Vince's and attract attention, and second to hopefully keep this agent from becoming involved in the same quagmire Vince stumbled into. It would be difficult, as Frank worked on the dossier and began the arduous task of determining who next to give this assignment to. He rubbed his forehead as if in pain, then got up and left the office. He needed some fresh air before he could continue business as usual.

Lexington, Kentucky

Macy made it back to Lexington in time to begin preparing dinner for George and Vince. She felt it was the least she could do since he had been nice enough to come get her and invite her into his home. She was in the middle of mixing the salad when her brother entered the house. As he came into the kitchen, Macy looked up, flashed a smile and a wink at him.

"I thought I would fix dinner," she said.

"Well, I'm glad to see you're feeling better," said George.

"Thank you," she said, smiling.

George sensed something was different. "Is there something you want to tell me?"

"You won't believe this," she said. "But I finally figured out what I want to do with the rest of my life."

"Well, don't keep me in suspense," said George, smiling back at her.

"I fell asleep on the flight back to Kentucky, and had this amazing dream. I dreamed I was a superhero and I was flying all over town rescuing people and fighting crime," she said with a giggle.

"But you can't really fly," said George.

"I know that, silly," said Macy. "But remember how I said I would like to be able to help people, especially since I really don't need the income from a regular job after what Mom and Dad left us?"

"Yes. But I still don't see how you can become a superhero."

"Well, I can't really fly. And if I go around wearing a costume, they will lock me up. But I can use my training and resources to help people who have suffered injustices. You even said yourself that you've seen people the system was not able to help because of self-imposed restrictions. That's where I can help."

"I'm still not following you," said George as he rubbed his forehead.

"Okay. Remember the lady whose husband skimmed money from their business then disappeared, and she had to pay all of those fines and almost went to prison?"

"Yeah, what about her?"

"I could have helped her track down her husband, or maybe even helped her disappear to avoid taking the rap for his indiscretions."

"That sounds illegal to me," said George.

"Not exactly. As long as the true bad guy pays in the end. At least, that's the way it works in the comics," she teased with a laugh.

"I don't know about all of this," he commented, shaking his head.

"As long as justice is served, everyone wins, right?" "Well, I suppose you're right, at least in theory."

"You know I'm right," she said, her eyes sparkling with excitement.

"And just how do you plan to find these people?"

"Well, I was hoping from you for starters."

"Whoa, wait a minute," he said, holding out his hands. "I'm not so sure I want to get mixed up in all of this."

"You already sent me one client, Vince Vrama, remember?" she reminded him. "Come on, George, where's your sense of adventure? Besides, all you have to do is give me their contact information once you encounter someone who has exhausted all of the normal options, especially people you've tried to help but can't. I'll take it from there. I also plan to talk to some old friends who are now attorneys. I'm sure they may have some clients who could use my services." She folded her arms and waited for his reply.

"Okay, I'll go along for now," he agreed. "But the minute it looks like I could get in trouble over this, I'm pulling the plug."

"Thanks, George," said Macy, letting out a squeal and throwing her arms around his neck. "You won't regret this. I promise."

"So what do you plan to call yourself?" he asked. "What do you mean?"

"Well, every superhero has an alter-ego," he said, with a laugh. "What you're talking about sounds kind of like that guy on TV back in the eighties, The Equalizer."

"Well I certainly don't want to copy Edward Woodward," she snickered.

"Superman, Batman, and Spiderman are already taken, too."

"They all end in 'man' too," said Macy, placing her hands on her hips. "Let's not worry about a name for now, I'll come up with something."

"I can't wait," said George, flashing a smile.

"Did I hear my name mentioned?" asked Agent Vrama, as he scrambled up from the sofa. George and Macy both looked at Vince with a stern expression of concern laced with fear. "What's the matter? You two look like you just saw a ghost."

"How are you feeling?" asked George.

"Not too good. But I guess it's all the travel and excitement."

"I'm afraid it may be more than that," said Macy, as she walked over to the sofa. She placed the back of her hand against his forehead, and quickly pulled it away. "You're burning up."

Suddenly, Vince began vomiting and shaking. George grabbed him up and carried him to the bedroom while Macy got a washcloth from the bathroom and began rubbing his forehead. George tried to talk to Vince but it was obvious he was unconscious. He looked at Macy and they both realized Vince had finally come down with bird flu himself. They knew it was too late for the vaccine, even if they had any. George placed a call to the CDC and requested they send a field team to take Vince in for analysis. They left Vince in bed and returned to the kitchen.

George turned on the television while Macy continued with the dinner preparations. After a few minutes, George called out from the living room. "Macy, come here, I think I just found your next case."

Macy walked into the living room as George turned up the volume. Senator Vanessa Jordan was discussing her recent husband's apparent suicide, when she said she did not believe he killed himself, but the authorities assured her he had. She vowed to continue to believe he would never do anything to harm himself, and began to discuss the suicide note. Her husband had mentioned misappropriating funds from the CDC budget for a special project he was involved in with some civilian investors, but did not name names or give any details of the operation. He did mention the amount of money was upward of one billion dollars, though. She assured the press her husband was not involved in such a scheme, or otherwise she would have discovered it before now since they were so close. She went on to say she controlled most of the financial dealings for the couple, and there was no record of any unusual deposits. She said she planned to have her husband's death investigated further by private means, since the police had officially closed the case. The rest of the press conference dealt with funeral arrangements and ended up being a tribute to her late husband.

George turned the volume down and looked at Macy. "Well, what do you think?"

"She seems steadfast in declaring her husband's innocence," Macy replied.

"You could investigate this for her and try to clear her husband's name," George suggested. "Who knows? He may not have committed suicide."

"That's true," she agreed. "I've seen enough fake suicides in special ops that I could write a book, if the cases were not classified."

"Vrama was a tough assignment," said George. "You really weren't fully prepared to deal with it."

"I still screwed up," said Macy.

"No one's perfect," he said. "Not even 'The Avenger.' I have some contacts who can probably arrange a meeting with you and the Senator if you'd like."

"What about Agent Vrama?"

"There's nothing you can do for him now. I'll wait for the CDC to call."

"The Avenger," Macy said almost under her breath. "That's it!"

"What's it?" asked George.

"Nothing," said Macy. "I'll tell you later. Just see if you can set up a meeting with Senator Jordan."

CHAPTER 18

LEXINGTON, KENTUCKY

Macy awoke the next morning feeling more refreshed, considering all of the flying she did. She sat up in bed, hoping today would be a better day and she would be able to meet with Senator Jordan soon. After a nice warm shower, she dried her body, and walked to the dresser where she retrieved a black thong and matching black bra, laying them carefully on the bed along with her leather pants and a black tank top. She knew she would have time to change if she were able to meet with Senator Jordan today. She enjoyed her bath so much she decided her body needed some lotion to keep her skin soft and supple. She grabbed the tube she had placed on the night stand and squeezed a generous portion in her palm, then rubbed her hands together and began to spread the warm silky liquid all over her body. She finished rubbing the remainder of the lotion in, then began to dress. She watched in the mirror as she slid on the thong then cradled her breasts in the lacy bra. She slid into a black pair of stockings, her leather pants, and black tank top. Lastly, she slid her stocking feet into a pair of high-heeled boots, and the transformation was complete. She walked out of the bedroom and headed for the kitchen.

George was already making breakfast when she appeared. She decided to read the newspaper and let him pamper her this morning. The front page article was about Senator Jordan's husband and all sorts of speculations as to why he committed suicide. There was a brief mention of the misappropriated CDC funds, but until a full audit was completed, there was no way to determine if it was true and exactly how much was missing. She grabbed a pad and pen and wrote down the name of the lead detective on the case, along with the words Holden Beach. She walked over to the table and sat down where George had placed a plate of eggs and bacon. George asked how she was feeling, to which she replied, "Great!"

Macy asked if Agent Vrama's conditioned had improved, to which George shook his head and informed her he had been up with him most of the night, but he remained unconscious. After breakfast, George started making some phone calls while Macy turned on the news channel to see if there was any more news of the suicide. The reports were the same as yesterday, though, so she turned the television off and waited patiently to see what George could come up with. Finally, he came into the living room and told her he was able to get her a meeting with the Senator tomorrow morning at nine o'clock. The Senator considered it to be so important she cleared her entire morning in case it took that long. Macy immediately called the airline to book a flight to Washington, and packed her grey pinstripe business suit and a few other clothes in case she needed to stay more than one day. George stayed at home to wait for the CDC while Macy left for the airport. At least the flight to Washington was much shorter than going to Hawaii, she told herself as she entered the terminal. After a couple of hours, the plane was airborne and she was on her way to Washington, DC to meet face-to-face with a United States Senator.

The next morning, Macy donned her business suit and took a taxi to the capitol building. The meeting was to take place in Senator Jordan's office to ensure privacy from reporters. No one knew she was meeting with the Senator, so there was no press camped out at her hotel. She had been given directions to Jordan's office so she would not arouse suspicion by having to ask where it was. She arrived at the senator's office at five minutes before nine o'clock. She knocked on the door and opened it, stepping inside. The administrative assistant announced her arrival, and instructed her to have a seat. She offered Macy some coffee while she waited, to which she refused. Senator Jordan emerged from her office and walked toward Macy, extending her hand.

"Vanessa Jordan," she said, smiling.

"It's an honor to meet you, Senator Jordan."

"Please call me Vanessa," she said. "If we're going to be talking a lot over the next several weeks, we may as well do it on a first name basis." She led Macy into her private office where she closed the door and asked not to be disturbed.

"I thought you were looking into several private investigators for this," Macy began.

"That was just fodder for the press, darling," said Vanessa. "You came so highly recommended there was no need to look further." She pulled out a file from her desk drawer and opened it.

"It appears you've been a busy woman, Macy," she said. "Special Operations with Naval Intelligence. I'm impressed. You had an affair with a superior officer and resigned your commission."

"Senator..." she began, before she was interrupted. "Vanessa," said the Senator.

"Vanessa, I don't see why we need to revisit old baggage."

"I don't either," said Vanessa, closing the file and tossing it aside. "I just wanted you to be aware I know your background and that is precisely why I want you to handle my case."

"I don't understand," said Macy.

"It's simple," she said. "You did nothing any other red-blooded American girl in the same situation would do. You simply got caught, and probably because you were honest enough to inform on a fellow Navy officer. I need that kind of honesty. Good or bad, I need to know exactly what happened to my husband and why."

"What makes you think your husband did not commit suicide?"

"We were very happy. There was no marital strife. We had a lot in common. Jack would never steal money from the government, or any company he worked for. I believe he was murdered and the note was written by someone else."

"Did the police analyze the handwriting?"

"No. They felt all of the evidence pointed to suicide, so they closed the case quickly. Too quickly, but that's how small time law enforcement works," said Vanessa.

"I see," said Macy, as she jotted down some notes. "Detective Josh Price was the lead detective on the case," said Vanessa. "He should be able to provide you with all the evidence. Here's a key to the beach house so you can investigate. I left it exactly like it was when the police got there."

"Do you have any idea who might want to kill your husband and why?" asked Macy.

"All politicians have enemies, if that's what you're asking," she replied. "But I'm not aware of any who hate me enough to kill Jack."

Macy reminded her that it was very possible she would come to the same conclusion as the police. Vanessa said she understood and would not get her hopes too high. She did believe, though, that once Macy began examining the evidence, she would find there was more there than what the police found. She thanked the senator for her time and assured her she would begin right away. Senator Jordan thanked her for coming and told her she looked forward to hearing from her soon. Macy left the capitol building and took a taxi back to the hotel. She immediately called the airline and booked a flight to Raleigh, where she planned to rent a car and drive the rest of the way. She checked out of the hotel and took a taxi to the airport. She was now glad she had packed extra clothes

HOLDEN BEACH, NORTH CAROLINA

Detective Josh Price had worked many suicide cases in his career, along with many homicides. The problem he was having with this case was his gut was telling him it was not a suicide, but the evidence said it was. He learned two things about gut feelings during his years as a cop. The first is that gut feelings are usually right. The second is that without any hard evidence to back them up, acting on gut feelings alone could get you in a lot of hot water. Josh looked through the evidence one more time, although he already knew what was there. The gun was registered to the decedent. His were the only fingerprints on it. The absence of gunpowder residue could be explained by the rain washing it away. Then there was the letter detailing the misappropriation of funds from the CDC and explaining his will to take his own life. The coroner believed it to be an open and shut case of suicide. Josh sealed the box containing the evidence and marked it closed before sending it off to be filed with the other closed cases. He left the station for lunch at the pizzeria. As he took a bite from the first piece of pepperoni pizza, his cell phone rang.

"Detective Price," he answered.

"Detective, this is Macy Merit. I've been retained by Senator Jordan to investigate the circumstances surrounding her husband's death and I'm on my way to Holden Beach as we speak."

"You're aware, ma'am, Jack Jordan committed suicide," said Josh.

"I understand that is the conclusion the coroner arrived at," said Macy. "However, Senator Jordan believes her husband may have been the victim of foul play and wants me to at least review the evidence and the crime scene to determine if there is any evidence to suggest another cause of death besides suicide."

"And I suppose you expect me to simply hand over our files to you," he said. "A total stranger whom I have never met before."

"I'll be sure to formally introduce myself when I get there," she said, then added, "certainly you want to cooperate fully with the senator's wishes."

"It's not so much I want to, but more that I want to keep the boss off my back."

"Thank you, Detective. I knew you would be most helpful."

"What time will you get here?" he asked.

"I should be there in about an hour and a half," said Macy.

"I'll have the file ready for you," he said, and ended the call. He finished his lunch before riding back to the station. He retrieved the box of evidence for Jack Jordan's case and placed it on his desk as he waited for Macy to arrive. About an hour and twenty minutes after she called, Macy Merit walked into the Holden Beach police department.

"I'm looking for Detective Josh Price," she informed the desk officer.

He motioned with his left thumb in the direction of Josh's desk saying,

"That's him in the yellow shirt."

She walked over and stood in front of Josh, clearing her throat to get his attention. He kept staring at the paper in front of him and said, "Ms. Merit, I presume. Have a seat. Everything you are looking for is in here." And with that, he lifted the box and let it fall hard to the desk in front of her. Macy opened the box and began examining the contents. She read the coroner's report first, repeating aloud the part about no gunpowder residue.

"It rained that night," said Josh.

Macy continued to look over the file as if she did not hear him. She stopped for a minute and said, "That's strange."

"What's that?" asked Josh.

"I assume this picture of the victim is accurate."

"Yeah, why?"

"The gun is still in the victim's hand. Usually in a suicide, the victim would drop the gun once he shot himself."

"Not necessarily," said Josh. "I've seen this before."

"But I'll bet not a lot," said Macy.

"No, this is more the exception than the rule." She continued with her study of the file. After reviewing it for an hour, Macy stood up and began to walk out.

"Hey, where are you going?"

"I need to see the crime scene."

"I'll go with you," he said, grabbing his jacket.

"Why?" she asked. "I thought you were through with the case."

"I am, but I don't want you to get hurt."

"I assure you I am quite capable of taking care of myself."

"Okay, then you can take care of me," he said with a laugh. "Seriously, let's just say I'm a little curious and leave it at that. Okay?"

"Fine, but I'm driving," she said, and they walked out of the station to Macy's rental car parked outside. They drove down to the far end of the beach and up to the gate. Vanessa had given her the code to get in, and after punching the sequence of numbers, the gate opened and they drove through. She stopped in front of the house, which was easily identifiable by the yellow police tape still around the door.

"I guess she hasn't been back since that morning," said Josh.

Macy nodded and walked to the front door. She placed the key Vanessa gave her into the lock, opened it, and stepped inside. Josh was right behind her, watching her every move to see how she would investigate the scene. She carefully examined every room in the house first, just to make sure nothing was out of the ordinary. She walked over to the deck to observe the crime scene. Examining the blood still on the chair, she made notes regarding blood spatter, direction and amount. She also looked at the broken glass to determine the trajectory of its descent before walking to the steps and down onto the sand, taking a few steps in each direction around the deck. Finally, she rejoined Josh next to the blood-stained chair.

"Well, are you satisfied now?" he asked.

"Yes, I am," said Macy. "I am now convinced it was murder."

"What? How did you come to that conclusion?"

"Easy," she retorted. "Just follow the evidence."

"Okay, Sherlock, just how do you figure it was murder?" he asked.

"The gun still in his hand is rare among suicides," she said. "Then look at the broken glass. How many people would not set the drink down before shooting themselves?"

"Go on," he nudged.

"Notice the overhang of the roof? Even if it had rained that night, the eave would have blocked the rain from washing off the gunpowder residue. I must admit, whoever did this is a pro. I can see how it would be mistaken for a suicide."

"You forgot one thing," said Josh. "What about the suicide note?"

"I was getting to that," answered Macy. "I would like to have it analyzed by a handwriting expert. I'll bet you a dozen doughnuts it's not his hand-writing."

"I don't eat doughnuts."

"I thought all cops ate doughnuts," she said, laughing. "Okay, I'll buy you dinner."

"You're on," he said, smiling back at her.

CHAPTER 19

Bob Gorman paced nervously in his office as he waited for news from Max. Finally after another hour, Harry interrupted him to inform him he had a call. "Yes?"

"It's Max, sir. We have the samples safely secured at our lab here in D.C."

"What about Lackland?"

"There is no trace of us ever being there," she answered. "Everything is sanitized."

"Excellent," he said. "Now it's time for the replicating process. You have my earlier instructions on how much of each we need, right?"

"Yes sir," she replied. "We're ready to go."

"Then proceed with Phase II," he ordered, and ended the call. For the moment he could relax, as the operation was still on schedule. The incident with Agent Vrama was unfortunate, but it appeared their security had not been compromised. Although it was only ten o'clock, he poured himself a scotch, partly to celebrate the progression of his operation and partly to finish calming his nerves, which were still somewhat shaky from his earlier bout of worry. He let out a huge sigh as he sipped his drink, reflecting on the next steps once Max and her lab rats had completed Phase II. "Patience," he told himself, as he reached for the phone.

"Did you get the info on Agent Vrama's location from our CDC friend?" he asked when the man answered. "This time don't mess it up." He abruptly hung up and drained his glass of scotch, unable to contain the smile that spread across his face.

Meanwhile, Macy was on her way to Washington to meet with three different handwriting experts. She had the suicide note carefully preserved in an evidence bag, along with some personal correspondence of Jack Jordan's Vanessa had given her. Macy had worked with one of the experts before when she was in Naval Intelligence. The other two came highly recommended by her brother. Between the three of them, they should be able to come to a conclusion as to whether Jack Jordan actually wrote the suicide note. Since she was in a hurry to get the results, she had George arrange for them to use the lab in Washington, and had all three of the experts meet her there. They passed through several security checkpoints before reaching the inner chambers of the lab. Once inside, they began examining the suicide note and comparing it to several different items of personal correspondence she gave them.

Macy paced back and forth until one of the men politely asked her if she could wait in another room. It seemed her nervousness was affecting their ability to concentrate. She decided to go to the employee break room for another cup of coffee. As she entered the room, she noticed another woman sitting at a table reading the newspaper. The lady had short spiked hair and glasses. Macy sat down at the next table and sipped her coffee. After a couple of minutes, her cell phone rang.

"Mace, it's George. The CDC boys just left with Agent Vrama."

"How was he?"

"Still unconscious. Are you having any luck?"

"I'm waiting on a call now," she said.

"Well, hang in there. I'll let you know if I hear anything about Agent Vrama."

"I've got another call coming in, George. We'll talk later." She pushed the button on her phone. "Hello."

"Any luck on the analysis yet?" asked Detective Price. "Not yet," she answered. "They're still working on it."

"So do I get to pick the place for this dinner you're going to owe me?"

"Sure, but after today I won't owe you a thing," she said, smiling. "I feel certain the handwriting on the suicide note is not Jack Jordan's. By the way, if I'm right, are you going to buy me dinner?"

"Why not," he said. "That sounds fair to me."

"I'll let you know as soon as I hear anything conclusive," said Macy, ending the call. She glanced in the direction of the next table just in time to see the other lady walking out the door. She figured her break must be over, and wondered how people could stand to work in a lab all day. She shook her head as she sipped her coffee.

The lady who left the break room quickly walked to the security station and asked to see the visitor's log. She found a private office and dialed a number on her cell phone. A man answered at the other end.

"We have a problem," she said. "I overheard some experts are analyzing Jack Jordan's suicide note to determine if it's his handwriting. Apparently, someone does not believe he committed suicide. The name on the visitor log is Macy Merit. I just thought you'd like to know." And with that, she ended her call and went back to the lab to resume her work.

Macy's cell phone rang again. It was the group of experts informing her they were finished with their analysis. She hurried back to the lab, pushing the door open and entering in a rush.

"Well, what do you think?"

"According to our analysis, the suicide note was not written by the same hand as these letters," said the first one, holding up the correspondence samples Macy gave them.

"We're all in agreement on this one," said the second.

"This is rare in our field." The other two nodded their agreement. They went on to show Macy some examples of both the note and the personal letters, explaining the characteristics they look for. Macy followed as best she could, but after they said Jack Jordan did not write the suicide note, she heard little else. They spent the next thirty minutes explaining every test they did to reach their conclusion. When they finished, the lead expert assured Macy they would prepare a written report based on their findings, and would forward it to George for her. She thanked them for their assistance, and turned and all but ran from the lab, eager to get back to Holden Beach to put the last piece of the puzzle in place and begin working on a potential suspect list. Macy headed straight for the airport and took the next flight to Raleigh. She decided to wait and tell Detective Price the results in person. Macy rented a car and left the airport, heading east on Interstate 40 toward the coast. Once Macy was out of the heavier traffic around Raleigh, she set the cruise control on seventy and cranked up the radio. She was feeling great after the news from Washington, as she rode along singing to Aretha Franklin's *Respect*. Macy was so engrossed in her thoughts she didn't see the other car coming up fast from behind her. Suddenly the car was alongside her, ramming her toward the side of the road. She took the next exit as she tried to elude her pursuer. The other car kept pace with her, ramming her from behind. She grabbed the steering wheel, trying hard to control the car, but was unable to stay on the small rural road, as her car hit the embankment on the right and flipped onto its top, skidding for several feet before coming to a stop. By the time, Macy climbed out of her car, the other vehicle had stopped a few feet in front of her. She crawled out and stood up, inspecting her body for any cuts or injuries. As she realized she was okay, she looked up in the direction of the other car when the driver suddenly struck her in the jaw with his right hand, sending her body crashing to the paved surface. She looked up, touching her bleeding lip, in time to see a man lifting his leg to kick her in then ribs. She went into self-defense mode, remembering her training, as she spun to avoid his kick, grabbing his foot and flipping him backward. The man landed on his feet saying, "I'll teach you to be so nosy." Then he moved in for a side kick, which she deflected as she landed her fist in his ribs causing him to groan in pain. She tried a side kick of her own, which he ducked, clipping her other leg out from under her. She sprawled onto the pavement as the man once again tried to kick her in the ribs. This time she was able to roll out of the way and jump to her feet. She landed a solid kick in the small of his back, sending him flying against her car. Then she grabbed the back of his hair and slammed his head into the metal of the car until he was unconscious.

Macy searched his body and found a hunting knife and a .45 caliber semi-automatic handgun. She held the gun on him until he came to. After a few minutes, he began moving his head from side-to-side, trying to collect his thoughts.

"Easy big fella," said Macy. "Tell me who you're working for."

"Screw you!" he replied.

"No thanks," she said, kicking him in the knee causing him to howl in pain.

"Now, let's try this again," she said. "Who are you working for?" The man said nothing, but instead spit at Macy. She kicked him again in the knee and across the face, sending the blood from his cut lip flying against the side of the car.

"I'll never tell you," he said. "You'll have to kill me first." He reached down toward his boot, pulling a small caliber pistol from underneath his pants. Macy saw the flash of the metal against the sunlight as he aimed the weapon in her direction. She instinctively fired first, causing his body to slump forward, dropping the pistol. She checked his pulse, but could tell before she touched him he was dead. She had seen her share of dead bodies in the Navy, and could remember every one she had killed as if it happened yesterday.

Macy grabbed his lifeless body and carried it to his car where she placed him in the trunk, wiping her prints from the gun and tossing it in with him. She stuffed his cell phone in her pocket, hoping it might hold some clues. She climbed in and drove back to Raleigh to the airport. She parked his car in the long-term lot, wiped her fingerprints from the car, and went inside the terminal to the rental car counter. She told them a deer ran out in front of her and the car was probably totaled, that she had called a friend to bring her back to the airport in order to report the accident to them. She gave the clerk directions to where the vehicle was, gave them her insurance information and handed them her platinum Visa with a credit limit of fifty thousand dollars. After they verified the credit limit with the card issuer, they gladly rented her another car. This time she paid the extra amount for the physical damage coverage just in case. Soon, she was back on the road headed toward Holden Beach.

Macy drove to the police station at Holden Beach and parked in front of the building in one of the visitor spaces. She walked in and went straight to Detective Price's desk, where he was busy filling out some paperwork. He was dressed very neatly, she thought, more so than the first time she had seen him. Macy thought his svelte five-foot eleven-inch frame was very becoming and he had a handsome face, covered with stubble, but rugged in a good sort of way. She especially liked his sky blue eyes that could be interrogative, but sensitive at the same time. Looking at his dark hair, she found herself wondering what it would feel like to run her fingers through it.

"Where can we get a good steak around here?" she asked, smiling at Josh.

"That depends," he said. "Who's buying?"

"You are, of course," she said, as she handed him the preliminary handwriting analysis.

"Well what do you know? It turns out you were right after all." He looked up at her and returned the smile. "I'm driving this time," he said, grabbing his jacket.

They headed to his unmarked police cruiser and sped off across the bridge in the direction of Myrtle Beach. Josh told Macy there were many good restaurants at North Myrtle Beach, She suggested he pick one since he knew them better than she did. He smiled, knowing exactly where he would take her. After a few minutes, he pulled into the parking lot of a place called Cagney's. He told Macy that it was famous for seafood, lobster, and Angus steaks. Her mouth began to water as she thought about how good some surf-n-turf would be. As they enjoyed their meal, she realized she had not been rattled at all by the earlier attack. She smiled as she thought, *I'm back.*

Josh ordered some wine, calling their dinner a mini-celebration, considering Macy had been right about her conclusion regarding the death of Jack Jordan. It seemed to her he was pouring more in her glass than his, and keeping hers full, but she was beginning to have such a good time she didn't really mind. *It was nice to have dinner with someone of the opposite sex who was not related to you,* she thought. After stuffing themselves on steak and lobster, they even ordered dessert, sharing a large piece of cheesecake.

Suddenly, Macy felt as if someone had turned the volume down, as her head began to spin from the effects of the wine. She started to lay her head on Josh's shoulder, which was his clue it was time to go. He paid the check and helped Macy to the car. They left the restaurant and headed back to her hotel.

CHAPTER 20

Vince gradually opened his eyes as he tried to discern his surroundings. He was still somewhat in a haze as he tried to make out the images of the people around him. He could tell by the jostling of his body he was in a vehicle apparently traveling on a dirt road or some other rough surface. He tried to sit up, but soon found he was strapped to a gurney. His movement alerted one of the people in the van, who walked over toward where he was lying.

"Well, well, it looks like sleeping beauty is finally awake," he said.

Vince didn't recognize the man's face, or the lady who was sitting beside the bed. Both were wearing camouflage military fatigues with black berets. Vince could tell his fever had broken, but he was still very weak. He asked who they were and where they were going, but they ignored him as if he were not there. After several minutes of the same questions, Vince began to raise his voice louder and louder until the woman stood up, retrieved a syringe from a medical bag, and plunged the needle into Vince's arm. After a few seconds, everything went black.

The next time Vince slowly opened his eyes and tried to focus on his surroundings, he could tell he was no longer moving, but was not sure where he was. He was strapped to a bed and hooked up to monitors. There was also an intravenous bag hooked up to him with some kind of solution being administered. The room was dimly lit, but he could tell there was no one else there. He decided to wait before he said anything in hopes someone would appear. He did not want them to knock him out again. As he lay there, he tried to see if there was anything within sight that would indicate who might be holding him or where he was. Unfortunately, nothing in the room had any discernible label, or wording he could decipher. Whoever was behind this certainly covered all the bases.

Thirty minutes lapsed before the door at the far end of the room creaked open. The lady from the van stepped inside and walked toward the bed. She scanned the monitors and wrote some information on a chart, turned and walked back out of the room, locking the door behind her. It took all of his strength not to speak to her, but he wanted to remain conscious in hopes of gaining some information that could help him. She never looked directly at Vince, and remained silent the entire time she was in the room. Vince had seen this type of behavior and training only once before when he was in the Army. He was very familiar with the training of special operation personnel and knew that unless he could find a chink in the armor, so to speak, there would be no way to dissuade them from completing their objective. Obviously, if they were not concerned about him seeing their faces, then part of their plan included his termination. Vince knew now his survival depended on whether or not he could find a way to escape.

He had no idea what time of day it was, or how long he had been unconscious. It was another two hours before the door opened again. This time the man from the van entered the room. He walked over beside the bed and scanned the monitors.

He glanced down at Vince and smiled. "It appears you're getting stronger."

"How long was I out?" asked Vince.

"A few days," the man said. "You seemed to have succumbed to a virus, but your immune system was strong enough to fight it off. I'm sure you're still weak from the effects, but your strength should return soon."

"Can you tell me who you are and what you want with me?"

"Just rest for now," he answered. "All in good time, but for now you should conserve your energy."

The man smiled at Vince, turned and walked out of the room without any further conversation. Vince pulled at the straps around his wrists, but they were securely in place. He was still so weak from the aftereffects of the virus, he immediately broke out in a cold sweat from the exertion. He relaxed his body, closed his eyes, and was soon asleep.

He was wakened by the lady from the van. She had brought some soup for him to see if he could keep food down. She pressed a pedal underneath the bed causing the head to rise and position Vince in a more upright position. He remained strapped to the bed while she fed him with a spoon. As he swallowed, he realized it had been a while since he had actually eaten solid food. The warm broth felt good as it warmed him from the inside out. He was able to eat half the bowl before indicating he was full. She took the rest of the food with her as she left the room.

Several days went by as Vince continued to gain both his strength and appetite. It was apparent to his captors he was almost back to full strength, and his two guardians came in one morning and approached the bed. The woman raised the bed to a more upright position while the man placed what appeared to be a medical bag on a table against the far wall and opened it slightly. He walked over to Vince and smiled as he sat down beside him.

"Agent Vrama, it appears you have recovered nicely," he said. "Thank you for your hospitality," said Vince.

"Now we would like a favor from you. Tell us what you know about the operation in San Antonio and who you have confided in about it."

"Well, I really don't know what was going on," admitted Vince. "All I know is that it looked like there were some experiments being conducted on some of the inmates from the Marion prison, but I'm not sure what they were for."

"Come now, Agent Vrama," he said. "You've attracted too much attention for me to believe you know nothing of the operation. I'm a reasonable man, but my reason goes just so far. Now I'll ask you again, what do you know and who did you tell?"

"You're probably going to kill me anyway," said Vince. "So why should I tell you anything?"

"You're correct. I *am* going to kill you. It's just a matter of how long I take and how painful I make it. That is up to you."

"Well, I'm not saying anything," declared Vince. "Now, go ahead and torture me."

"Agent Vrama, you mistake me for a common thug. I don't intend to torture you. At least not until I get what I want. No, I believe a little memory juice will change your statement," he said.

He smiled at Vince, turned to the table, and retrieved a syringe and vial from the bag. He drew some of the liquid into the syringe, tapped it to ensure there was no trapped air bubbles, and walked back to the bed. He injected the substance directly into Vince's bloodstream and waited for it to take effect. When he was certain, Vince was under the influence of the sodium pentothal, he resumed his questioning. With the drug running through his system, Vince was helpless at the mercy of the man. He told him everything he knew about the Asian influenza experiments, including the deaths he had witnessed. He admitted he had confided in Macy Merit, the only one he'd told his story to. Satisfied with the information, the man left the room and dialed a number on his cell phone. When the man on the other end answered, he relayed what Vince had told him, including the name Macy Merit and listened for a couple of seconds for instructions before ending the call. He returned to the room and motioned for the woman to join him outside.

"Prepare him for transport," he told her, then walked off while she went back into the room. She removed the straps from his wrists and ankles since the drugs had greatly limited his ability to move. She bound his wrists together in front of him and eased him into a chair. She sterilized the room, removing all bedding, linens, and anything else that might indicate anyone had been in the room recently. She pushed the bed against the wall and carried the linens to the van, tossing the bag into the back and returned for Vince. She led him out to the back of the van and helped him inside, sitting him on the floor, climbing into the passenger seat while the man started the engine.

"Where are we going?" she asked. He turned to her with an expression that let her know she was not to ask any questions, but simply follow orders. She remained silent for the remainder of the trip. Slowly, Vince began to regain his faculties, and could tell they were once again on a bumpy road. He felt certain they were driving him out to a remote location to kill him and dump his body. Probably the only reason they had not killed him back in the room was because they did not want the possibility of any trace evidence of the murder left at the scene. After several minutes of traveling, the van came to an abrupt stop. Vince had to brace to keep from being thrown toward the front. The driver got out and walked to the back, pulled open the door, and grabbed Vince by the arm, pulling him from the van. He led him around to the front to a small clearing, moving a couple of steps away from Vince as he raised his gun until it was pointed directly at Vince's head.

"Do you have any last words?" he asked.

"I have some," said a voice from behind him. "Place your weapon on the ground, back toward the van, and place your hands against the sides in plain sight." Vince recognized the sound of Frank Pickard's voice. Suddenly, they were surrounded by several agents in full gear with automatic weapons. The man began laughing as he spun around in the direction of Frank's voice. The agents emptied their weapons into both suspects, killing them instantly. They quickly made their way to Vince, where they freed him from the bonds and began giving him medical attention. Frank walked over to him and placed his hand on Vince's shoulder. He looked up and tried to smile.

"I knew you'd come for me," he said.

"Don't count on it next time," said Frank. "If George hadn't called us, we wouldn't have known where you were. I'm glad now I put surveillance on you before these goons got here, or we would have lost you again—for good. Those CDC uniforms they used were pretty convincing, until we noticed they were wearing combat boots. That's when I decided to follow you and we wound up here. Now get some rest. That's an order," said Frank, motioned for one of the agents to escort Vince to a waiting car before walking back to his car.

He phoned the office and told Agent Phipps that Vince had been recovered safely. He also spoke with the Director, who told him to clean up the scene, turn the bodies over to Homeland Security as possible terrorists, and close the case file. Frank was puzzled by all the secrecy, but gladly complied. After all, he had his agent back, safe and sound.

After a few days in the hospital, Vince was released for light duty. The Director debriefed him about the case, and instructed him not to talk to anyone about what he saw or heard. He told Vince it was a matter of National Security and could never be discussed. He assured him the two who were killed were the main leaders of the group, and the others had all been rounded up and dealt with. It was officially a closed case. He advised Vince to take three weeks off to relax and regain his full strength before returning to the office. Vince was grateful for the time off, especially after the ordeal he had been through. It would give him time to take stock of his situation and decide if he really wanted to remain in his current occupation.

CHAPTER 21

Macy awoke in her hotel room at Myrtle Beach, still foggy from the night before. Josh had insisted they have a little wine to celebrate Macy's accurate prediction about Jack Jordan's death. As she tried to clear her head, it was obvious she had a little too much wine the night before. In fact, she was having trouble remembering much of the evening after the meal. She rolled over in bed to find Josh sound asleep beside her, suddenly sparking her memory of last night's events. Now she remembered Josh carried her back to her hotel and helped her to her room. Once inside, he pulled her to him, placed his mouth over hers, and gave her a long probing kiss. The effects of the alcohol combined with the kiss had aroused her, and before she knew it, she was kissing him back. They began shedding clothes as they made their way to the bed, groping blindly for each other, their lips locked together with their tongues intertwined. Macy remembered how surprised she was at his strength as he pulled her on top of him, holding her firmly in his grip. He was strong yet gentle, paying special attention to her needs and desires above his own. They seemed totally in sync as their bodies writhed together as one. They continued making love until their energy was spent, and they collapsed in each other's arms, drifting off to sleep as they basked in the afterglow.

Macy got out of bed and walked to the bathroom, trying not to disturb Josh. When she came back into the room, she almost shrieked as she tried unsuccessfully to cover her naked body with her hands. He was propped on his elbow looking at her, smiling at her sudden modesty.

"Relax, Macy," he said. "You've got nothing to hide."

"I could take that as either good or bad," she said, as she climbed back into bed and pulled the covers over her.

"I meant it as a compliment," he said, chuckling. He reached over and grabbed her, causing her to shriek and begin giggling. He pulled her close to him, kissing her deeply as her body went limp in his arms. She shoved at him and pushed him to his back so she was on top of him. She kissed him softly as he ran his hands down her back. They made love again, their bodies convulsing together in waves of passion. Reaching the point of near exhaustion again, Macy rolled off and closed her eyes, still breathing heavily from the exertion. Josh placed his arm around her and pulled her to his side as she laid her head on his chest. They remained like this for a while, comfortable with the silence of the moment. Finally he got up and walked to the bathroom, announcing he had to go to work. She gripped his pillow, breathing his scent deeply into her nostrils as she lay there listening to him in the shower. Suddenly, she shuddered, wondering what she was doing as she realized she really didn't know this man at all. How could she let herself become such an easy woman? Sure the sex was great, which helped her make the decision to know him better. Who knew? Maybe he could be the one.

Josh gave Macy a kiss as she passed him on the way to the shower. She showered, dried off, and dressed quickly. Since she had left her rental car at the station the day before, she had to ride with Josh to pick it up. She had reserved the room for the week in case she needed—or wanted, to come back. She told Josh he was welcome to stay while she was gone, and gave him a key just in case he wanted a change of scenery from Holden Beach. She carried her note pad with her in order to organize her thoughts while they rode. She was thinking about the details of the case when she had a sudden revelation. If someone came after her in North Carolina, he must be in on Jack Jordan's murder as well. Apparently, Agent Vrama's ordeal and Jordan's death were somehow connected, especially by his statement she should not be so nosy. The only question now is what were they both involved in that would get them killed? Macy told Josh about Agent Vrama and how she thought the two cases were connected. He agreed it certainly looked that way.

Josh looked up in the rear view mirror in time to see a black sedan speeding toward them. "Looks like we've got company," he said, as he pressed the accelerator harder. The sedan pulled up alongside them and began ramming into the side of their car, trying to knock them off the road. He did a good job of keeping his vehicle on the road as the sedan kept coming. Finally, he became fed up with the situation and slammed on the brakes. The black sedan traveled a few feet ahead and stopped, went into reverse and started backing quickly toward them. Josh climbed out of the vehicle and trained his service revolver on the car, squeezing off several rounds. The sedan swerved sideways, then flipped over and over until it came to rest on its top a few feet behind Josh's car. He and Macy walked over to the driver's side where the driver was lying halfway out the window. He was dressed in a black outfit with a matching ski mask. Josh reached down and felt for a pulse, and looked up at Macy, shaking his head to indicate the man was dead. He pulled the mask off revealing the driver's face and asked, "Is this a friend of yours?" Macy just shook her head no and walked back to the car. Josh called it in and waited for a uniform patrol car to arrive. He gave them a report, before they continued on their way back to the station.

"Is it always this exciting whenever you're around?" he asked.

"Maybe you should hang out more with me and find out," she said, smiling.

When they got to the station, Macy kissed Josh goodbye and told him she needed to go to San Antonio. He said he understood and asked if he would see her again. She winked at him and said she hoped so then drove off in the direction of the highway on her way to Raleigh.

Macy called the airline from her cell phone and booked a flight to San Antonio. She remembered Agent Vrama had escaped from a military base near there where a group of prisoners were subjects for some kind of lab experiment. She hoped she'd be able to gain access to the base to snoop around some and hopefully find some clue as to what exactly they were doing at that facility.

She returned the car to the rental agency and made her way through the security checkpoint to her gate. The flight began boarding about ten minutes after she made it. A few minutes later, the plane was in the air and she was on her way to Texas.

SAN ANTONIO, TEXAS

Macy left the plane and headed into the terminal at two o'clock Central time. She rented a car and asked for a map of the area. She questioned the clerk about any military bases nearby. The clerk made a big circle in red around Lackland Air Force Base on the map he had just given her. She thanked her for her help and headed out of the terminal to the rental car lot. She found the mid-sized Chevrolet, climbed inside and drove out of the airport, following the map directions to a nearby hotel. She checked into a room and carried her luggage onto the elevator to the second floor. Once in her room, she quickly changed into her old uniform and clipped her Naval Intelligence identification badge onto the jacket, just in case. She was hoping it would gain her access to the base without anyone calling to verify her credentials.

Macy left the hotel and headed in the direction of Lackland. It was not very far from the hotel, and she made it in a matter of minutes. She drove up to the guard gate and quickly flashed her I.D. The guard looked at it briefly, and waved her through. *So far so good*, she thought, as she made her way to the parking area outside the main office.

Macy walked into the base commander's office and told the airman on duty she was with Naval Intelligence and was investigating a smuggling operation that involved leaking chemical warfare secrets to China. She added a lot of legal and technical jargon, hoping to confuse the airman and asked about what type of laboratory facilities they had on base. The airman pulled out a map of the base and pointed out their main labs and the types of testing and experiments that typically went on in each. She asked where any top secret experiments, if any, would be held. The airman nervously pointed to the small lab located by itself, but added there hadn't been any activity in that facility for the last three years. Macy thanked him for his assistance and headed off in the direction of the main laboratory. Once she was out of sight, she doubled back and carefully made her way to the lone isolated lab. Judging by the airman's reaction, she felt it must be the one where the prisoners were kept.

As Macy approached, she noticed the guard shack in front of the building and the razor wire around the perimeter. Since there was a barracks located close by, Macy decided to take a look inside to see if she could find any trace of Agent Vrama or the other prisoners. Finding the barracks unlocked, she carefully opened the door and stepped inside. She looked around at the empty bunks, noticing no linens on the beds. Obviously, the barracks wasn't in use at the moment. She sneaked a quick look under each bed for any evidence, but the floor had been scrubbed clean there as well. She moved into the bathroom, and surprisingly, found it in pristine condition like the room she'd just vacated. She walked over to the trash can and opened the lid. It had a new liner in it, but there was no trash inside. She pulled out the liner and checked inside the can. She knew sometimes trash got between the liner and the inside of the can, where it could have been overlooked by a cleaning crew. She reached in and pulled out a small piece of paper that had been folded several times. She unfolded the paper to reveal a list of names. She stuffed the paper in her pocket and glanced into the can again. Seeing nothing else, she placed the liner back in the can and replaced the lid. Taking one more cursory look around, she slipped outside.

She made her way back toward the lab, but saw someone in the guard gate. She knew from experience the guard would be of no value to her, and decided to use a different approach. She made her way back to the commander's office and asked the airman if the labs kept any video surveillance of activities within the lab itself. The airman again appeared nervous, and Macy snapped at him before he could answer, informing him this was a matter of national security and he had better produce those tapes ASAP. He retreated to a back office then emerged with a box full of videotapes, each one labeled with the date and the number of the lab. As Macy searched through the box, she noticed there were none for the isolated lab. When she asked the airman where the tapes were for that lab, he replied there were none, since it had not been used for the past three years. Macy seized the opportunity to push him farther.

"Listen airman, you and I both know there was recent activity in that lab. Now, if you want your next assignment to be in Alaska, remain silent," she barked.

"Okay, okay," he said, lowering his voice. "There was a group of scientists brought in from somewhere off base a few weeks ago, but they didn't record any videos of their work. They left a few days ago and there has been no activity in that lab since."

"Did you happen to get any names of the lab people that were brought in?"

"No, but I remember seeing one of them," he said. "She wore glasses and had short spiked hair. I remember her because I made a comment to her in passing about how pretty I thought she was and she slammed me up against the wall and told me not to speak to her again."

Macy remembered the lab technician in Washington who fit his description perfectly. She thanked the airman for his cooperation, and advised he keep their conversation confidential if he wanted to keep his current assignment. She hurried back to her rental car and drove through the gate and off the base. She knew if this was the professional job she thought it was, there would be no evidence left in the lab. She thought about the lab technician in the break room in Washington, and then it hit her. She must have overheard Macy talking with Josh about Jordan and called that man to intercept her. *How else would he have found her so easily? And how else did he know she was investigating this case? It had to be her,* thought Macy as she sped toward the hotel.

Colonel Wagoner stepped out of his office and said to the airman, "Well done, son." He picked up a phone and placed a call. When the voice answered on the other end, Wagoner said, "This is Wagoner. Macy Merit was just here asking questions." There was a slight pause before Wagoner responded, "Just keep it from coming back on us." He hung up and returned to his office, closing the door.

As Macy was packing to leave the hotel, the attacker's cell phone rang. She looked at the display to get the caller's number, but it was unavailable. She decided not to answer it for now since she had a plane to catch. She checked out of the hotel and drove to the airport for her flight to Washington. On the way she called George to update him and see if he could pave the way for her to get back into the lab. He told her he would do better than that. He had to go to Washington anyway, so he would meet her there. She told him what flight she was on, and he agreed to meet her in baggage claims. Macy dropped off the rental car and made her way to the gate just in time to catch her flight. She was so wired with adrenaline she didn't even think about how much she had traveled recently.

She left the plane in Washington and headed down the corridor to claim her luggage. George was already waiting for her. She gave him a big hug and a kiss on the cheek. After a few minutes, her luggage appeared, they grabbed it and headed for his rental car parked outside. Soon they were on their way to the hotel for the night. He assured her the lab technician would still be there tomorrow since she had no reason to suspect anyone was on to her. Macy reluctantly agreed, but still felt they should go to the lab tonight. They grabbed some dinner and settled in their rooms for the night. Macy decided to give Josh a call before going to sleep. She dialed his cell and he picked up on the second ring.

"Detective Price," he said.

"You sound so professional," said Macy, with a slight giggle.

"Hey you," he said. "How's San Antonio?"

"Well, what little I saw of it seemed okay," she said. "I just happen to be in Washington at the moment."

"Wow, you really get around. What's up?"

"Too much to get into over the phone. I'll fill you in when I get back."

"I like the sound of that. Any idea when that might be?"

"Not yet," she answered. "I'll call you when I know something more definite."

"You better," he said, smiling. "Oh, by the way, I'm sleeping in your bed tonight. I can still smell you on the linens."

"Have a good night," she said, and hung up.

She smiled at the thought of him in her bed, but wished she were there with him. She was wide awake now after talking with Josh, so she decided to grab a beer from the mini bar and watch a little television. She flipped through the channels as she sipped her beer, but nothing really interested her. She was frustrated by being away from Josh, and decided to call him again. As she reached for her cell phone, it started to ring.

"Hello."

"Hey," said Josh. "I couldn't sleep after talking to you, so I decided to call you back. Did I wake you?"

"No, I'm having the same trouble sleeping."

"Well, we certainly didn't have this trouble last night."

"At least not afterward," said Macy, with a giggle.

Their conversation quickly turned into phone sex as both Macy and Josh were able to satisfy each other as best they could, given the distance between them. Afterward, they felt more relaxed, said goodbye for the night. Macy felt warm all over, her skin glowing with perspiration, as she drifted off to sleep.

Chapter 22

Washington, DC

George met Macy in the hotel lobby and together they rode to the lab in Washington. They walked inside and up to the security guard. He flashed his I.D. and the guard instructed them to sign in before entering the lab areas. Once past the guard, they searched through the different lab rooms, and realized it would take too long to simply go from room to room. Macy found one of the technicians on his way back from break and stopped him in the hall. She described the woman they were looking for and the man said the description sounded like Max, but she was not working today. She asked if he knew where they could locate her. The man told them her full name was Maxine West and he thought she lived in Georgetown, but was not certain about that. They thanked him for the information and quickly exited the building. George immediately grabbed his cell phone and dialed his assistant to request a location for a Maxine West living in Georgetown. They climbed into the rental car and sped off in the direction given them by the technician while George waited for the information. When his assistant gave him the address, he relayed the information to Macy, who wrote it down on her note pad. He thanked her for the information and ended the call.

Maxine West's apartment was in an older mixed neighborhood

approximately seventy-five percent black and the rest white. She lived alone in a modest one bedroom apartment on the second floor of her building. George and Macy carefully climbed the stairs to the second floor and made their way to her apartment. When he knocked on the door, it jarred slightly open. He drew his gun and motioned for Macy to get behind him. He called out and identified himself, but there was no answer from inside. Pushing the door open quickly, he stepped inside, looking from side-to-side in the first room. He carefully moved from room-to-room until he determined no one was there. He and Macy began searching the apartment for clues, but it looked as if whoever stayed there had moved out. The furniture was still there, but it was very old and worn. No clothes hung in the closet or taking up space in the dresser, and no personal items. It was obvious Maxine West had skipped town. The question was where did she go?

George called the local field office and requested a forensic team to come and thoroughly go over the apartment in case he and Macy missed anything. They went downstairs to the superintendent's apartment to see if he could provide any information. He knocked on the door and identified himself. The super opened the door and immediately began to proclaim his innocence without waiting to hear what they were there for. George asked if he knew anything about the lady in Apartment 210. The super said she left in a hurry yesterday, paid him through the end of the month in cash, and left no forwarding address. Macy asked if he had any idea where she might have gone. All he knew was she sometimes hung out at a local club called The Wild Side. Apparently it was a gay and lesbian bar. George and Macy drove back to their hotel to regroup and decide what their next move should be.

After lunch, Macy called Josh's cell phone, but was directed to voice mail. She left him a message that she was just checking on him and there was no need to call her back, unless he wanted to. She called the hotel and asked for her room in case he was still there, but there was no answer. He was probably at work, she thought. George called information and got the address of the club Maxine West frequented. They decided to go undercover in hopes they would find her at The Wild Side. Macy told George she remembered what Ms. West looked like well enough to make a positive I.D.

Since they had the rest of the afternoon to kill before time to go to the club, Macy decided to call Senator Jordan's office and see if she could meet with Vanessa to give her an update on her investigation into her husband's death. Senator Jordan's assistant informed her that the Senator's schedule was completely booked today, but she would check with her and call Macy back with an appointed day and time they could meet. Macy told her fine and thanked her before hanging up. She called the Holden Beach police station and asked for Detective Price. After a few minutes, the desk officer told Macy he had not reported to work. She tried his cell again, but was transferred to voice mail. She didn't leave a message this time, but called the hotel again. Still no answer. She began to worry about him, wishing she were back in North Carolina, but they needed to find Maxine first. She and George grabbed an early dinner before heading back to the hotel to get ready for tonight.

She had brought her leather pants and tank top along, which would be perfect for going out. All George had were business suits. Macy selected the one that was closest to the current style without a tie for him to wear. They left the hotel and headed to The Wild Side for some surveillance work. The club was located close to the university, the majority of the crowd younger than George and Macy. A few older customers were scattered throughout the place, probably with a taste for the younger ones, she thought. She had described Maxine to her brother as best she could, in order to split up and work the crowd. They planned to sit at opposite ends of the bar where they could scan the crowd easier. George was approached by several men the first hour they were there, but simply said he was waiting for someone. Macy was only approached by one woman, an older lady who was looking for a submissive girl. She informed the woman she was far from submissive and not interested in older ladies. The woman turned and left in a huff.

Two hours passed and Macy wondered if Maxine would even show tonight. It was a little after ten when she finally walked in the door. Macy immediately caught George's eye and nodded toward where the woman stood. Max walked over to the bar and sat down near the middle. Macy got up and moved toward her while George eased away from the bar and walked toward the door in case the woman ran. Macy sat down beside her and asked if she could buy her a drink, feigning a British accent to hopefully keep her from recognizing her. The outfit and the accent seemed to work as Max smiled and ordered a Cosmopolitan. She bought three drinks before suggesting they go to her place. Max was feeling good by now, and agreed, flashing a big smile at her. Macy winked at George as they stood up from the bar and he immediately walked outside. She led Max to their car where she opened the back door and shoved her in. She jumped in beside her and George cranked the engine, speeding out of the parking lot. At first Max thought she might be the victim of some gay bashers, but when Macy spoke in her real voice, she recognized her from the lab.

"Relax, Maxine," she told her. "We're not going to hurt you."

"What do you want?" she asked.

"We want to know about your recent experiments in San Antonio."

"I don't know what you're talking about."

"Look Max, we have an eyewitness that places you at Lackland Air Force Base three weeks ago," said Macy. "Two people are dead because of whatever went on in that lab, so you need to cooperate."

"Why?" asked Max. "What's in it for me?"

"It could mean the difference between life in prison and the death penalty, depending on how deeply you're involved."

"I had nothing to do with killing anybody."

"Okay, then tell us what went on in that lab."

"You don't understand," said Max. "If they find out I even looked in your direction, I could wind up dead myself."

"Who's 'they'?" asked Macy. "Look, I've said all I'm going to."

"We can offer you protection," George said from the front seat.

"Not from these people you can't," said Max. "Now let me go!"

"At least give us some idea of where next to look." urged Macy.

"All I'll say is it goes a lot higher than you two," said Max, then added, "a lot higher."

She refused to say anymore, and they drove around the city, eventually returning to the club. Macy let Max out of the car and climbed in the front seat beside George. They sped off in the direction of their hotel. He placed a call to the local field office on his cell requesting surveillance be placed on Maxine West to see if she would lead them to anyone else. They returned to the hotel for the night, each retiring to their separate rooms.

Once inside her room, Macy tried to call Josh again, but was not able to reach him. She yearned for his touch as she glanced around the empty hotel room, thinking about the night she spent with him. Although it was late, she wasn't tired, and grabbed a small bottle of orange juice and some vodka from the mini bar and mixed a screwdriver. She stripped and climbed into bed, propping her shoulders on the pillows. She turned on the television and flipped through the channels as she sipped her drink. Suddenly, she came across a movie that interested her and began watching. It was not long before the combination of a long day and alcohol got the better of her and she fell sound asleep with the television still on.

CHAPTER 23

Macy awoke the next morning to the sound of white noise coming from the television. Apparently, the movie channel she'd been watching stopped after a certain time and didn't start again until the next night. She grabbed her cell phone and tried calling Josh again, but there was still no answer and his voice mailbox was full. Evidently, she wasn't the only one trying to reach him, she thought. She climbed out of bed and headed for the shower. As she was drying off, her cell phone rang. She ran to get it, hoping it was Josh, but it was Senator Jordan's aide to tell her the Senator was available this morning if she could come by at ten o'clock. Macy told her that was fine, and after the call ended, she finished drying her body and dressed. She pulled on a pair of sexy bikini panties and matching bra, and black stockings. She decided to wear a business suit since she was meeting with the Senator, but the underwear was for Josh. She planned to fly back to North Carolina as soon as she was finished meeting with Senator Jordan.

Macy had just finished dressing when there was a knock at her door. When she peered through the peephole, George was standing in the hallway. She was a little embarrassed by having her intimate apparel lying around, and slid out the door before George could see in. They walked downstairs to the hotel restaurant for breakfast.

George accompanied Macy to Senator Jordan's office. It was exactly ten o'clock when they entered the Senator's office. She came out immediately and invited them in, closing the door after instructing her aide she was not to be disturbed. "We have reason to believe your husband did not commit suicide," Macy informed her.

"I knew it," Senator Jordan said with satisfaction. "How did you arrive at that conclusion?"

Macy proceeded to describe her visit to the beach house and her review of the evidence. She went into detail about the inconsistencies between her husband's crime scene and that of an actual suicide victim. Finally, Macy got to the part about the lab in San Antonio and Agent Vrama, believing somehow the agent's situation and the Senator's husband's death were related.

"That's very interesting," said Senator Jordan as she stood up and walked across the room. She made her way to a wooden file cabinet, pulled a key from her jacket pocket, and unlocked the bottom drawer. Reaching into the drawer, she pulled out a folder, pushing the drawer closed again.

"I found this the morning I discovered Jack dead," she said, handing the file to Macy. "It was on the table where he left it. I believe he was reading it that night, which is why it was left out."

"Why didn't you give this to the police?" asked Macy. "Because I knew they believed he committed suicide and wouldn't look any further into Jack's death. I didn't want to start a panic if it turned out not to be connected, but after what you just told me, I believe it may be of importance."

Macy opened the file and began to look over the contents. There was a report on top that was titled 'Bird Flu: What Avian Influenza Means.' Macy went on to read the following:

The Asian strain of avian influenza is highly pathogenic. There have been one hundred ninety confirmed human infections, with one hundred seven deaths to date. Human deaths have been restricted to Southeast Asia and the Middle East. To date, the virus has appeared in forty-eight countries.

The rest of the file contained charts and graphs related to migratory bird patterns, locations of outbreaks of avian influenza, and illustrations of diseased birds and humans. When she turned to the last page, Macy's eyes were drawn to something he had circled in red that read:

While there have been cases of transfer of the virus from birds to humans, there are no cases of transfer from human-to-human of the virus to date.

Macy slowly lifted her emerald green eyes up to meet Senator Jordan's.

"What do you think this means?" asked Macy, handing the file to George.

"There have been concerns ever since the discovery of avian influenza that one of our enemies, or even terrorists, would develop a strain of the virus that could be spread from human-to-human," said Senator Jordan. "Such a virus could be used as a biological weapon against us."

"Do you really believe someone could do this?" asked Macy.

"It's not so much a matter of whether they can do it," said George. "It's more a matter of *when* someone will."

"Exactly," said Senator Jordan. "That's why the CDC, and particularly Jack, has been concerned about this for years. But the government has been reluctant to provide funding for research into a possible vaccine against such a virus."

"That seems like an easy decision," said Macy.

"One would think so," said Vanessa, "But until the virus is actually mutated to where it can be spread from human-to-human, there is no way to isolate it in order to establish a vaccine."

"So what you're saying is the disease has to appear before we can begin work on a vaccine," said Macy.

"Unfortunately, yes," she replied. "Of course, every year the flu vaccine is tweaked somewhat to hopefully take care of newer strains, but we can't be sure there will not be an epidemic, or even a pandemic, once the high pathogenic Asian strain mutates to where it can be easily spread among humans."

"The end result could be very catastrophic," said Macy. "Yes, that's why Homeland Security is keeping a close watch on this."

"Tell me, Senator," began George, "do you have any idea how all of this could be connected to your husband and Agent Vrama?"

"Not really," she answered. "I was hoping Macy would be able to find out." She looked at Macy with a pleasant smile.

"Well, we know at least one person who was involved," said Macy. "We have her under surveillance, so hopefully she will lead us to the others."

"In the meantime, I'll see if I can find out anything about top secret experiments from some of my colleagues whom I can trust to keep this between us," said Vanessa.

George and Macy shook the Senator's hand and excused themselves, walking from her office and leaving the capitol building. They discussed possible suspects that could benefit from such an experimental breakthrough, but Max's comment kept haunting them. *It goes a lot higher than you two.* Exactly what did she mean by that? Sure, they had heard horror stories about abuse of power among high ranking politicians, but what would anyone in the political arena of the United States have to gain from developing a mutated strain of avian influenza? They agreed to keep thinking about it and see if they could come up with any ideas. George headed back to Kentucky, while Macy was on her way back to North Carolina. They planned on comparing notes the next time they got together.

Macy was able to book a flight to Raleigh leaving at one o'clock that afternoon. George had already left for Kentucky before her flight began boarding. She had a pleasant flight from Washington to Raleigh, and arrived on time. She rented another car from the same clerk as before, who informed her her insurance company was settling the claim on the totaled rental and there were no hard feelings. She flashed a smile and headed out of the terminal to the rental car lot. She hopped in and left the airport in the direction of Interstate 40. She drove east on I-40, trying to make the best time she could. She tried to call Josh again, just in case he had a problem with his cell phone, but there was still no answer.

She decided to drive to Holden Beach first to check if Josh was at the station. She arrived in front of the Holden Beach police department at four-thirty in the afternoon. Walking in, she immediately glanced in the direction of Josh's desk, but he was not there. She continued on to the desk officer and asked if he was on duty. The officer informed her he'd called in sick and would be out the rest of the week. She thought that strange, especially since she hadn't been able to reach him on his cell phone. Maybe he felt so bad that he was in bed and could not talk, she thought. She left the police station and drove toward Myrtle Beach. Even if he wasn't there, she needed to freshen up and change from her trip. She was glad she'd reserved the room longer so she didn't have to go through the hassle of checking in again.

She arrived at the hotel thirty minutes later, walked straight to the elevator and up to her room. When she inserted the key card in the lock and opened the door, she noticed the lights were off. The room was totally dark, and it took her a minute for her eyes to adjust. She closed the door and walked into the bedroom. She could tell someone was lying in the bed, but as she drew nearer, she noticed something else that caused her to catch her breath. There was a figure sitting in a chair in front of the window.

"It's about time you got here, Macy," he said. She recognized the voice.

"What the hell are you doing here, Gordon?" she demanded.

"I just came to see you," he said, a smile spreading across his face.

"Well, now you've seen me, so just leave."

"I'm afraid it's not that simple. You've been a naughty girl, Macy, poking your nose into things that don't concern you." As he stood up from the chair, Macy saw the glimmer of a gun barrel trained on her.

"What do you plan to do with that?" she asked, pointing to the gun.

"I'm sorry, Macy, but you gave me no choice. I tried to warn you so you would stay away, but you're so stubborn. You've always been stubborn."

"Listen, Gordon, I don't know a thing yet. Why don't you just leave and I'll forget you were here?"

"I wish I could, but now there's the matter of your new boyfriend."

"Where's Josh? What did you do with him?" she asked. "Why don't you see for yourself?" he said, turning on the lamp beside the bed.

Macy brought her hands to her mouth to keep from screaming as she saw Josh in the bed, his head lying in a pool of his own blood. She could tell by the position of the body it had been a stealth attack. He never knew what hit him. Tears rolled down her cheeks as she realized now why she hadn't been able to reach him. Although she hadn't known him long, she knew he was too good a person to die this way. She started to blame herself for getting him involved, but realized there would be time for that later, if she got out of this alive. She rushed to the bed and held Josh's lifeless body, crying and rocking back and forth. Her plan worked as Gordon lowered the gun and walked toward her. It was just the opening she was looking for. When he drew close enough, she jumped from the bed and thrust her fist into his ribs, knocking the wind out of him. As he reeled backward, she grabbed the gun and wrestled with him, trying to get him to drop it. He pushed her off and pointed the gun directly at her, firing one shot. She lunged sideways onto the floor, avoiding the bullet. Immediately, she swung her legs outward, sweeping him off his feet. She jumped on top of him, grabbed his hair, and bashed his head into the hard floor several times until he was unconscious. She took a moment to gather herself, then pulled Gordon upright into the chair and walked across the room holding his gun.

She waited patiently for Gordon to come to, pointing the gun at him. She had turned on all of the lights, fully illuminating the room.

"Do you still think civilian life has made me soft?" "

Why don't you put that gun down and find out?"

"Tell me about Jack Jordan," said Macy. "Why did you kill him?"

"I was just being a good soldier and following orders," he answered.

"Whose orders?"

"I don't know. After the Navy, I started mercenary work. Landreau gave my name and number to this guy, but I never met him. He would deposit money into my bank account anonymously when I did a job for him."

"What's his name?"

"He never said and I never asked."

"Well you can tell it to the police," she said, standing up from the chair. As she walked toward the phone, Gordon suddenly lunged toward her. She stepped back and fired; the bullet landing squarely between his eyes. He fell forward across the bottom of the bed, dead. Macy stood for a moment looking at him while she collected herself. She thought somehow she would feel more remorse, but after what he'd put her through, she was almost relieved he was dead.

Since the room was registered in her name, Macy was afraid this would all come back to her. She walked over to the adjoining room door and opened the door on her side, carefully picking the lock of the adjoining room and eased it open. She could tell by the way the beds were made and the lack of luggage the room was vacant. She dragged his body into the other room and propped it upright in a chair. Wrapping Josh up in the sheets and blanket, she carried him to the other room. When she went back to her room, she noticed the blood from Josh's head wound had bled all the way through the sheets and into the mattress. She compared the mattress in the other room with the one in hers to make sure it was a match and wrestled with her mattress, taking it into the other room, where she removed that mattress and placed it in her room. Once she had the beds in place, she took the linens from the other room and placed them on her bed. Going back to where she left Josh, she hoisted him up onto the bed and spread the linens out, making the bed as best she could. She stood back and surveyed what she had done satisfied the police would believe there had been a struggle. She placed the gun in Gordon's right hand, called in an anonymous report of a disturbance and the sounds of gun fire to the police. Given their recent attention to detail, she figured they would probably rule it a murder suicide. She grabbed Gordon's cell phone and stuck it in her pocket. She locked the two doors back that linked the rooms, gathered any personal belongings she had left in the room, and walked out. She hurried downstairs and checked out at the front desk, handing the clerk her room key. Macy left the hotel parking lot and drove south on Ocean Boulevard for a few miles, and turned into the parking deck of a resort hotel. She booked a room for the night, not wanting to drive back to Raleigh that same evening. Once inside her room, she called George to make sure he arrived in Lexington okay. He told Macy the flight was fine and he was relaxing in front of the television. She didn't want to go into all the details of her afternoon, so she just told him she would fill him in when she got back. She was planning on flying back the next day, and told him she'd see him when he got home after work. They said goodbye and ended the call after which she took a shower, and went to bed. She couldn't sleep after what happened at the other hotel, and decided to head downstairs to the bar. She hastily threw on a pair of jeans and a polo shirt, checked the mirror and was off.

Only a handful of people were in the bar when Macy arrived. She took a seat at the closest end and ordered a vodka martini. A basketball game played on the television behind the bar, and she turned her attention to watch the screen, not really interested in the game. She was on her third drink before she could feel the numbness easing the pain from the day's earlier events. Sure, she wanted to get even with Gordon, but not kill him. Yet, deep down she knew she had no choice. He was planning to kill her, so it was self defense. Still, it was never easy taking another person's life. She thought about Josh and what was done to him. Although she hadn't known him long, she definitely had strong feelings for him. Why did all of her relationships seem to end badly? She killed another martini and staggered back to her room. Once inside, she collapsed on the bed and passed out without even removing her clothes. It would take all night for her to sleep it off.

CHAPTER 24

Macy awoke the next morning in a stupor. Her head felt like it was going to explode, as it throbbed incessantly from the previous night's drinking binge. Although it helped her sleep and forget about yesterday for a while, now she not only was haunted by the memories of yesterday, but that was compounded by a raging headache. The pain seared through her brain so sharply she stumbled to the bathroom and vomited, heaving what was left of the contents in her stomach into the toilet. She wiped the remnants from the edge of her mouth with the back of her hand, and turned the shower on, hoping a hot shower would help dull the pain. Her eyes were only half-open as she tried to lessen the pain in her head the light exacerbated. She dried off, and brewed some strong coffee in the in-room coffee maker. She drank the bitter potion, hoping it would soon take effect and ease her pulsating headache. She also took a couple of aspirin, washing them down with another vile swallow.

Macy finished off several cups of coffee before the pain in her head began to ease somewhat. She needed some food, and made her way downstairs to the restaurant. The mere thought of eggs sickened her, opting for a bagel and more coffee. She was able to keep the bagel on her stomach, which satisfied her hunger for the moment. She went back to her room and packed her bags. With Gordon and Josh now dead, there was no need to stay in North Carolina. She felt certain the answers she needed were not here. She called the airline and found out she could actually fly from Myrtle Beach to Lexington with one stop through Atlanta. The fare was more expensive but it would save her driving to Raleigh and with her head still hurting, she was not looking forward to a long drive. She reserved a seat on the flight, leaving at twenty minutes after one. That would give her plenty of time to check out, return the rental car, and get through the security checkpoints. She grabbed her luggage and headed downstairs to the front desk. Handing the clerk her room key, she asked for directions to the airport, and left the hotel, walking to the parking deck. She climbed into the rental car and drove to the airport. Luckily the rental company she booked the car through had an office here, making it easy to turn the car in without any trouble. She was charged extra for a one way rental, but she didn't mind, rubbing her still pulsing temple. She was looking forward to getting back to Kentucky and comparing notes with George. She knew she could count on him to help her sort through all of this mess and determine what her next move should be.

Macy arrived at the airport in plenty of time to make it through security and grab a sandwich before her flight left. She was feeling better and starting to get her legs back. She ate while she waited for them to announce the boarding of her flight. Once on the plane, she found she was sitting next to a handsome gentleman in a business suit. At first she wondered why anyone would be flying here on business, but realized you could usually find some type of business traveler on any flight. She smiled at the man as she sat down in the aisle seat, since he was already in the window seat. As the plane pushed back from the gate, it became apparent there was no one seated between them. The gentleman started in on Macy before the plane took off.

"Good afternoon," he said. "My name is Bob Tyler."

"Hi. I'm Macy Merit," said Macy, shaking his hand. "Were you here on vacation, Macy?"

"Yes," she said, looking down at her magazine, hoping he would get the hint.

He did not, though. "I was here the last two days on business. I'm a sales associate for a meat company. We supply beef, particularly steaks, for many of the finer restaurants in the area. You probably ate one of our products while you were here on vacation." He flashed a big smile her way.

"I'm afraid I stuck with the seafood," Macy lied, hoping that would discourage him.

He pressed on. "What line of work are you in, Macy?"

"Actually I'm a homemaker. My partner brings home the bacon, so to speak. She works in advertising," said Macy, feeling that if he believed she was gay, he would definitely end the conversation. He didn't.

"Wow, that sounds interesting," he said. "Do you live in Kentucky?"

"Yes. Lexington," said Macy.

"What a coincidence," he said. "So do I. Hey, maybe the three of us could hook up sometime. I'm what you would call a metro-sexual, and am very open minded."

Macy had enough. "That's great, Bob, is it? Bob, I've been trying to be nice, but you don't seem to be able to take a hint, so I'm going to give it to you straight. I'm not gay, I'm not married, and I'm not interested in 'hooking up' with anyone right now, especially you. Now, can I please enjoy the rest of the flight in peace?" she asked coldly.

He sat back with a surprised look on his face, struggled for something to say, but all he could stammer was, "Sorry." His face turned as red as a tomato from embarrassment. It was obvious Bob was not a veteran at the pick-up game, and being shot down in flames like this may have permanently damaged what was left of his fragile psyche. Macy didn't really care about that. She was too busy with more important matters, like trying to figure out who was behind several deaths, and now might have the ability to launch a bird flu epidemic. Bob would heal over time, she told herself, and if not, maybe he would find a higher respect for the opposite sex. Either way, she turned her attention to her inward thoughts and began to sift through the facts of the case, making mental notes she could bounce off George.

Macy had to change planes in Atlanta to continue on to Lexington. She wasn't sure if Bob remained on the plane because his business was taking him elsewhere, or because he was trying to give her plenty of space. She didn't see him board her flight, so either he changed flights back to Lexington, or he had business elsewhere. Either way, she was certain she had seen the last of him. The flight to Lexington was about half-full, and she had the row to herself. She settled in the window seat to watch the white clouds go by as she continued to analyze the case in her mind. She thought about Josh a couple of times and tears began to well up in her eyes. She told herself it probably wouldn't have worked out anyway since they lived so far apart, trying to trick her mind out of its sadness. Before long, the plane was setting down on the runway and Macy was back in Lexington.

She had called George from the airport to let him know what time she would arrive and the flight number, so when she got to baggage claim, he was waiting on her. She walked over to him and kissed him on the cheek, holding him in an embrace that seemed longer than normal to her brother. He knew immediately something was wrong, but decided not to pry until they got home. He grabbed her luggage and they left the terminal on their way to his car. They made small talk on the drive home, saving the important dialogue for when they were settled in.

When they got home, George began preparing spaghetti for dinner while Macy took a shower and changed into something more comfortable. She let the warm water run over her, as she tried to wash away the past several days. She felt so dirty after all that had happened and her recent plane flight. After twenty minutes in the shower, she stepped out and toweled off. She decided to simply put on her robe since she wasn't going anywhere. By the time she made her way back to the kitchen, dinner was ready. They ate in silence, waiting until they both were completely finished before resuming their conversation. He poured a glass of bourbon while she settled for a soda. They sat down at the table and began to compare notes.

Macy filled George in on what happened at Myrtle Beach, conveniently leaving out the part that she slept with Josh. He could tell by the way she almost cried when she mentioned what happened to him, there was more to the story. He especially wondered why Josh was sleeping in her hotel room while she was in Washington, but decided he would wait and let his sister tell him later if she wanted to. He vowed many years ago to be a lov-

Dale Crotts

ing and understanding brother who did not pass judgment on his sister. He listened intently as she described the details of her encounter with Gordon, making mental notes about what he said to her. He was impressed with the way she handled herself in the field, wishing some of his agents were more resourceful. He had tried unsuccessfully to recruit Macy to work with the Bureau, but he understood her determination to help those who the system did not.

After she finished, George spoke. "Well it looks like two people involved in this have refused to talk," he said. "One is now dead and the other refuses to talk to us."

"Looks like we may be at a dead end," said Macy with a long sigh.

"I wouldn't necessarily say that. You're just going to have to dig a little deeper. Is there anyone else you know who is involved?"

"Surely the officer over the entire base in San Antonio would know what's going on in his own back yard," said Macy. "I wonder if I could persuade him to talk."

"Maybe," he replied, "But you know how tough those military people can be."

Macy smiled back at George and said, "Yes, I know. I was one of the toughest."

"Let's assume you get nowhere with him. Where do you think you should look next?"

"Well, I'll probably have to go back to Maxine West and see if there's some way I can get her to change her mind. She obviously knows something, if I can just get it out of her. She seems very afraid of whoever's pushing all the buttons. And her comment about it going a lot higher than us makes me really curious as to who is behind all of this."

"Me too," said George. "The deeper we get into this, the more dangerous it seems to become. I'm beginning to get a little worried about you, Mace."

"I've got to see this through, besides, The Avenger isn't afraid of a little danger," she said with a laugh.

"Oh, so that's what you meant the other day when I said The Avenger and you said that's it," said George, smiling. "You picked that for your alter ego?"

"Why not?" asked Macy. "I thought it fit, given what I'm trying to accomplish."

"Whatever," said George, as he shook his head. "I still want The Avenger to be careful. I love my sister, just the way she is."

"That's so sweet," she said. "I love you too."

"Okay, back to the case," said George, blushing.

"Do you have any information from the surveillance on Maxine West?"

"We know where she's staying," he said. "But that's about it." Macy could tell by the way he hesitated that something was wrong.

"What are you not telling me?"

"I'm afraid I have some bad news."

"She's not dead too, is she?" asked Macy, her voice rising.

"No, not that," said George. "It's just... I can't help you any more with this case."

"What do you mean?" she asked.

"The Director asked what operation I was working on that required field agents to be following Maxine West."

"What did you tell him?"

"Well, I certainly didn't tell him I was helping my sister," said George. "I told him about Agent Vrama and how the OCB had asked for any assistance I could give them. My Director proceeded to tell me he had spoken with the Director at OCB, and they had informed everyone to drop the case. Needless to say, he was a little angry, but thought that perhaps the message hadn't been communicated to me by the OCB. He told me to cease and desist immediately."

"I hope you're not in any trouble because of me."

"No. I spoke with him later that day and he was okay."

"So you can't help me anymore," said Macy.

"Not on this case," he said. "Of course, that doesn't mean a brother can't talk to his sister about her work, so you can still discuss it with me here at home. I just can't help in the field with any agents, or myself."

"I understand," said Macy. Then she remembered the list she found at the base. She ran to the bedroom and went through her pockets until she found the piece of paper. She ran back into the kitchen holding the paper in her hand.

"What's that?" asked George.

"This is a list of names I found inside the trash can of a barracks near the lab at Lackland when I was there the other day," she said. "I hoped you could look the names up for me and tell me who these people are. I believe Agent Vrama may have seen the names on their I.D. and copied them before he escaped. Under the circumstances, though, I guess I can't ask you to help me with this."

"Let me see the list," he said, taking the paper from her. "I believe I said we could still talk at home. Let me see what I can find out on public records. If it is a matter of public record, and I'm on my own time, the Director shouldn't have a problem with me doing a little research."

"Are you sure about that?" she asked.

"Don't worry about me," said George. "Now go find something to do, like watch television, while I work on this list."

She retreated to her bedroom while her brother began working on his laptop, busily punching keys as he went over the list of names she gave him. She flipped through the channels, deciding to watch a movie and give George a little time to work alone. When the movie finished, she turned the television off and walked out of the bedroom. He was busily typing away when she walked into the living room.

"Any luck yet?" she asked.

"Actually, I believe you were right about Agent Vrama making this list," he said. "I've been able to locate all but the last two, and I'm in the process of pulling their information as we speak. It seems they're all lab technicians with impressive credentials, and each one has done research in infectious diseases."

"Interesting," said Macy.

"That's not all," said George. "Every one of them recently left their current position for a job at the lab in Washington working for guess who?"

"Maxine West," said Macy.

"Bingo. I believe Agent Vrama saw their I.D. just like you said, and made a list of the lab team."

"Great! Were you able to find out the name of the officer in charge at

Lackland?"

"His name is Colonel Wagoner," he answered. "He's a career military man who is very close to retirement. Good luck getting him to talk."

"I have my ways," said Macy with a sly laugh. George looked up and smiled. Then he disappeared into his room, returning with a garment bag and an envelope.

"This may come in handy," he said, handing her both. She opened the zipper to reveal a Navy Lieutenant uniform, complete with a fake I.D. with her picture on it. The envelope contained pictures of who she assumed was Colonel Wagoner in very compromising situations.

"I believe the artwork may come in handy. Besides, you didn't think you could just walk onto the base a second time in your Seaman outfit, did you?"

Macy bit her lower lip. "Oops, I guess in my haste I overlooked that detail. Now I'm ready to head out to San Antonio tomorrow."

"Okay. By the time you get back, I'll have the last known address for each person on this list. Hopefully Wagoner will tell you everything you need to know, but if not, I guess you can work on the lab techs one-by-one until someone breaks. Surely out of this many people, there's at least one you can intimidate into rolling over on their co-conspirators."

"Let's hope so. Otherwise we'll be at a dead end."

George continued working on the last two names on the list while Macy called the airline and booked a flight to San Antonio for the next day. The flight left at eleven in the morning, which gave her plenty of time to get ready without having to rush. She sat down and made a list of items she would need once she got to San Antonio, then told George she was going to bed. He said goodnight, not looking up from his computer screen. She closed the door to her bedroom, slipped out of her robe, and lay down on the bed uncovered. She turned on the television to catch the news, but there was nothing about the murder/suicide in Myrtle Beach. She figured it probably only made the local news there. Most likely the police would think they were gay lovers, and Gordon killed Josh because he was sleeping with someone else at the hotel. One question that would most likely come up would be how they got in the room without a key and no record of registering it in either name. Of course, if the last person who rented the room was male, they might believe he was the third party. It would give the police a little work to do before they closed the case and filed it away. Anyway, that was not Macy's concern now. She needed a good night's rest before her trip tomorrow.

CHAPTER 25

Macy awoke the next morning feeling refreshed after a relaxing evening. She showered and dressed, and walked to the kitchen for some breakfast. George had left a note on the counter saying he had already left for work and would have her list ready by the time she got back. She poured cereal into a bowl, along with a little milk, and sat down in the living room to eat while she watched the morning news. Again, no mention of the deaths in Myrtle Beach. Nothing about any flu outbreaks. Just a lot of coverage about Jack Jordan's funeral as the commentators discussed who was there. Since Mrs. Jordan was a senator, most of Congress turned out. With the President out of the country, the Vice President attended the funeral on his behalf. The President was in the middle of peace talks in the Middle East that were considered vital to the nation's oil industry and the security of military bases abroad.

Macy finished her breakfast and returned to the bedroom to pack some clothes. She packed extra, just in case, but really didn't expect to be away long. She drove to the airport, parked her car in the long-term lot, and entered the terminal. There was a long line at the security checkpoint, making the wait longer than usual. Eventually she made it through and walked to the gate her flight would leave from. Even with the longer lines, there was still thirty more minutes before her flight would begin boarding. To kill time, she read the newspaper she took from her brother as she waited. There was another article in the paper about Jack Jordan's funeral, and on the next page, coverage of the President's visit to Saudi Arabia.

After about thirty minutes, the flight to San Antonio began boarding. The first leg of the flight was on a fifty seat jet to Cincinnati, where she would change planes and board a 737 to San Antonio. The sky was cloudy, with thunder showers in the forecast. As the plane took off, Macy could feel the wind beginning to whip the plane around as it climbed toward its cruising altitude. The plane was only about half-full, and she had the seats to herself. Once they reached cruising altitude, she noticed the pilot failed to turn off the fasten seatbelt sign, which usually indicated the presence of turbulence or wind shear. Suddenly, the jet dipped quickly and began bouncing like a car driving down a dirt road. It bumped along for a while, before dropping for a long time causing several of the passengers to panic. The remainder of the flight went the same way, one of the roughest domestic flights Macy remembered in a long time. The pilot came on every so often to reassure the passengers everything was okay and it was simply turbulence from the storms. As the plane descended toward the Cincinnati airport, she could see the pavement was wet and it was still raining. The jet lurched sideways from a strong crosswind on approach to the runway. It seemed to Macy every time she had flown to Cincinnati, the wind was always strong.

The plane touched down without incident and taxied to the gate. She walked off the plane and into the Concourse C terminal. She took the tram to the other terminal where Concourses A and B were to catch her connecting flight. By the time she reached the gate, the flight to San Antonio had just begun boarding. Handing the airline attendant her ticket, she made her way down the ramp to the plane. After an initial bout of turbulence, the remainder of the flight was smooth, as the jet cruised above the storm clouds. It was raining in San Antonio by the time the plane touched down on the runway.

Macy made her way through the terminal to the rental car counter. This time, she rented a sport utility vehicle for her trip, just in case she needed the extra room.

Driving from the airport to a nearby hotel, she booked a room for the night. After she placed her luggage in the room and washed her face, she went to a local fast food restaurant for a burger and fries, made a stop at an automotive store, and purchased a battery and jumper cables. She drove on to a local hardware store and purchased rope, a hammer, some nails, and a nail gun. She bought a tool box to carry everything in, then left the store and drove back to the hotel. In the parking lot, she carefully inventoried the contents of the tool box to make sure she had everything she needed. She closed the box and locked the vehicle before returning to her room.

Back inside her room, Macy phoned George to let him know she had made it to San Antonio okay and everything was on schedule. He informed her he had the list of lab technicians ready when she returned. She thanked him for his help, and asked him to wish her luck with Colonel Wagoner. He assured her she would be fine, but insisted she be careful. He reminded her again this was a career military officer she was about to confront. She laughed and told him not to worry, she knew how to handle herself around career military men. They said goodnight and ended the call. Knowing tomorrow could be a very long day, she reviewed the file George gave her on Wagoner, and slipped into bed early for a long night's rest.

The next morning Macy was wakened by the hotel phone relaying her wake up call. She showered and dressed, and headed downstairs for breakfast. She decided to go with the pancakes and sausage to make sure she had plenty of carbohydrates. After all, she would probably need the energy before she was finished today. Afterward, she went back to her room and changed into her new Navy uniform, complete with I.D. badge, then headed to the rental car, and drove away from the hotel in the direction of Lackland Air Force Base.

Macy pulled up to the guard gate and flashed her I.D. to the guard. He looked at the badge, then up at her, comparing the photograph with her face. Handing the I.D. back, he waved her through. She decided to begin at the same place as she had when she was here before, parking outside the main office and walking inside. The airman she spoke with before was sitting behind his desk when she walked in. He immediately began to fidget and look nervous as she moved toward him. She told him she was there to see Colonel Wagoner, causing the airman to disappear for a few minutes before returning to escort her to the Colonel's office. Once she entered, the airman excused himself and closed the door.

"Lieutenant Waxman, (the name George had placed on the I.D.), it's refreshing to have someone with your beauty visit our base," said the Colonel, flashing a full smile at Macy while extending his hand.

She grasped his hand firmly and said, "Thank you, sir."

"Now, what can we do for you today?"

"For starters, you can tell me what you know about the experiments that took place in the small lab in H sector a few weeks ago," she insisted, her smile quickly erased.

"You certainly get right to the point, Lieutenant," he said with a half laugh.

"I don't have time to waste, Colonel."

"Very well. I know nothing of any experiments in that lab for over three years. Besides, even if there were, I'm sure it would be of a sensitive nature that I could not discuss with you. Why is Naval Intelligence interested in what the Air Force is doing here?"

"They're not," said Macy. "But I am."

"Then on whose authority are you acting?" he asked. "This is my authorization," she said, pulling her .45 and pointing it directly at him.

"You realize, Lieutenant, you're wading in serious waters right now."

"From where I stand, Colonel, it looks like you're the one doing the wading."

"Okay, Lieutenant, just what do you want?" he demanded.

"The truth about what went on here a few weeks ago," she stated firmly. "What exactly was going on in that lab, and who's giving the orders?"

"I'm afraid I can't help you, Lieutenant, that information is classified."

"I was hoping to do this the easy way, Colonel," she responded easily. "But I had a feeling you wouldn't cooperate, so we're going for a little drive." She motioned with her gun for Wagoner to walk out in front of her, hiding the gun under her jacket so the airman wouldn't see it as the Colonel told him they were going out for a little while. Once outside, she took his side arm and placed it in her belt, insisting the Colonel drive his vehicle, as she grabbed the tool box from her rental and climbed into the passenger seat. She trained the gun on him and demanded he drive from the base and head south. They drove for several miles out into the countryside until they came to an abandoned barn. She directed Wagoner to park the jeep inside the building to conceal it from the road, told him to get out and turn around, facing away from her. She brought the butt of the gun down hard across the back of his skull, rendering him unconscious.

When he came to, he was tied to a chair with rope, completely naked. She was waiting patiently for him to awaken, still holding the gun on him.

"You'll pay for this!" he barked.

"Calm down, Colonel," she said, smiling. "All you have to do is tell me what I want to know and I'll let you go."

"Never!" he shouted.

"I was hoping you would say that," she said smugly, as she walked over to the tool box. She reached in and pulled out the hammer, and crossed back to where he sat. She lifted the hammer into the air and brought it down swiftly on his right index finger, crushing the bone and causing him to howl in pain. She continued her interrogation.

"Now, Colonel, tell me about the lab experiments."

"Go to hell!" he shouted.

She just shook her head in disapproval and lifted the hammer again, this time landing it squarely on the top of his left hand. Colonel Wagoner screamed and cursed in pain again as his hand began to swell immediately.

"Okay, Colonel," said Macy. "Let's try that again."

"I'll never talk," he said. "You might as well kill me."

"Now, Colonel, we don't want to rush things. If you continue to stay this stubborn, I assure you, you will wish you were dead long before I'm done."

She raised the hammer a third time and bashed his right hand. Afterward, she continued until she broke every finger on his left hand. He could no longer control the stream of tears flowing down his face. His survival training had been several years ago, and at his age, he was not prepared for such trauma.

"Colonel, I have been easy on you so far," said Macy. "Now tell me about the lab."

"You call this easy?" he asked. "What more can you do to me?"

"I'll take that as a 'no,'" she said, walking toward the tool box. She retrieved the battery and cables, placing them beside the chair.

"What are you going to do with that?" he asked, suddenly beginning to shake.

She connected one end of the cables to the battery, touched the other ends together, causing a spark and moved closer to Wagoner with the cables extended in front of her.

"No! Don't!" he started to scream, as she touched the cables to his nipples, sending a shock throughout his body. He screamed in agony, as the current flowed through the sensitive area of his chest. After a few seconds, she removed the cables. His head slumped forward and he was panting heavily. His body was completely soaked with sweat, as a mixture of tears and perspiration streamed down his cheeks. "How about that lab now, Colonel?" she asked.

This time Colonel Wagoner simply shook his head 'no' as if he were unable to speak. Macy placed the cables against his genitals, making him jump in his seat from the jolt. As the electricity shot through the most sensitive parts of his body, he screamed again. He bit his lip until the blood ran down his chin. He was unable to keep his bladder or his bowels from moving, as the shock from the current caused him to lose all control. Wagoner sat there humiliated in his own urine and excrement, while being stared at by a female.

"Go ahead and kill me!" he demanded. "If I tell you anything, they will."

"Who are they?" she asked.

"I can't say. Please, just kill me and get it over with."

"All you have to do is tell me what I want to know, Colonel. I can protect you."

"Not from them you can't."

"So you still won't tell me anything?" she said.

"If I do, I'm a dead man," he said. "And if I don't, I assume you're going to kill me. So if you are, please go ahead and do it."

"I'm not going to kill you," she promised. "However, after you see this, you will probably not want to live." She removed a file from her bag and walked directly in front of him. She opened it for him since his left hand was useless and his right hand not much better, and held it up for him to see. After looking at it for a few seconds, he began to cry.

"Why are you doing this to me?" he begged.

"You did this to yourself, Colonel," she said. "These pictures prove your homosexual relationship with the airman at your barracks. I assume that's why he's continued to work for you for years, because of the fringe benefits."

Macy removed the rest of the rope holding him to the chair and placed all of the items back into the tool box. She took his gun and removed all the bullets from the clip, leaving one in the chamber. She walked back over in front of Wagoner.

"As you can see, Colonel, once word of this gets out your reputation and marriage will be ruined," she said. "Are you sure you can't tell me about the lab?"

He just shook his head no as he continued to stare at the photos. Macy pointed her gun at him as she handed him his sidearm. He dropped the file and grabbed the gun.

"I left you one bullet in the chamber," she said. "Please don't waste it trying to shoot me." She turned and walked out of the building. Just as she passed through the door, a shot rang out. Macy kept walking until she reached the road. She dialed a number on her cell phone, and after a brief conversation, ended the call. She ran through the woods on the opposite side of the road until she reached a clearing at a rural intersection. There was a small convenience store where a taxi was waiting. She climbed into the back seat of the cab.

"Hope you haven't been waiting long," she said.

"Nah, I just got here," said the driver. She instructed him to take her to Lackland and drop her off in front of the guard gate. Macy paid the fare and tipped the driver, then walked up to the guard. She flashed her I.D., told him the Colonel's jeep broke down and she came back to get her car.

She walked to her car, climbed in, and drove off, leaving the base and heading back to the hotel.

Macy arrived at the hotel within minutes and grabbed her bag, which she had already packed in case she needed to leave in a hurry. She wanted to get away from San Antonio as soon as she could just in case the airman decided to give out her name. Of course, given the information that was about to leak out about him and Colonel Wagoner, he probably would not be considered very credible at this point. Macy was glad she was able to get an old friend to do her the favor of procuring the photographs. When she had mentioned she was working on something involving Colonel Wagoner and was looking for any information she could use, her friend was able to retrieve the photographs that had been taken as part of an internal investigation. They had placed surveillance on Wagoner in response to an allegation of improper behavior by a female officer. Since the Colonel was close to retirement, the military had decided to shelve the pictures in order to avoid public embarrassment as part of their 'don't ask, don't tell' initiative. Her friend left the photos with George just before her last trip to San Antonio. Lucky for Macy, the photos were just what she needed. She felt sorry for the Colonel's family, who would have to suffer the indignity of his actions. At least now they would know the truth.

As she made her way back to the airport, she couldn't help but feel a little down. She had hoped Wagoner would give her something she could use, even if it was only the name of the person in charge of the operation. George was right when he said it would be difficult to extract information from a career military man. Even after being exposed, he still preferred to take his own life rather than betray a confidence. In some sort of way, he felt suicide was the only way to maintain his reputation. A reputation that would soon be tarnished by scandal and lies, unless, someone cleaned up the scene and destroyed the photos. His death would still be ruled a suicide, but no one would know the reason why. Macy believed that would probably be what happened, depending on who found the body first. She suddenly had an idea, and placed an anonymous call to the local sheriff's department from one of the airport pay phones. Afterward, she stood in line and waited to book a flight back to Kentucky. After twenty minutes, the clerk summoned Macy to the counter. She inquired about flights to Lexington and the clerk began typing on the keyboard. In checking the flight schedule, she found a flight that went through Cincinnati and continued to Lexington would be leaving in exactly forty-five minutes, informing Macy she should be able to make it if she hurried. She paid for the ticket and took off in the direction of the gates. The line at the security checkpoint was short, and she breezed through in a matter of minutes. Rushing to the gate, she arrived just as they were making their final call. She stepped onto the plane and quickly found her seat. In no time, the plane pushed back from the gate.

Once in the air, Macy breathed a sigh of relief. At least this task was over, but now she was back to square one. Hopefully, the list of technicians George had worked on would give her something, she thought. It would have been easy for her to get discouraged and give up, but she kept reminding herself she had to prove Jack Jordan did *not* commit suicide. Even though the evidence pointed to murder, there was still not enough proof to satisfy the authorities. And her client was counting on her to deliver. She definitely did not want to fail Senator Jordan.

Macy eased the seat back and ordered some bourbon for her cola from the flight attendant. She paid the attendant and emptied the contents of the bottle into her glass, picking it up and taking a sip, hoping it would relax her, while she nibbled on pretzels. Before long, the plane was landing in Cincinnati. She changed planes and settled in for the short flight to Lexington. She was just beginning to relax when the plane began its descent. Once on the ground, Macy made her way through the terminal to the parking area where she climbed in her car and sped off toward George's thinking Kentucky was feeling more and more like home every day. As she entered the house, he looked up from the sofa. He could tell by the look on her face it did not go as well as she had hoped. He decided to take her out for pizza and beer while she told him all about it. George told her he had the list ready for her, but advised she wait until morning to begin on it. Macy agreed, seeing how exhausted she was. All she wanted was a good night's sleep.

Chapter 26

Lexington, Kentucky

M acy awoke the next morning, blinking her eyes from the bright sunshine beaming through her window. Glancing at her watch, she jumped out of bed, when she realized it was eleven o'clock. She had slept much longer than she wanted, and now felt rushed as she made her way to the bathroom. She tossed on a pair of sweat pants and a t-shirt. She walked to the kitchen, picked up a banana from the counter, and grabbed a cup of yogurt from the fridge. She poured a glass of orange juice and peeled the banana while she looked around for the list George left for her. She spotted it on the far edge of the bar, and made her way over to take a closer look, tossing the banana peel into the trash along the way.

Macy stuffed a spoonful of yogurt into her mouth as she picked up the paper, leaving the spoon clutched between her lips. Scanning down the page, she carefully reviewed the names and addresses on the list. There were nine others along with Maxine West. Unfortunately, no progress had been made with Maxine, which caused Macy to worry the others may be as tight lipped as she. Macy finished the cup of yogurt and tossed the empty container into the trash. She carried her juice and the list over to the table. She grabbed a blank piece of paper and began making an itinerary of the best route to follow based on where the people lived. Three of them were in the Washington, DC area, two lived in Charlotte, North Carolina, two lived in Detroit, Michigan, one lived in Columbus, Ohio, and the last one on the list lived in Allendale, Michigan. She decided to check out the ones in Washington first, since three of the hopefuls lived there. With any luck, at least one of them would give her what she needed and there would be no need to go traipsing over half the country. She called the airline and booked a flight for that evening to give her time to check into a hotel and get one night's rest before beginning her search tomorrow.

Macy retreated to her bedroom to pack enough clothes for a week, just in case one of the listers was able to give her some valuable information that would require her to stay a few days to check out. She stuffed the list George made into her carryon, then called her brother on her cell phone. He answered after a couple of rings and she asked him to meet her for lunch. She changed into a less casual outfit and finished getting ready for her trip. Afterward, she watched the news channel until it was time to meet George.

She picked a local Chinese restaurant to meet at. George arrived ten minutes late, and looked like he was having a bad day.

"What's wrong?" she asked.

"Don't ask," said George. "The Director was in the office when you called, and proceeded to remind me I was not to get involved in the Agent Vrama case."

"What did you tell him?"

"I told him I was simply meeting my sister for lunch. I was late because I took a few extra turns getting here, just to make sure I wasn't being followed."

"I'm sorry, George. I didn't mean for you to get into any trouble."

"Don't worry about it, Mace," he said. "I'm not mad at you. I want you to find out what is going on here. Someone is definitely hiding something and I'd like to know who and what it is."

"Well, with a little luck we'll get some answers soon," she said, smiling.

"Where are you planning to start?" he asked.

"Since most of them are in the D.C. area, I thought I'd start there. My plane leaves this afternoon."

"Just remember, no one has your back now," warned George. "Please be careful."

"Relax big brother," she said with a giggle. "I believe I can take care of myself."

They finished their meal and George left to go back to work. Macy had already loaded her luggage in the car to go straight from the restaurant to the airport. Since her flight left at three o'clock, she had plenty of time to pass through security and make it to the gate before boarding. Her flight would stop in Cincinnati before continuing on to Washington. This time, though, she would not need to change planes and was relieved to hear that, especially since changing planes in Cincinnati often meant taking a tram from one terminal to the other.

Macy arrived at the airport and parked in the long term lot. She entered the terminal and checked her bag, and headed through the security checkpoint. Since most of the business travelers were on the morning flights, the line at the security checkpoint was very short. As she passed through the metal detector, the guard directed her to bring her carryon bag and step into one of the side rooms. Since 911 some passengers were randomly selected for search of their carryon luggage to ensure the safety of the other passengers. Some people were on a watch list, while others were just selected by security for search. As the guard looked through her bag for anything that could be considered a weapon, she concluded she must have been placed on a watch list by whoever was behind Senator Jordan's death. Perhaps they felt if they inconvenienced her enough, she'd simply give up and stop her investigation. What they didn't know about her was such impositions only served to fuel her passion, not extinguish it.

After the guard finished his search, he left Macy alone in the room to place all of her items back into the bag. She walked out of the room and proceeded through the concourse to her gate. It was a forty-five minute wait before they began to board the plane. Once on board, she noticed she was alone in her row again, as the plane was not even half full. This time the flight to Cincinnati was much smoother with no turbulence. After the plane landed, she sat patiently while most of the passengers departed the plane. Once they began boarding again, it was clear this flight would be full. She was seated in the window seat when a young girl sat down beside her. She looked like she was in her teens and Macy wondered if she was a college student.

As the plane took off, Macy glanced over at her and noticed she seemed nervous.

"First time flying?" Macy asked the girl. "Yes," she answered, managing a shaky smile.

"Relax," Macy advised. "It's actually the safest way to travel. Are you a college student?"

"Yes, a freshman at Cincinnati."

"Are you flying back home to Washington?"

"No, I'm from Georgia. I'm going to Washington for the summer to be a page for Senator Jordan."

"Senator Jordan's from Georgia also, isn't she?" asked Macy.

"Yes, and she usually selects her pages from there each year," she said.

Macy continued her small talk with the girl for the remainder of the flight. She asked about the page program and what exactly they did. The girl was so eager to talk about herself, she never asked Macy any personal information, which was fine with her. It seemed like very little time had passed when the plane began its descent into Washington. In minutes, the plane was on the ground and Macy looked over at the girl, smiled, winked, and said, "See, I told you everything would be fine." As they left the plane and walked into the terminal, Macy suddenly realized she hadn't even asked her name.

"Kimberly Morgan."

Together, they both headed toward baggage claim, retrieved their luggage, and said goodbye as Macy headed off in the direction of the rental car counter while Kimberly walked outside to hail a taxi. She smiled as she thought about how young and innocent the new page was, and hoped the Washington legal system would not corrupt her before she had a chance to enjoy life a little.

Macy drove out of the rental lot and away from the airport as she glanced at the map the clerk gave her. He had circled her hotel and drew a crude route for her to follow. His directions were good, and she found the hotel without any trouble. She checked in and carried her luggage to her room. When she made her reservation, she'd requested a king, non-smoking room, but upon arrival, the hotel clerk told her there was a mistake and the only rooms they had left were smoking. She punched some keys on her computer and advised her they would give her a Jacuzzi suite, which was non-smoking, for the same rate since it was the hotel's error. She didn't complain since she was being upgraded at no additional cost.

Macy unpacked her bags and washed her face to revive herself from the trip. She left the hotel and drove around the area for a little sight seeing. While she was out, she found what appeared to be some sort of steakhouse, and decided to stop there for dinner. After she ate, she drove around a little longer, but when dusk began to settle on the city, Macy made her way back to the hotel. She called George to give him her room information and let him know she was okay. Since the room had a Jacuzzi, she decided she might as well put it to good use. She grabbed the bath oil she brought with her and placed it on the side of the tub. Searching the bathroom for bubble bath, but found none, she went back downstairs to the hotel gift shop. She found what she was looking for at twice the price she normally paid back home, but decided it was okay to splurge once in a while. Back in her room, she ran hot water into the tub, pouring some of the bubble bath and bath oil into the water. She knew it would take just a small amount of the bubble bath, since the motion from the jets would churn up a lot of bubbles.

Macy closed the curtains on the large panoramic window, and walked back to the tub to check the water temperature. Slowly, she undressed, kicking off her shoes and unfastening her slacks, letting her pants fall to the floor as she lifted her top over her head, exposing her hot pink bra and matching panties. Stepping out of the pants, she slowly rolled the stockings down each leg, carefully removing them at her toes. She unfastened the front of her bra and let it fall to the floor, revealing nice, supple breasts. Lastly, she used her index fingers to slide under the sides of her panties and ease them down her body until she could step out of them. Macy walked over to the tub, tested the temperature and stepped into the hot water. She turned off the tap once it reached the right level, and turned on the jets. She eased back into the roiling water as the jets massaged her back and legs.

After about fifteen minutes of relaxing to the pulsating streams of water, she turned off the jets and eased her head back against the edge of the tub to simply bask in the warm water.

After a few minutes, Macy opened her eyes and climbed out of the tub, her legs a little shaky from the day's journey. She dried off, pulled back the top sheet, and lay down on the bed. Still totally relaxed from her bath, she fell asleep. She napped for two hours before the noise from people talking outside her room woke her up. The room was almost completely dark now, except for the bathroom light. She listened as the voices continued from the hall into the next room behind the head of her bed. She could tell by the tone and volume that it was not a fight, but instead the effects of too much alcohol causing their normal voice volume to rise. Macy slid out of bed and walked to the bathroom to relieve her bladder, realizing she might not get much more sleep until her neighbors passed out.

She turned on the television and flipped through the channels, hoping to drown out the noise from next door. She soon found herself unable to concentrate, as she was trying to listen to the voices in the next room over the television. She could tell by the sounds they were beginning foreplay, and turned the volume up a little more to drown out the sound. After several minutes, she couldn't hear any noise coming from next door, turned off the television and curled up for the night.

She woke feeling relaxed, as she climbed out of bed and made her way to the bathroom. She slipped on a pair of jeans and a sport shirt, shot a couple of squirts of Beautiful behind her ears, and stepped into her boots and headed downstairs to the hotel restaurant for breakfast. While she sipped her coffee, Macy thought about the night before and wondered if the couple next door was hurting from a severe hangover. She hadn't heard a peep out of them so far this morning, and figured they must be sleeping it off.

After breakfast, she walked over to the hotel gift shop to purchase an area map. She went back to her room and grabbed the list of lab technicians. She searched on the map for the street names on the list and carefully planned out a route that would take her to each one as efficiently as possible. It would be great if the first one was all she needed, but after her conversations with Maxine and Colonel Wagoner, she was beginning to wonder if she would ever find the answers she needed. She smiled as she looked toward the wall behind the head of her bed, still hearing no sound from the couple next door. She feigned a tip of the hat in their direction and walked out of the room to begin her day of hunting down the people on her list. The first stop was just a couple of miles away at the apartment of Arlene Grant.

Chapter 27

Washington, DC

Macy parked on the street outside the apartment building that was first on the list. She walked up to the entrance, but it was one of those that remained locked and could only be opened with a key, or if someone from inside buzzed you in. She scanned the row of buttons, but most didn't have a name beside them, just the apartment number. She found the number to Arlene Grant's apartment and pressed the button. After a few seconds, a sleepy voice came over the intercom.

"Who is it?" she asked.

"Max," said Macy, hoping to deceive her into letting her in. The door buzzed indicating the lock had been disabled. So far her little trick had worked. She made her way to apartment 2B and knocked. She was careful to keep her head turned away from the peephole so Arlene wouldn't be able to recognize she was not Maxine West. Macy heard the turning of several locks before the door opened.

"You're not Max," she said.

"I'm sorry for the deception. But I need to talk to you. It's important," she said, brushing past Arlene and walking into the apartment. She closed the door, looking at Macy in bewilderment. Macy turned and looked directly into Arlene's eyes.

"I know you were on a team of lab technicians performing some top secret experiments at Lackland Air Force Base in San Antonio a few weeks ago," she stated firmly. "I need to know what you were working on there. It's a matter of life and death."

"You know I can't tell you about any government operations."

"Listen Arlene, five people are dead because of whatever went on in San Antonio," said Macy. "You could very well be in danger yourself."

"And just where did you get your information from?" asked Arlene.

"Maxine West and Colonel Wagoner, just to name a couple." Arlene did not need to know she actually obtained no real proof from either of these two. She hoped the mere mention of their names would cause Arlene to open up.

"I'm afraid I can't help you. Now, please leave," she said, opening the door.

"Arlene, please don't make this mistake. Someone will eventually blow the lid on this, and when they do, anyone who was a part of it and did not cooperate will be facing serious jail time."

"Jail's better than dying," said Arlene. "I'll take my chances."

She again motioned for her to leave. Macy handed her a piece of paper with her cell number scribbled on it and told her to call if she changed her mind. She walked out of the apartment and back to her car. She placed an 'X' beside Arlene Grant's name on the list and looked over her map for the location of her next subject. She pulled away from the curb and drove six blocks before turning left. After two blocks she turned right and parked a few feet down the street in front of another apartment building. The second name on her list was Anne Mathers.

Macy walked to the entrance door to the building and pulled, the door opening easily. No security lock or buzzers on this building, which she was glad to discover. She made her way to apartment 1-G and knocked on the door. There was no peephole, so whoever was inside had to crack the door at least a little to see who was knocking. She was surprised, however, when the door swung wide open and she stood face to face with Maxine West.

"Maxine, I was looking for Anne Mathers," said Macy.

"Surprised, Ms. Merit?" asked Max. "Anne is not here right now, but I can assure you she isn't interested in anything you have to say."

"Please Maxine, five people are already dead because of whatever went on in San Antonio," Macy implored. "Colonel Wagoner was the last one to die."

"I never was fond of him," said Max. "He got what he deserved."

"Maxine, I'm worried about you."

"How sweet," said Max, and continued, "but you're not really my type. I believe we discovered that from our last meeting. Now if you'll excuse me, I have to go."

"Wait," she said, handing Max a piece of paper. "Here's my number in case you change your mind." Maxine took the piece of paper and closed the door. Macy was feeling more helpless as she had made no progress with the first two on her list. She kept telling herself that all she needed was one person to tell her the details of the operation. She just hoped she found someone willing to talk before she ran out of names.

Macy returned to her car and drove off in the opposite direction. She drove across town before she came to a rather run down neighborhood. There were several apartment buildings along the street, but they were in disrepair, and much dirtier than the first two she had visited this morning. She drove slowly as she read the numbers on the buildings until she found the one she was looking for. There was definitely no security locks on the buildings in this neighborhood. She entered the building and walked to the door of apartment 1115. Since there was no doorbell, she knocked firmly. Macy heard the sound of locks turning before the door opened slightly and a woman peered through the small opening. Shirley Jennings was a petite black single woman, twenty-five years old, who lived alone.

"I know what you want," she said. "Max just called me to tell me you were probably on your way here."

"What else did Max tell you?" asked Macy.

"She said I shouldn't tell you anything, or I would be in trouble."

"What kind of trouble?"

"She said she would kill me if I talked to you," she said, her voice trembling. Macy could sense the fear in her voice and thought this might just be the opportunity she was looking for. She decided to press on.

"Miss Jennings, I'm here to help you," said Macy. "But I need you to cooperate with me on this."

"But if I say anything, I'm as good as dead," she said, her voice still shaking.

"I can protect you if you cooperate."

"I don't know what to do. I'm so scared. I wish I had never agreed to this assignment, but the pay was good and I really needed the money."

"Then let me help you," said Macy.

"They may be watching," she said. "So you can't stay here long. Where are you staying in town?" Macy gave her the hotel name and room number.

"I'll meet you tonight at eight o'clock," she said. "We'll talk then." She closed the door and locked it securely. Macy walked out of the building and climbed into the rental car. She drove back toward the hotel and parked in the hotel parking garage once she arrived. Those were the only three members of the lab team in the Washington area, so all she could do now was to wait until tonight and hope Shirley showed up.

Macy went back to her room and turned on the television to see if there was any news about Colonel Wagoner. Surely the death of someone that high up in the military would attract the attention of the press. She watched the headline news as they ran through the major stories. Suddenly, a picture of Colonel Wagoner appeared on the screen, and she pressed the button on the remote to increase the volume. The reporter said Colonel Wagoner died apparently from a self-inflicted gunshot wound to the head. He went on to say the Air Force disclosed Wagoner had been severely depressed for some time over personal and health issues prior to taking his life. There was no mention of the file or the pictures of the Colonel and his aide. It was just as Macy had suspected. The Air Force would cover up the information about the Colonel's homosexual activity in order to preserve his dignity and prevent tarnishing theirs. It was a case of typical political spin, which the public would easily accept as the entire story, especially since Colonel Wagoner was not a household name. Macy smiled and shook her head as the news moved on to other stories, having spent an entire twenty seconds on Colonel Wagoner's death.

She decided to leave the hotel for lunch. It was a beautiful sunny day, and since she had nothing else to do for the rest of the day, she wanted to at least get outside and enjoy the weather. As she started to walk out of the room, she heard the familiar ring of a cell phone. She went over to her bag, she reached in and pulled out Gordon's cell phone. When the display indicated the number was unavailable, she didn't answer the call. After a few rings, the phone went silent. The phone she had taken from the guy who tried to run her off the road rang. The number didn't display on his phone either, and she let it ring until it stopped. This was the first time Gordon's phone rang since she took it.

Suddenly, Macy had a sharp pain in her stomach as if someone had knocked the wind out of her. She shuddered as the thought crossed her mind that someone may be trying to order a hit on Shirley Jennings. She went over her visit with Shirley, convinced she hadn't stayed there long enough to arouse suspicion. Surely it was just a coincidence, she thought, as she walked out of her room and to the parking garage. Her stomach continued to gnaw at her, though, but she attributed it to needing to eat. She assured herself Shirley would not be in danger at this point since no one knew she was planning on cooperating.

She left the hotel parking deck and headed south in search of a restaurant. There were many to choose from, so Macy pulled into a neat-looking chain restaurant where she felt confident she could get a good salad. She didn't want to eat anything too heavy since she wanted to make sure she was alert. After her last few brushes with Gordon and his men, she never knew when she might have to react quickly to sudden danger.

Macy finished her lunch and decided to call and update Senator Jordan. She also wanted to see if the Senator heard anything from her colleagues regarding any military or top secret government experiments surrounding virus research. After a couple of rings, her aide answered. She asked to speak to the Senator, but was informed Senator Jordan was not in. Macy did not leave a message, but instead asked when the Senator was expected back. Her aide said she would not be in her office again until tomorrow. Macy thanked her and ended the call.

She decided to drive around Washington and see the sights for a couple of hours. She drove by the White House and the Capitol Building, as well as Washington Monument and the Lincoln Memorial. It was nice to relax and enjoy the day without having to be at a particular place at a given time. As long as she was back at the hotel in time for her meeting tonight, she had nothing else on her agenda.

Macy made it back to the hotel by five o'clock. Although she hoped Shirley would provide the information she needed, she retrieved the list of lab technicians and began planning where she would go next in case Shirley didn't provide enough evidence. She could fly from Washington to any of the other areas, and decided the next place she would go if her meeting failed to yield sufficient information would be Detroit. Macy grabbed a small vodka bottle from the mini bar and mixed a drink while she waited until time for her meeting.

She was watching the news channel when she glanced down at her watch. It was fifteen minutes after eight o'clock, but so far Shirley was a no show. She decided to give her thirty more minutes before going out to find her. She called downstairs to the front desk to see if there were any messages for her, but the hotel clerk told her there were none. She began to grow more anxious as the time passed. Finally at forty-five minutes past eight, Macy walked out of the hotel room and headed for her car. She drove back out to Shirley Jennings' street, hoping she would be able to speak with her there. As she turned onto the street, Macy could see flashing lights from emergency vehicles ahead. She could only get as close as the block before Shirley's building since the rest of the street was blocked off. There were fire trucks, police cars, and rescue personnel.

Macy got out of her car and walked up to the police line to see if she could find out what happened. As she came closer, she could see smoke coming from Shirley's building as firemen were spraying the building with water. She walked over to one of the policemen and asked, "What happened here?"

"Do you live here?" he asked.

"No, but my friend lives in that building," she said, pointing to Shirley's building.

"I'm sorry, ma'am, but it appears a fire started inside one of the apartments around seven o'clock. It spread through the entire building so fast it's taken this long for the fire department to get it under control. Unfortunately, only two residents made it out alive," he said, pointing toward a middle-aged couple.

"They lived in the front apartment and were lucky enough to smell smoke and get out before the entire building went up."

"What about Miss Jennings in 1115?" Macy asked.

"Let me see if I can find out anything," he said, grabbing his radio. He spoke into the radio for a couple of minutes, then turned back to Macy.

"I spoke to the fire chief," he said. "The fire apparently started in Miss Jennings apartment. It looks like she fell asleep while smoking. I'm sorry miss, but she didn't make it," he said, shaking his head.

Macy raised her hand to her mouth in disbelief as she watched the firemen continue putting out the blaze. She thanked the officer as she processed the fact a woman she had seen earlier that same day was now dead. She couldn't help but feel somewhat responsible for her death, since whoever did this must have followed her and knew she was talking to Shirley. Once she composed herself, she carefully scanned the crowd to see who was watching. She was not buying the smoking in bed story, given her earlier conversation with the woman. She knew from experience that most arsonists liked to observe the results of their work, often blending into the crowd as a spectator. As she looked around from face to face, Macy suddenly recognized a familiar face in the crowd. It was Maxine West!

She worked her way through the crowd to where Maxine was standing. As she closed to within twenty feet of where her target stood, Max looked over at her, flashed an evil smile and a half wave, and disappeared before Macy could reach her. Either someone was watching Shirley's building, or Maxine followed Macy when she left her apartment. Now Shirley Jennings was dead and she felt responsible.

Macy left the scene and drove back to the hotel. Once inside her room, she called George to tell him about her day and the fire at Shirley's. He became concerned when she told him about her meeting with Maxine and the fire. He reminded her again to be careful, although he realized she was quite capable of taking care of herself. After all, she had successfully made it through several missions while in Naval Intelligence, which was no small task. George asked Macy what her next move would be. She told him she would go to Detroit next, hoping for better results. He told her to keep him posted, and wished her a good night's sleep as he ended the call.

She sat motionless for a few minutes contemplating the day's events and wondering if there was anything she could have done differently so that Shirley Jennings would still be alive. She realized if she was ever going to learn the truth about what went on in San Antonio and who was behind it, several more lives would probably be put in danger along the way. She couldn't blame herself for what happened to Shirley. It was Maxine West who killed her. The only thing that kept haunting Macy was the fact there never seemed to be any proof to link anyone to these deaths.

Macy stood up just as a loud blast echoed through the hotel hallway. She looked toward the door and saw smoke pouring under the bottom. She quickly crossed the room and grabbed the doorknob, letting out a shriek of pain as the heat of it burned her palm. She ran to the bathroom and wet a towel, wrapping it around her hand, then grabbed another towel and soaked it with water, placing it around her nose and mouth to avoid breathing in too much smoke. She heard the sprinklers turn on, flooding the floor with enough water to extinguish the fire. As soon as Macy felt certain the flames were out, she cracked the door and looked outside. Several of the hotel patrons were rushing about, while firemen tried to escort them downstairs to a safer location. Apparently some explosive device was placed outside her room causing a flash fire. Most of the damage was restricted to the carpet and wall, and of course, the room door. One of the firemen saw Macy and rushed to her, asking if she were okay. She held out her burned hand as he motioned for a paramedic to come and look at it. The paramedic treated the burn and wrapped a bandage around her hand. She asked the fireman if they had any idea who started the fire, but he said any evidence such as fingerprints was destroyed. He went on to say that what was left of the incendiary device was common material that could be purchased anywhere, and would be of no value in determining who set it. Macy nodded her head in agreement, but believed she knew who was responsible. The hotel manager offered to move her to a suite on another floor, but she decided since Maxine obviously knew where she was, it would be best to leave.

She packed her bags and checked out of the hotel, deciding to drive over to the airport to check on flights to Detroit. If she couldn't find one leaving tonight, she'd spend the night in the airport and catch the first flight out in the morning.

Macy arrived at the airport around ten o'clock. There was no line as she approached the ticket counter. She asked the clerk if there were any flights leaving for Detroit, but was told the only thing left this evening was a flight to Cincinnati which was leaving in thirty minutes. She decided to go ahead and take this flight, knowing she could leave from Cincinnati first thing in the morning to Detroit. The airport looked almost deserted as Macy made her way to the gate. With the exception of the few people waiting on the same flight as she, there were just a few others scattered throughout the airport.

She called George to let him know she had decided to fly to Cincinnati tonight and continue to Detroit in the morning. When he asked if everything was okay, she told him yes, conveniently leaving out the hotel fire, and advised he call her on her cell should he need to get in touch with her for anything. She assured him again that everything was okay before hanging up.

They began boarding the plane a few minutes later. This flight was only half full, and she stretched out along two seats and tried to take a nap during the flight. She was actually able to doze for a little while, but the flight wasn't very long. Macy was awakened by the flight attendant who told her to fasten her seatbelt and remain seated while they landed. Once the plane arrived at the gate, she walked into the terminal and made her way to the shuttle area. She decided to take a shuttle to one of the nearby hotels for the night in order to ride the shuttle back tomorrow for her flight to Detroit. She felt she would be safe now since Maxine probably stayed behind in Washington.

Catching the shuttle to the Holiday Inn, she booked a room for the night. She took her luggage to the room, laid the bags on the floor, pulled the covers back, and lay down on the bed. She was so exhausted she curled up and went to sleep, never turning the entire night.

CHAPTER 28

Macy slowly opened her eyes as she tried to clear her head. Her limbs felt like logs from sleeping so hard the night before. Her neck popped as she moved her head around, obviously still tense from last night. She could really use a massage, she thought as she sat up on the edge of the bed. She stood and walked to the bathroom, peeling off the clothes she slept in as she went. She climbed in the shower and let the warm water flow over her body, hoping to give her aching muscles some relief. Afterward, she dried off, dressed, and headed downstairs for some breakfast. After she ate, Macy called the airline and booked her flight, departing in a couple of hours. She went back to her room, packed her bags, and checked out, taking the shuttle back to the airport. The airport was buzzing with people, mostly business travelers, taking the early flights to the cities where they would spend the day doing whatever it was they did for a living.

Macy was seated beside a man in a business suit, who worked on his laptop most of the way to Detroit. She was glad he was so engrossed in his work that he didn't try to talk her up. Two of the lab technicians she planned to see were in Detroit, and she spent the flight organizing her thoughts and developing a plan to contact them. She was concerned after yesterday's misfortune she could be endangering their lives, but hoped since these two were further away from Washington, they were far enough from the source to be afraid of threats. All she needed was one person with enough information to expose the operation who was willing to talk to her. Shirley Jennings seemed ready, but they got to her first. Macy was anxious to get to Detroit and get started, hoping for better results than what she got yesterday.

When the plane reached the gate, she walked up the ramp and into the terminal. She knew it would take a few minutes before the luggage would be transferred from the plane to the conveyor, and hurried to the rental car counter first and rented a car. Baggage claim was next on her agenda and she retrieved her luggage, leaving the terminal and heading to the rental car lot. She climbed into the vehicle and sped off in the direction of the interstate. Macy drove down Interstate 94 heading east toward the city. She had called ahead and reserved a room at the Omni Hotel, and wanted to go ahead and check in if she could, even though it was early. That way she would have a base of operation to work from.

When she arrived at the hotel, the clerk told her there was a room ready and allowed her to check in early. She grabbed her luggage and headed to her room, which was actually a small suite with a king-sized bed. There was a desk in the room where Macy laid out her maps and address list. She went to the bathroom to freshen up before beginning her mission, splashing water on her face and patting her face dry with a towel as she moved back into the bedroom. She sat down at the desk and began to look over the list of lab technicians. Luke Stanfield lived on Five Mile Road in Livonia. Albert Winfield lived on Big Beaver Road in Troy. Each one was on opposite sides of Detroit, so it really didn't matter which one she went to first. She decided to go to Troy then if she wasn't successful there, she'd stop back by the hotel before heading to Livonia.

She took the interstate up to the Big Beaver Road exit and headed east, passing several office buildings and other businesses before she located the apartment complex Albert Winfield lived in. She entered the complex and drove around looking at the building numbers. According to the information George gave her, Albert was in building 11201, Apartment H. She continued to drive slowly until she found the right building. Parking out front, she climbed out of the rental and walked through the open breezeway to

Apartment H. She knocked on the door loudly and waited for someone to answer. After a few seconds when no one came, she knocked again, this time louder. When again no one responded, she knocked a third time. No one was home, it seemed, and she made her way around the back of the building to where the patio was. Since Mr. Winfield's apartment was on the first floor, she could walk up to the sliding glass patio door and peek inside. As she approached, she could see the door was opened slightly. A faint odor came from within, which she recognized as soon as she reached the door. She had encountered the same odor before on more than one occasion during her stint in special ops. Once you smelled a rotting corpse, you never forgot the scent.

Macy eased open the door and entered the apartment. The odor was not strong enough yet to alert the other tenants, but it soon would be. She could tell it was coming from the side of the apartment most likely where the bedroom was located. Carefully moving in the direction of the odor, she covered her nose with her hand. When she reached the bedroom door, she could hear the sound of flies buzzing about. Cautiously, she pushed the door open to find Albert Winfield, his hands and feet tied to the four corner posts of the bed, completely naked, with cut and burn marks all over his body. Macy could tell by his condition he'd been dead for about a week. The cuts, burns, and bruises he'd endured indicated he'd been tortured before his throat was slit. The blood from the wound had pooled around and under his neck, but was now dried. His eyes were fixed in an open position, expressing the fear that resulted from torture, and the knowledge he was about to die.

Macy took a quick glance around the room, and noticed his laptop was sitting on the desk open. She decided to take it in case any valuable infor- mation were on it. Exiting the apartment as quietly as she could, she made her way back to the car. As she drove out of the apartment complex, she called information for the number of the local police station and reported a strong odor from Winfield's apartment, as if she were a neighbor, so at least they would find him and put him to rest before the decomposition got any worse. It was bad enough to die like that, but to be left to rot all alone was cruel. She was convinced his death was definitely connected to the San Antonio operation. If that were the case, then Maxine West was in danger also. She hoped she could get to Luke Stanfield's place in time before something happened to him.

Macy drove back to Interstate 75 and took I-696 West, and headed south on 275 to Livonia. The traffic was always heavy, but it moved at a quick pace. She had no trouble navigating her way around the loop, and once she reached 275, the traffic thinned out a little. She took the Five Mile Road exit and turned right, heading west. Macy searched the street numbers until she reached the 5000 block. The apartment building was located at 5050 Five Mile Road. After a few minutes, she realized she had passed it, and turned around. She slowed as she neared where the building should be, then figured the number must have been removed. She found the number before and the number after, and concluded the building in between must be the one she was looking for. As she turned into the drive, she could tell it was a small apartment building with probably no more than thirty units. She parked the rental car and climbed out, looking at the door numbers for apartment 2D.

She located the apartment on the first floor of the second unit, knocked on the door, but heard no sound from inside. As she raised her arm to knock again, she felt the cold metal of a gun barrel against the back of her neck.

"Don't move," a voice ordered from behind her. She felt a strong hand grab her arm and pull her across the breezeway and into the apartment across from 2D. The man shoved her onto a sofa and shut the door, locking it securely, pointed the gun at Macy and asked, "Who are you and what do you want?"

"My name is Macy Merit," she said. "I'm looking for Luke Stanfield."

"What do you want with him?" he asked.

"I need to talk to him about something that happened in San Antonio a few weeks ago."

"Who sent you?"

"I can't say."

"Then I guess I have no choice but to kill you," he said, cocking the trigger.

"Wait!" shouted Macy. "There's no need to overreact."

"Listen, lady. You come around here asking questions without telling me what you're up to. I don't call that overreacting. I call it self-preservation. Now, you've got exactly three seconds to tell me who sent you and what you want with Luke Stanfield, or I'm gonna blow a hole in that pretty little head of yours."

"Okay," said Macy. "I'm working for the EPA. We're investigating a tip we received about a top-secret viral experiment in San Antonio."

"Did Maxine West send you?"

"No. I told you, I'm working for the EPA."

"Are you some kind of P.I.?"

"Sort of," she said, nodding her head.

"And you think this Luke Stanfield knows something?"

"I hope so. I'm trying to find out who is behind all of this and why."

"Well, lady, I'm afraid you're out of luck. Luke Stanfield doesn't know a thing."

"What makes you so sure?" asked Macy.

"Because I'm Luke Stanfield," he said and lowered his gun. "Please excuse the rough treatment, but I had to be sure you weren't one of them."

"One of who?" she asked.

"I'm not sure," he said. "But ever since we finished that assignment, people have started dying. I went over to see Al in Troy and found him dead, tied to his bed. The poor guy had been tortured. Since then, I talked the super into renting me this apartment under a different name so I could see if anyone came looking for me. So far you're the only one who's come knocking," he said.

"What makes you so sure Mr. Winfield's death had anything to do with the assignment in San Antonio?" asked Macy.

"Because one of the members of the team called to tell me Shirley was killed last night and Colonel Wagoner committed suicide," he said. "That was enough to convince me their deaths were not just a coincidence."

"And you have no idea who was behind the San Antonio experiments, or what they're planning?"

"I wish I did, lady. Everything was top secret. We weren't even allowed to talk about it among ourselves. But I can tell you one thing, Max knows."

"What makes you think that?"

"Because she was in charge of the lab when we were in San Antonio," he said. "And you could tell this was not her first rodeo, if you know what I mean."

"I believe I do," she said. "Here's my number if you think of anything that might help." She handed him a slip of paper with her cell number written on it. He apologized once again as Macy walked to the door. She assured him she understood and told him to watch his back. He told her to do the same as she walked out the door. She walked back to her rental car and climbed in, sat for a moment collecting her thoughts then cranked the engine and drove off toward the interstate.

Macy drove back to the hotel and went to her room. Since it was already the afternoon, she decided to stay for the night and leave tomorrow morning. She called George and filled him in on her day and the latest details. She was discouraged she was unable to get anywhere with the investigation. It seemed whoever was behind the experiments had been able to keep a tight lid on it. George reminded her that many of their investigations started out the same way. Many times it took a while before they finally got a break in a case. He told her to keep at it, and surely something would turn up. She thanked him for being so supportive and listening. She asked about his job and if he had taken any more flack from the Director about her. He told her everything seemed to be back to normal, and advised her not to worry. She said goodbye and ended the call.

After the day she had, she had no desire to get back out in the traffic when she felt certain she would be able to find something good to eat in the hotel restaurant. She went downstairs for dinner, found a seat and a waiter took her order. She was sipping a glass of wine as she waited for her steak, when she noticed a man at the bar staring at her. When she looked over at him, he smiled and stood up from the barstool. He moved over to where she was sitting and asked if he could join her. She didn't mean to be rude, she told him, but she was very tired from a long day and was not interested in any company. He smiled and told her he understood, and walked back to the bar. By the time her food came, she noticed the man was gone.

She was beginning to wonder if there was a big sign across her forehead say-ing 'hit on me,' especially considering the attention she had received from strangers over the past few weeks. That was one thing her old uniform was good for, she thought. It usually intimidated most men from approaching. Of course, back then she wanted to be approached more. And if it was not for the fact she was so involved in this case, she probably would have at least had dinner with that guy. Oh well, that's life she thought as she placed a bite of steak in her mouth and began to chew.

After dinner, Macy returned to her room to relax. She turned on the television and watched the local news channel. A picture of Albert Win-field flashed on the screen as the reporter related how the police had re-ceived a tip earlier about an odor coming from his apartment. The news station showed footage of the bagged body being removed then displayed the crime stoppers number on the screen in case anyone had information related to the murder. She continued to listen to the news as she walked over to the desk and pulled out the list of lab technicians. She placed a big red 'X' beside Shirley Jennings, Albert Winfield, and Luke Stanfield. There were now only four left on the list, two in North Carolina, one in Ohio, and another in Michigan. Since she was already in Detroit, it made sense to visit Allendale next.

Allendale, Michigan is a small town just west of Grand Rapids, approxi-mately fifteen miles from Lake Michigan, the home of Grand Valley State University, which enrolls approximately twenty-four thousand students each year. Macy looked over her map and decided she could drive from Detroit to Allendale tomorrow. Since, it would take a little less than three hours to get there, there was no need to fly. Macy mapped out her route, and organized her papers for the trip.

Deciding to watch television before going to bed, she flipped through the channels. Finding nothing of real interest, she turned off the T.V. When she closed her eyes, all she kept seeing were visions of Albert Winfield. The dreams she was having about Gordon had stopped since his death, but now Macy found she was haunted by the images of death she seemed to be en-countering almost every day. She consoled herself with the fact that as long as they remained only images in her mind, and didn't become nightmares, she would be able to discern reality from mind tricks.

After a couple of hours spent tossing and turning, Macy searched for the remote and turned the television back on. She was so wound up from the day's events, she was afraid she would never get to sleep. And with a three hour drive ahead of her tomorrow, she definitely needed her rest. As she flipped through the channels, Macy found one of the movie channels and stopped to see what they were showing. It was one of those documentary-type films describing an archaeological dig in one of the ancient Egyptian tombs. After an hour of listening to the monologue voice of the narrator, she became sufficiently sleepy. She turned off the television and curled up in a fetal position, drifting off to a sound sleep for the rest of the night.

CHAPTER 29

M acy awoke the next morning around eight-thirty. She climbed out of
bed, showered, and tossed on a pair of jeans and a sport shirt. She
ate breakfast in the hotel restaurant before checking out then drove out of
the parking deck and headed toward the interstate. She took Interstate 75
south to Interstate 94 west, where she drove for just a short time before
bearing onto Interstate 96 headed west. Interstate 96 took her all the way to
Grand Rapids, where she would exit just past Grand Rapids to Allendale.

The traffic was fairly heavy with morning commuters until Macy crossed
275, then began to thin out. Once she passed Lansing, the scenery was very
rural and peaceful. As she drove along, she noticed a few dead deer lying
on the side of the road. She was about thirty minutes from Grand Rapids
when a deer suddenly ran out of the brush on the left side of the interstate.
She saw it out of the corner of her eye, and slowed as the deer leaped across
the opposite lanes. Time seemed to stand still as the majestic creature ran
just in front of her and disappeared into the brush on the right side of the
road. She could see the outline of its muscles underneath its sleek coat as
it loped gracefully along. After it passed, Macy cruised along slowly, taking
time to catch her breath. She was glad she saw it in time to avoid hitting the
animal. Not only would it have caused significant damage to the car, but

she didn't like to see wildlife killed in that manner. She wasn't opposed to hunting for food, but every time she saw an animal on the side of the road, a victim of urban sprawl, she thought it was such a waste. She continued on her way as she noticed a road sign indicating twelve more miles to Grand Rapids.

Macy continued on Interstate 96 as it traveled just north of Grand Rapids until she came to the 68th Avenue exit. Her map indicated this was where she should go, so she exited and headed south. She was beginning to feel hungry, and looked for somewhere to grab a bite. When she reached the intersection of 68th and Lake Michigan Drive, she saw a sign for a local restaurant with an arrow pointing east on Lake Michigan Drive. She turned left and drove about a mile before spotting the restaurant on her left. The sign blinked 'The Corner Kitchen,' as Macy pulled into the parking lot. They seemed to have a good crowd, but there was still plenty of room.

She ordered a burger and fries, and glanced around the restaurant to observe the people while she waited for her food. After a few minutes, she noticed a man in the back corner who kept stirring his coffee over and over, causing the cup to clink noisily as he continued stirring incessantly. He began talking aloud, even though no one was there. She believed he must be schizophrenic, and decided not to stare for fear of making him feel more paranoid than he seemed to be.

Macy hadn't eaten since breakfast, and hungrily devoured the burger and fries in record time. Leaving a couple of dollars on the table for the waitress, she paid for the meal, and walked out of the restaurant full and satisfied. She climbed into the car and drove back in the direction of 68th Avenue.

The address she was looking for was 1521 Creekview Street. Macy followed her map as she turned left onto 68th heading south. She drove for a couple of blocks until she reached Noel Street. There she turned right and followed Noel to Creekview Street, where she made a right. She cruised down Creekview, searching the house numbers until she located 1521 on the left side of the street. It was a two story house on a small lot, with a large wooden privacy fence in the back. They must have a dog, she thought as she pulled into the driveway. Macy made her way up the walk to the front door. She stood on the small cement porch and rang the doorbell. She could hear a dog barking inside the house, obviously alerted to the noise of the bell. It was not long before she heard the latch on the door click and someone open the inner wooden door, peering out through the storm door at Macy. It was a lady in her late twenties, and there at her feet, jumping at the door, was a Bichon Frise. It was white all over and looked like a powder puff, probably only weighing about twelve pounds. She was surprised such a large bark could come out of such a small dog.

The lady spoke to Macy through the storm door, trying to be heard above the barking dog.

"Can I help you?" she asked.

"I'm looking for Martin Vandifer," said Macy.

"I'm sorry, but he's not home," she said. "What do you want with him?"

"I need to speak to him about a recent assignment he had in San Antonio."

"Had? I thought he was still there," she said, looking surprised.

"May I come in?" asked Macy.

The lady took her foot and pushed the dog back, opened the storm door and invited Macy inside. Sensing from the lady there was no imminent danger, the dog came over to Macy and began wagging its tail for attention. *What a guard dog,* she thought.

"I'm Jean Vandifer," said the lady, extending her hand. "I'm Macy Merit," Macy said, introducing herself, grasping her hand and shaking it firmly.

"My husband has been in San Antonio for over a month," Mrs. Vandifer informed her.

"I hate to tell you this, Mrs. Vandifer, but the mission your husband was on concluded a few weeks ago. Have you heard from your husband?"

"No, not since he left, but that's not unusual when he goes off on one of these operations. Why did you need to speak to Marty?"

"It's a long story," said Macy. "The operation your husband was on involved some sort of top secret experiments."

"Oh no, is Marty okay?" Mrs. Vandifer asked, rather alarmed.

"I don't know. But I won't lie to you. Two of the lab technicians have been killed so far. I was hoping to speak with your husband about the San

Antonio experiments to see if he had any idea who was behind them and what they planned to do with the results."

"Like I said, I haven't heard from Marty since he left," she said. "What should I do?"

"At this point, I would file a missing person report," said Macy. "Have you talked to his boss or anyone he works with?"

"No, do you think I should?"

"It wouldn't hurt. But I doubt they will give you any information. If you hear from your husband, please have him call me," she said, handing her a piece of paper with her cell phone number written on it.

Mrs. Vandifer assured Macy she would have Marty call when she heard from him. She thanked Macy for stopping by and at least giving her the news the operation her husband was on was finished. Now she needed to find him and make sure he was okay.

Macy left the Vandifer house and retraced her route back to the interstate. There was no one left to visit in Michigan, so she decided she might as well catch a flight from Grand Rapids back to Lexington. She could easily drop the rental car off at this airport, instead of driving all the way back to Detroit. She headed east on Interstate 96 to the 28th Street exit, driving west on 28th until she came to Patterson Street, where she turned left and followed it to the Gerald R. Ford Airport.

Macy dropped off the rental car and entered the terminal, heading for the ticket counter. The line was average, so she waited ten minutes before she was called to the counter. She told the ticket clerk she wanted to fly to Lexington, Kentucky. The lady busily punched away at her keyboard, then looked up at Macy with a pleasant smile, letting her know there was a flight leaving in one hour going to Cincinnati, before continuing on to Lexington. Macy handed her a credit card, checked her luggage, and after the clerk handed her the ticket, headed off toward the security checkpoint. Thankfully most of the crowd had already passed through, and she didn't have long to wait. She had plenty of time before the flight left, but didn't like to stand in line. It was one of her pet peeves.

Macy grabbed a soda and a magazine from one of the gift shops to have something to read while she waited. She thought about carrying the laptop she picked up at Winfield's with her, but decided to pack it away securely in the luggage she checked before she left the hotel. Since 911, people traveling with laptops and other electronic equipment were often asked to turn them on and change the display at the security checkpoint, and since it was not hers, she was afraid it might be password protected, which would make it easy for the guard to conclude the computer was not hers. Besides, there would be plenty of time to look at it when she got back to Lexington.

Macy flipped through the pages of the magazine, unable to concentrate on reading the articles because her mind was still processing her visit with Mrs. Vandifer. This was the first lab technician she was not able to locate, alive or dead. There was nothing in the communications Agent Vrama left that pointed to any of the technicians being killed while in San Antonio. She began thinking of different scenarios that would account for Martin Vandifer's whereabouts. The fact he hadn't even phoned his wife since the project was finished had Macy wondering if he was still alive. After all, these people proved they had no conscience when it came to cold-blooded murder. She stared out the window, lost in her thoughts, when the airline began boarding the plane. She found her seat and sat down near the window. The flight was fairly full, as an elderly lady sat down beside her. The lady smiled at her, so Macy smiled back, then immediately dove into her magazine as if she were avidly reading something extremely interesting. She wanted more time to concentrate on her thoughts without having to make idle small talk with a stranger. Thankfully, the lady pulled out some knitting and began earnestly working on what appeared to be a shawl. Neither of them spoke the entire flight.

Macy remained on the plane after it landed in Cincinnati, but the lady beside her got off. She smiled at her again as she gathered her belongings before walking toward the exit at the front of the plane. There were only a handful of people on the flight to Lexington, and she relaxed a little more as she had the entire row to herself.

There were only three of the lab technicians left, assuming Martin Vandifer was dead. Macy was beginning to feel a little discouraged at not having made any more progress than when she started. This investigative work was definitely not as easy as it seemed on television, she thought.

The flight from Cincinnati to Lexington lasted about forty-five minutes, and soon the plane was on the ground. Macy retrieved her luggage and made her way to the long term parking lot. She tossed the bags in the back and climbed in, heading off in the direction of George's house. He should be home by now, but she had been so wrapped up in her thoughts she forgot to call him and let him know she would be back this evening. She could see the look of surprise on her brother's face as she walked through the door.

"I didn't know you were coming back tonight."

"I didn't either until a few hours ago."

"Why didn't you call so I could have dinner ready?" he said. "You must be tired."

"I'm okay," said Macy. "Let's just call in a pizza."

"Fine by me," he said as he stood up and walked to the kitchen to grab the phone.

Macy carried her luggage to her room while George called in their order. She washed her face and cleaned up a little before the food arrived. She was hungrier than she realized when she took a big whiff of the pepperoni and cheese. They both dove in, eating in silence until the last piece was gone. Then George spoke up.

"So, how did it go?" he asked.

"Don't ask," she said, rolling her eyes. "Everywhere I looked was a dead end."

"Did you find them all?"

"No. I found one dead, one who swore he knew nothing, but was very scared and paranoid, and the third one was not home and hadn't spoken to his wife since the project began. My guess is he's probably dead, too," she said with a sigh.

"The one you found dead," said George. "Were there any clues?"

"Nothing visible," said Macy. "But I took his laptop hoping I can find something on it that will explain why he was killed."

George nodded his approval, told Macy he was going to watch some television and asked if she wanted to join him to unwind a little, but she told him she wanted to take a look at the laptop she got from Winfield's and see if it would give up anything.

Macy opened her luggage and removed the laptop wrapped up in a couple of towels to keep it from being damaged. There were no disks on his desk, so she figured he must have stored anything important on the hard drive. She plugged in the power cord and turned it on, crossing her fingers in hopes it would work. The computer whirred as it began to boot up and Macy let out a small sigh of relief. She sat on the bed with her legs crossed and the computer resting on her lap. Once it finished its initial start up, she began looking through the files. Everything appeared to be generic, with a few personal games and programs he used for household management. She located his email folder and scanned it for anything he'd saved or sent any emails that would give her a clue as to who killed him. She was surprised to find nothing in the email folder. It was too clean, leading Macy to believe whatever had been there before had been erased.

She began to smile as she started punching the keyboard. She had received special training while in the Navy regarding computers and how to find and restore erased files. Most people believed that once they erased something, it was gone forever. She learned these files were usually still somewhere on the hard drive, you just had to know where to look.

She continued working away at the laptop until she suddenly sat back and said, "Ah-hah!" She resumed typing until she pulled up a file of Winfield's sent emails. She scanned through them until she came across one that was titled 'information.' She opened the email and read the contents. It was addressed to Max, and said he wanted to be paid extra for his silence regarding their last mission together. She searched for a reply in his received emails, and found her response saying she would meet him at his place the following evening. The dates on the emails coincided with the estimated time of death Macy crudely calculated based upon the degree of decomposition. So, Winfield was killed by Max, or someone she sent, to keep him quiet. She thought that might be the case when she first discovered his body, but now this confirmed it.

Macy continued looking through the computer for any other important information, but found nothing else. Whatever Winfield knew about the operation, he kept it in his head and not in his computer. She stretched and left her room and walked back to the living room, to tell George what she found.

"No wonder we didn't get any information from Maxine," said George. "It sounds like she's the most ruthless one of them all."

"Maybe," said Macy. "But I wonder if she would remain silent if she thought her own life was in danger."

"What are you planning?"

"Nothing for now. I still want to talk to the other lab members first."

"And if you get no information from them?"

"Then I guess I'll have to improvise," she said, smiling at George.

He shook his head as Macy walked back to her room. She shouted in his direction she was going to take a bath and turn in early. He called a goodnight back, and resumed watching his television program.

She curled up and went to sleep, not even thinking about the case or her next step. Tonight she just wanted to sleep.

CHAPTER 30

LEXINGTON, KENTUCKY

The next morning Macy got up, wrapping her robe around her and made her way to the kitchen. George had already left for work, she noticed, as she poured a bowl of cereal and sat down at the table to review the list of remaining lab techs and decide who to call on next. So far she was doing a lot of leg work with nothing to show for it. At least after last night, she knew what happened to Albert Winfield and why.

There were two technicians living in North Carolina, and one in Ohio. Macy decided to fly to Charlotte first and see if one of those two would be able to provide the information she was looking for. As she sat eating her breakfast, her cell phone rang. It was George.

"Mace, just thought you would want to know, we just received a bulletin about a killer on the loose in Michigan. Luke Stanfield was tortured and killed last night, the same way as Albert Winfield. The local police suspect a serial killer and have called in the FBI. Of course, you and I know better, but I can't tell what I know since I'm not supposed to be involved in your case."

"Thanks for the info."

"It looks like whoever is behind this has decided to go ahead and eliminate the team. Be careful."

"I will," said Macy, and hung up.

She went to the bedroom, tossed her robe on the bed, and stepped into the shower. She made it short, quickly dried off and walked to the dresser. She quickly pulled on her underwear, and decided on a grey pantsuit. Once dressed, she stepped into a pair of pumps, packed her tennis shoes just in case she would need to do any running along with enough clothes for a week in case she needed to fly straight from Charlotte to Columbus. Time was critical now since it appeared each member of the team was in jeopardy. She only hoped she could reach them before the killer did.

Macy phoned the airline as she drove out of George's driveway. She booked a flight to Charlotte that left in forty-five minutes, which would be cutting it very close. She arrived at the airport and practically ran into the terminal. She rushed through the security checkpoint as quickly as she could, and barely made it to the gate for the final boarding call. She squeezed past the seated passengers, walking all the way to the back of the plane. That was the only seat left on the flight when she called. She tossed her carry-on bag into the overhead compartment and sat down beside a flight attendant who was on her way to Cincinnati to work a flight from there.

Macy talked with her about her career and what it was like to be a flight attendant. When she was younger, she had toyed with the idea of becoming a flight attendant, but joined the Navy instead. It was a pleasant flight to Cincinnati, and before she knew it, she was headed to the terminal to catch her connecting flight to Charlotte. The flight to Charlotte was two-thirds full, she had one person seated in the same row as she was, leaving the middle seat open.

The man close to her was a school teacher returning from a vacation trip while school was out for summer. He taught in the Charlotte Mecklenberg School System, and had been to Kentucky to see the horse farms. He told her that one day he would love to see the Kentucky Derby in person. She thought it was neat to see someone appreciate something so close to her she never bothered to go.

As soon as the plane touched down and stopped at the gate, Macy was up gathering her bag and heading through the terminal to baggage claims, then hurriedly rented a car and sped off away from the airport. She was in a rush to reach the two technicians before someone else beat her to it. She grabbed a map the rental car clerk had given her and quickly circled the areas she needed to go.

Both of the technicians were single, and Macy assumed they lived alone. The first one she planned to see was on Sharon-Amity Road. She left the airport and headed from the interstate to Independence Boulevard. She traveled south until she came to Sharon-Amity, and turned left. She was looking for number 5301, when she realized she had several blocks to go. She sped along as fast as she could without bringing attention to her speed by an officer if she passed one until she reached the 4900 block. She slowed to enable herself to read the numbers better. Up ahead, she saw 5301 on a building in large white letters, and turned into the drive. It was an apartment complex with probably one hundred units.

Macy drove through the complex until she saw building M, parked the car and walked up to the first floor breezeway, looking for apartment 10. She walked up to the door and rang the bell. She could hear a baby crying inside, but no other sounds. She punched the bell again, but still no one came to the door. Macy walked around to the back of the apartment and placed her face up against one of the windows, hoping to see inside. She could still hear the baby crying, but could not see anything from the window. She walked to the next window and looked in, seeing the baby in its crib standing and crying. Then when she glanced over at the bed, she saw a woman lying face down. Macy rushed to the front door and kicked it open. She ran to the bedroom to where the woman lay, felt her neck for a pulse, but there was none. She could tell by the body temperature the woman had probably been dead for several hours.

Macy quickly surveyed the scene and saw a needle sticking out of the woman's arm. Apparently, her death was supposed to look like a drug overdose, but she found no other needle marks on either arm. Walking over to the crib, she tried to quiet the distraught baby. She picked up the woman's phone and dialed 911 to report the death. After she hung up, Macy wiped all traces of her fingerprints from the phone. She patted the baby's back again, and hurried back to her car. She climbed in and drove out of the apartment complex and down the street to a convenience store. There she parked for a few minutes to collect her thoughts and try to form a plan on how best to proceed. She pulled out her list and placed a big red 'X' beside the name Betty Allred.

Betty must have been a single mother, thought Macy, and worried who would take care of the baby. Then she realized Betty must have had family nearby because someone would have had to take care of the baby while she was in San Antonio.

The next person on her list was Gretchen Cole. She lived on Idlewild Road. Macy raced down Sharon-Amity to Harris Boulevard, turning right and taking Harris to Idlewild Road, where she turned left. The address was 1510 Idlewild Road, apartment 2C. She almost jumped the curb turning into the apartment complex. She hoped she would reach Gretchen in time to save her. The car had barely stopped moving when she leaped out and headed in the direction of the apartment. She raced up the walk, and pounded loudly on the door. She was just getting ready to kick in the door when the click of the lock turning caught her attention, and the door began to open.

"Can I help you?" asked Gretchen, swinging the door wide.

"Are you Gretchen Cole?" asked Macy. "Yes. And you are?"

"My name's Macy Merit," she replied on a rush of breath. "I have reason to believe your life may be in danger."

Gretchen seemed a bit confused as she motioned her inside. She closed the door behind her and offered Macy some coffee. They sat on the sofa while Macy explained everything she knew up to this point. Gretchen listened patiently, her face showing no emotion as Macy went into detail about the recent deaths. After a few minutes she asked Macy to excuse her while she went to the bathroom. She continued to sip her coffee while waiting for Gretchen to get back. When Gretchen returned, she was holding a gun in her right hand.

"That was a very interesting story, Miss Merit," she said. "But you see, I already knew about Betty. I'm the one who killed her."

She raised the gun and pointed it at Macy, squeezing off a shot. The gun was equipped with a silencer so as not to attract attention. Macy leaped from the sofa just in time as the bullets ripped through the fabric and took up a position behind the bar. Gretchen continued to talk as she moved after her.

"Max told me what was going on and how we needed to silence the rest of the team in order to keep our mission a secret," she said, as she neared Macy's hiding place.

As she peered around the bar, Gretchen squeezed off another shot, which she was able to dodge. She ran to the back of the apartment, her assailant firing several shots in her direction. She ducked into the bedroom opposite the master suite. Gretchen walked slowly down the hall.

"There's nowhere to hide in this small apartment, Miss Merit. You might as well come out. I promise I won't torture you like Al. Besides, that was Max's doing."

She laughed as she threw open the master bedroom door. Macy made a lunge across the hall and knocked the woman to the floor. She found Gretchen to be surprisingly strong considering how thin she was. She was only five feet two, with a very pale complexion. She had mousy brown hair pulled back into a pony tail. To look at her, one would think she was sickly, but Macy soon realized she was a very formidable adversary.

They struggled for the gun, rolling back and forth over each other. Finally Macy was able to knock the gun from

Gretchen's hand, sending it flying across the floor. As she tried to crawl in the direction where the weapon lay, Gretchen pulled a small knife from her waist, raised it above her head, and then thrust it downward toward Macy. Out of the corner of her eye, she saw the descending swoop of a hand, and Macy rolled to her right to avoid the blade. The knife buried into the carpet, missing its intended target. She jumped onto Gretchen and pinned the hand that held the knife with her knee. She began hitting Gretchen in the face until she finally rendered her unconscious.

Out of breath, Macy rolled off Gretchen's still body and stumbled over to where the gun rested. She grabbed it off the floor and was turning around when Gretchen raised to her feet, knife in hand, pulling back her arm as if to throw the weapon. She quickly fired off two shots, striking Gretchen in the chest. The force of the slugs knocked her backward into the hall, and the knife dropped to the floor. By now, Macy was thoroughly pissed at so many people trying to kill her over the past several weeks. Instead of stopping to check for a pulse, Macy walked with angry steps over to where Gretchen lay and fired another round into her brain at point blank range. Wiping her prints from the gun, and everything else she had touched in the apartment, she strode out of the apartment and back to her car, rage in every step.

Macy climbed in the car, keyed the engine and drove out of the complex, heading west to Independence Boulevard. Since there was nothing left for her to investigate, she headed to the airport. She booked a flight to Columbus, Ohio with one stop in Cincinnati, and took a minute to grab lunch at one of the restaurants in the airport while she waited for her flight to leave. With time to kill, she enjoyed her meal and read the paper before walking to her departing gate. Macy convinced herself Gretchen was already dead before she fired the last shot. Besides, either way you looked at it, it was still self defense, especially the way Gretchen kept coming after her. It was obvious to Macy now that Maxine knew she was trying to see everyone who was in the lab. Max must have told Gretchen she would eventually show up, and instructed her to kill her.

While Macy waited for her flight to begin boarding, she heard a cell phone ringing—the one she'd taken from Gretchen's counter. If she was right, it would be Maxine calling. She pushed the button and spoke into the phone, trying to sound like Gretchen.

"Yes?"

"Has she shown up yet?" asked Maxine. "Yes."

"I assume then since I'm talking to you she's no longer a threat?"

"Yes," she said, remembering Gretchen was a lady of few words.

"Excellent," said Max, and hung up.

It worked, Macy thought, relieved. Now to see if she could reach the last person on the list in time. This time she didn't bother to call the police about Gretchen's body. Eventually someone would report the smell. She wiped her prints from the cell phone and dropped it into a trash can. She took a seat and waited to board.

Thirty minutes later her flight was called and she made her way to the gate. Finding her seat, she leaned back and closed her eyes, remaining that way for most of the trip, trying to rest from the altercation with Gretchen, while avoiding conversation. The flight to Cincinnati was smooth and uneventful, helping her to relax a little. She didn't have to change planes for the flight from Cincinnati to Columbus, and spent the time napping. A flight attendant woke her once they reached the gate in Columbus. She had never slept that soundly on a plane before, and shook the cobwebs from her head. For some reason, she usually felt worse after a nap than if she had not slept at all.

Macy slowly walked off the plane and into the terminal, headed to baggage claims and the rental car counter. She was beginning to feel like she was on a treadmill. On a plane, off a plane, rent a car and hit the road again.

After she signed the paperwork, Macy carried her luggage to the rental car lot and dumped her bags in the trunk. Sliding under the steering wheel, she opened up the map of the area. The last person on her list lived at 1103 Winchester Pike. The name was Stanley Houghton.

Macy sped away from the airport and followed the map to Winchester Pike, driving south in search of the house numbers until she found 1103. She pulled into the driveway and slowly climbed out of the car, hoping that since Max thought she was dead, Stanley Houghton would still be alive.

She walked up to the door, rang the bell and waited. After a few seconds she heard the familiar sound of the lock turning. She almost crouched in defensive mode after what happened at Gretchen's place, but regained control of her emotions and stood erect as the door swung open. A man peered at her through the storm door.

"Hello, I'm looking for Stanley Houghton."

"I'm Stanley Houghton. What can I do for you?"

"I need to talk to you about your recent trip to San Antonio."

"What do you know about that?" he asked. "That was supposed to be top secret."

"I realize that," said Macy. "But I'm afraid the mission was compromised. Several of your team members are dead."

"Dead?" he said in disbelief. "May I come in?"

"I guess you'd better," he said, opening the door and motioning her inside.

Playing it safe, she turned and locked the door behind her as Stanley watched in confusion. They sat on the sofa and he turned off the television he had been watching.

"What can you tell me about the experiments in San Antonio?"

"Wait a minute," he said, holding out his hands. "First tell me who you are and why I should say anything about a top secret mission."

"My name's Macy Merit," she said. "I'm with Naval Intelligence and we've been working on a case where we believe terrorists are planning some kind of biological sabotage."

She flashed her I.D., hoping he would buy her lie. He studied the I.D. badge carefully before handing it back.

"I'm afraid I can't help you," he said. "Don't get me wrong, I want to help. It's just that I don't really know anything to tell you. I simply helped in the lab, but none of the samples we worked with were labeled in any way, so we had no idea what we were working with."

"Can you tell me who authorized the operation?"

"Colonel Wagoner was the only one we saw at the base. Of course, Maxine was mostly in charge. Have you spoken with her?"

"Yes," said Macy. "I'm afraid she wasn't much help either."

"Well, she would be your best bet," said Stanley. "If she doesn't know anything, then I don't know who else would. Now, what's all this about members of the team dying?"

Macy told Stanley about the members who were dead, leaving out the part that Max was behind the murders. She asked a few more questions about their routine while in San Antonio, just to make it seem like she was actually conducting a Naval Intelligence investigation, asking about the prisoners, if he had any contact with them. He mentioned they were instructed not to fraternize with the test subjects, but were to treat them as if they were lab mice. She thanked him for his time and advised he may want to take a little vacation and get away, just in case someone thought he might know anything about the operation that was important enough to kill for. He thanked her for the advice and said he probably would go visit his sister in Chicago.

Macy drove out of his driveway and headed back in the direction of the airport. She had traveled a lot today, and would like nothing better than to find a hotel and crash for the evening, but she decided to return to Kentucky instead, and the comfort of George's place.

She turned in the rental car and made her way to the ticket counter. She was in luck, as there was a flight leaving for Cincinnati in thirty minutes, where she could catch a connecting flight to Lexington. She checked her luggage and hurried to the gate. Once on board, she laid her head back and closed her eyes, but this time she wasn't able to doze off. By the time the plane landed in Lexington, she was thoroughly depressed. George could see it all over her when she walked in the house. She had finally reached a dead end.

Chapter 31

M acy barely spoke to George as she headed straight for her room, closed the door behind her and threw her luggage on the floor in disgust. Never in all of her years in Naval Intelligence had she worked a tougher case. Usually someone broke before now and gave her valuable information, but this 'Avenger' thing appeared to be much harder than she envisioned. After a few minutes, there was a soft knock on the door.

"Mace, are you okay?" asked George.

"Yeah, I'm fine," said Macy, letting out a big sigh.

"Can I come in?"

"Sure."

He stepped inside, crossed the floor and sat beside her on the bed. "I take it things didn't go well."

"That's an understatement," she said grimly, furrowing her brow in frustration.

She went over the details of her trip and her encounters with the others on the list. Based upon what little information she was able to get, it seemed Maxine West was the only member of the team who really knew anything, but had no luck getting her to talk before.

"I'm sorry I can't help you any more with this," said George.

"That's okay," said Macy. "Thanks for all you have done.

"I just believe there's got to be a way to lean on Maxine enough to get her to talk. If only you knew the right button to push.

"I agree. But right now I'm fresh out of ideas."

"Just try to relax tonight and sleep on it," said George. "Maybe things will look differently in the morning. "You need to eat something, though. I got some Chinese take-out tonight." He gestured toward the kitchen.

Macy slowly pushed to her feet and followed George. She ate a very small amount, just enough to stave off her hunger, not having much of an appetite after her experiences the last few days. Unable to fork in another bite, she said goodnight to her brother and went to bed early, hoping to-morrow would be a better day, as she lay down on the bed and curled up, grasping a pillow in her arms.

The next morning Macy awoke to the light from the sun illuminating her room. She glanced at her watch, and saw it was ten o'clock. Not having anything planned for today, she was in no hurry to get dressed. She pulled her robe around her body and walked to the kitchen. George had left her a note before leaving for work, telling her he loved her and to cheer up. She couldn't help but smile as she read his words. He was certainly a very good brother to her and she decided she needed to do something special for him one day soon.

Macy poured a cup of coffee and grabbed a bagel as she headed into the living room to watch some news. Of course, there was no coverage of the deaths she had witnessed. No one knew how any of them were connected, or how serious a matter any of this was. At this point, she was even begin-ning to question the seriousness of things herself. Maybe it was time to simply throw in the towel. She could tell Senator Jordan she was certain her husband didn't commit suicide, but that would be as far as she could go. She wouldn't be able to present the Senator with enough concrete evidence to completely vindicate her husband, which would leave the dark cloud of embezzlement hanging over his death. Senator Jordan wanted to clear her husband's name and restore his good character. She suddenly felt saddened at the thought of telling Vanessa there was nothing more she could do.

As she watched Senator Jordan giving a press conference regarding some piece of legislation being debated in Congress, she came up with an idea. It was extremely risky and unconventional, but it might just work.

She reached for the phone and dialed Senator Jordan's office. Her aide answered and Macy explained she needed to see the Senator as soon as possible. After a brief silence, her aide came back on the line and informed her the Senator had an opening at ten the next morning. Macy told her that would be great, and to please pencil her in. She hung up, and devoured the rest of her bagel. She walked quickly to her room, tossed her robe on the bed, and stepped into the shower.

Macy finished her shower quickly and dried off. She grabbed a pair of black bikini panties and matching bra, and carefully slid into them, shoved her long legs into a pair of jeans and dropped a t-shirt over her head. Once she was completely dressed, she packed her suitcase and was ready to get on the road again. She called the airline, booked a flight to Washington, DC, leaving from Lexington at two.

She drove to the airport early to have plenty of time to check her bags and grab a sandwich before the flight left. At two, the plane pushed back from the gate and taxied toward the runway to get ready for takeoff. Soon the plane was in the air, and headed to Washington.

Macy was excited once again as she tried to work out the details of the plan she devised in her head. It was a last ditch effort at finding out the identity of the person or persons behind the lab experiments and the subsequent deaths that resulted from her investigation. She was confident that if she could learn the 'who,' that would give her the 'why.'

She struggled to calm her nerves as she played her plan over and over in her mind. It consumed her thoughts so much the plane was touching down in Washington in what seemed like a matter of moments. She rushed to baggage claim to retrieve her luggage, straight on to the rental car counter, quickly renting a dark sedan and drove off with no time to lose, in the direction of the hotel she booked, checked in, and started to get ready for tonight.

As Macy watched the clock in her hotel room display eight o'clock, she knew it was time to begin the first phase of her new plan. She pulled on her leather pants and matching tank top, applied a lot of makeup to make her look different than normal. She spiked her hair and put on sunglasses to further disguise her appearance. She sprayed on some cologne and walked out of the hotel to her car.

She drove to 'The Wild Side,' and parked close to the front, walked in and made her way to a booth in the back, where she ordered a drink and patiently waited. After about an hour, Macy saw her walk in. Maxine West walked up to the bar, sat down, and ordered a Cosmopolitan. It was now time for Macy to make her move.

She slid out of the booth and moved toward the bar. As she drew close to Max, Macy grabbed one of the ladies who was standing nearby and asked her to take a few pictures of her and her girlfriend at the bar while they talked, handing the lady a fifty dollar bill and a small digital camera she pulled from her jacket pocket. The lady smiled at Macy, and nodded her approval.

She walked over to where Max was seated and sat down on the stool next to her, placing a hand on Max's back. Maxine turned around, flashing a large smile, which soon melted at the sight of Macy.

"What are you doing here?" she demanded.

"Relax, Max," said Macy, smiling. "I just came by for a friendly little chat."

"Oh, yeah? Well I know how you usually 'chat.'"

Leaning closer in, she whispered, "Easy, Max, I came as a peace offering. Can't I at least buy you a drink?"

Without waiting for a reply, she motioned to the bartender, putting up two fingers and pointing to the Cosmo in front of Max. She resumed their conversation without interruption.

"I've got to hand it to you, Max. You're good. I mean, remaining so steadfast in your resolve to maintain your silence about San Antonio. My hat's off to you," she said, lifting a hand and tipping an imaginary hat.

Max smiled at her and placed her hand on Macy's arm, giving her a squeeze. "Does this mean you're going to leave me alone about San Antonio?"

"Absolutely," said Macy. "I just wanted to tell you that you won. No more hassle."

"That's sweet of you to come all the way here just to tell me that," said

Max as she placed her hand on the small of Macy's back and began to caress her gently. "You know, now that we are not enemies, care to hook up tonight? I always did think you were hot."

"I'm sorry. But I've never thought about being with another woman."

"Well, think about it. I think we would really have some fun together."

"You may be right, but not tonight," said Macy. "I'll have to think about it."

"Here's my number." She handed Macy a small piece of paper. "Just give me a call whenever you're ready," she whispered, leaned over and gave her a long wet kiss full on her lips. It was all Macy could do to keep from vomiting, but she held her ground, not wanting Max to see how repulsed she was, repeatedly reminding herself why she was doing this.

Max leaned back on her barstool and winked at Macy.

She smiled back and stood up, heading for the door. The lady who took their picture was waiting with her camera. Macy grabbed the camera, and the drink the lady was holding, chugging it quickly to wash away the taste of Maxine from her lips. Handing the empty glass back to the lady, she smiled, and walked out of the club. She climbed into her sedan and sped out of the parking lot in the direction of the hotel.

Once back at the hotel, Macy looked through the pictures on her camera the lady at the club had taken. As she flipped through them, she was pleased with some of the shots. When she came to the one of her and Max kissing, she quickly deleted it. There were a total of ten pictures of the two of them talking, which Macy thought should be sufficient. After all, she only needed one good one if everything worked out like she planned. She dialed George to let him know where she was, since she did not leave him a note.

"Hello," said George.

"Hey, it's me," said Macy.

"Where are you?" he asked, sounding alarmed.

"Calm down," she said. "I'm fine. I'm sorry I didn't leave a note, but I left in such a hurry I didn't really think about it until after I was gone. I'm in Washington."

"Why? What are you doing there?" he asked.

She told George about watching the Senator's press conference and the revelation that suddenly hit her. She laid out what she was planning to do in detail, and waited for his reaction.

"Well, it sounds to me like The Avenger still has a few tricks up her sleeve," he teased.

"I hope so," said Macy. "Keep your fingers crossed." They said goodnight, and Macy slipped into bed.

Chapter 32

Macy reached across her body for the phone when it rang for her wake up call for the next morning, eagerly jumping out of bed to get the day started. Depending on how her meeting with Senator Jordan went, she could be on her way to actually breaking this case wide open. Excitement powered through her at finally bringing it to a close.

She quickly showered and dressed in a conservative business suit. To keep from being seen in case anyone was watching, she ordered room service and ate there. She finished her meal, and prepared to leave. She walked out of the hotel, took a quick glance around and climbed into the car, heading toward the Capitol building.

She arrived at Senator Jordan's office at exactly five minutes before ten o'clock. While she waited patiently for the Senator to finish with her first appointment, she went over her plans once more in her head. A few minutes passed before she was ushered into the office. They exchanged pleasantries, and Macy got right to the point.

"Senator Jordan, I'm at a dead end on your husband's case and I need your help," she said bluntly.

"I'll certainly help in any way I can," Senator Jordan promised.

"Great. I know your husband didn't commit suicide, but I still don't have enough evidence to prove it. I need you to hold a press conference."

"A press conference?" she asked, a bit confused by the request. "Why?"

"I need you to go on national television and tell the world your husband was killed as part of some sort of conspiracy. And show one of these pictures." She handed the camera to Senator Jordan.

"What's this?" she asked.

"Those are pictures of me and Maxine West meeting in a club," Macy responded. "I need you to state the woman pictured here, without using her name, is speaking with an undercover agent in the photos, and is currently working with the authorities to identify and apprehend the guilty parties responsible for your husband's death."

"I don't know about this," she said slowly. "I could be sticking my neck out, and exposing myself to lawsuits and negative press."

"That is a possibility," Macy agreed. "But I believe you won't have anything to worry about. You see, everyone I talked to about this case was either too scared to talk, or ended up dead—everyone except Maxine West, who was probably behind more than one of the murders. If we make it look like she's cooperating with the authorities, maybe it will flush out the unknown perpetrators in an attempt to keep her quiet."

"Oh, I see," Senator Jordan replied. "You're hoping to smoke them out, so to speak."

"You've got it, Senator."

"Vanessa, please."

"Okay, Vanessa," said Macy. "Can I count on you for this?"

"Anything to clear my husband's name," she returned. "I'll make the press conference this afternoon at three o'clock. Will that give you enough time?"

"That will be perfect, Vanessa," said Macy. "Thank you for your cooperation."

"Just get the bastards who killed my husband," said Vanessa firmly.

Macy left Senator Jordan's office, stopping for a quick bite before heading straight for Max's apartment. She needed to locate Max's whereabouts to tail her once the press conference aired. There was no way to predict when or where she may be confronted, and she needed to be within sight of Max to shadow her every move. She just hoped her plan would work. Otherwise, she was out of options and the Senator may be out of office.

She was sitting outside Maxine's apartment when Gordon's cell phone rang. She checked the time. It was exactly four o'clock. The number display showed unavailable again, but this time she decided to answer it, pressed the button, and waited. After a few minutes, a man's voice growled into the phone, "Mr. McCain, I have another assignment for you."

"I'm sorry," Macy said a bit snidely. "But I'm afraid Mr. McCain is permanently out of commission. Who's calling please?"

The man hung up without saying another word. Now all she could do was wait and see if he would do his own dirty work. Apparently Senator Jordan's press conference hit a nerve. Max suddenly appeared from across the street and headed into her apartment building. Macy waited patiently, keeping her eyes fixed on the apartment, settled into the seat and prepared herself for a long night.

Around eight, Max emerged from her apartment and hailed a taxi. Macy followed the cab, and soon realized where it was headed. The cab pulled up in front of 'The Wild Side' and Max exited. Macy parked toward the back of the lot, hiding between some cars, hoping not to look suspicious. She waited for several hours, watching people enter and leave the club. Every time a taxi pulled up, Macy peered through her binoculars to see if it was Max leaving. Before long, she realized Max could easily leave with someone else, so she made sure to scan every face coming and going. At fifteen past one, Max appeared outside the club. Macy watched as she lit a cigarette and waited. A few minutes passed and another taxi pulled up. Max climbed in and it sped away from the club. Macy followed at a safe distance but the cab drove straight back to Max's apartment building without making a stop. Max got out, paid the driver, and hurried inside.

Macy leaned back and settled down for what appeared to be a long night.

The sun was just beginning to rise, spitting pale colors across the sky. Macy sucked in a quick breath and slinked down in her seat to avoid being seen when Max walked out of the building. She watched as Max hailed a cab and rode toward the city.

She followed, recognizing again where she was going after a few blocks—the route to the lab. The cab pulled into the private drive and let Max out at the front door. Macy parked in the lot of an office complex across the street where she could watch the comings and goings without fear of being discovered by the guards. Her stomach growled, reminding her she needed to eat and she took the time to go grab a quick meal while Max worked. She felt certain no harm would come to Max at the lab.

Macy sped off and angled the car through a fast food drive-thru, returning to the same spot to keep an eye across the street and consume her biscuit and coffee.

At five o'clock, she watched Max exit the building and climb into a waiting taxi. As the cab pulled out of the driveway, Macy fell in behind and followed as Max returned to her apartment. Macy waited patiently for several more hours, beginning to wonder if her plan was actually going to work. So far, no sign of anyone coming after Maxine. At fifteen minutes before eight, Max suddenly appeared and began walking north up her street. Instead of following in her car, Macy decided to trail her on foot and climbed out of her car. Keeping a few feet behind Max, she did her best to avoid being seen.

Max continued for five more blocks before changing directions and going right. Macy, close behind, wondered where she was going. They crossed two streets before coming to a small secluded park. Max entered the park entrance and Macy kept a safe distance behind.

Max walked to a bench underneath a wooded area and sat down. Not wanting to get too close, or be seen, Macy circled around the trees until she was behind Max, hidden by the darkness and the foliage. They remained where they were for a few minutes before someone appeared from the left side of Max out of the trees. The person walked over to where she was and sat down beside her on the bench. Judging by the size, Macy figured it to be a man. He was wearing a hat and a dark coat.

She watched as they talked, but she was too far away to hear what they were saying. Suddenly, the man's hand shot out of his coat pocket and made a stabbing motion toward Max. She slumped forward, falling off the bench as the man stood up and glanced around in all directions. Seeing no one, he slowly and carefully walked back into the woods.

Macy ran quickly to where Max was laying. As she approached, she could tell she was still breathing. Max looked up at her, blood running from the corner of her mouth.

"Max, who did this to you?" she asked. Max was only able to whisper the words "white house" before she exhaled her last breath, her eyes fixed open in the cold stare of death.

Macy placed her hand over Max's eyes, closing them for the last time. She pushed to her feet and quickly hurried into the woods in the direction where the man re-entered. She was running as fast as she could trying to catch the killer. The park lights, along with the moon, were just enough to keep her from running into trees as she raced along in pursuit. She went on alert when she heard a noise directly in front of her and quickly came upon a dark figure. The glint from the blade in the moonlight was her only warning moments before it swung at her. She tried to dodge, but was too late, the blade slicing her right arm. She winced from the pain, but remembered from her training not to utter a sound in order to keep her adversary unaware he had been successful in his attempt.

She lunged to one side and swung her legs out, clipping the man's legs out from under him and sending him to the ground with a thud. She jumped on top of him for a look at his face, trying to identify who he was. As the man pushed her backward, she wrestled the knife from him and plunged it deep into his left leg, causing him to howl in pain. She fell back onto the ground with a bone-jarring thump, her head hitting a rock. As she began to lose consciousness, through the haze she saw the man struggle to his feet and limp off, blood pouring from his leg. Just before she passed out, she took note he only had four fingers on his left hand. Then everything went black.

* * *

Macy opened her eyes, her body feeling damp from the morning dew. She started to raise her head but a sharp pain searing through her skull quickly changed her mind. She groaned in pain, closing her eyes to gain control of her faculties. She struggled through the pain, rolled slowly to her side and gently tried to sit up. It was barely twilight as Macy looked around. In a few more hours, she would have been discovered by some jogger or park officer, but at the moment she was alone. She remembered Max back at the bench and struggled to get to her feet. As she stood, trying to get her balance, she became aware of something in her hand. Looking down, she found she still held the knife she'd grabbed during her struggle with the stranger. She felt certain it was the same knife used to kill Maxine West. She wiped her fingerprints from the handle on the tail of her shirt and carefully hid it in a hole inside an old tree stump. Once more, she walked off in the direction where she last saw the killer. She knew she needed medical attention, but didn't want to be found in possession of the murder weapon, or be anywhere near the body when it was found.

Macy walked for about fifty more yards before she emerged from the woods onto another street. She followed along until she came upon a patrolman, who she flagged down and reported she'd been mugged. The officer immediately transported her to the hospital emergency room where she was diagnosed with a concussion from the blow to her head. The doctor put five stitches in her head and prescribed something to take for pain, advising her to stay awake and alert for the next several hours and to get lots of rest.

Once the hospital released her, the police officer asked her for a statement. Making it up as she went along, she told him she was here on vacation seeing the sights and was walking in the park when someone ran up behind her and hit her on the head. She used the name and address of Max's roommate, claiming she was an old college friend whom she was staying with. With her purse still in her car when she went out to follow Max, she said it had been stolen in order to cover why she had no I.D. The officer took her statement and offered to give her a ride home. She quickly took him up on the offer, hoping Max's body had not been discovered yet.

The police officer pulled up in front of Max's apartment building and Macy got out. She was relieved to see no other police in the area and waved goodbye to the patrolman as he drove away. Once he was out of sight, she crossed the street and climbed into her car, keyed the engine and let the car idle a moment. Thank goodness no one had broken into it, she thought as she pulled away from the curb. As she drove back to the hotel, she turned on the news, but there was no story about Max's murder yet.

Once inside her room, she found she was famished. Electing to stay inside for a while due to her condition, and the fatigue that was swiftly bearing down on her, she ordered room service. The pain reliever they gave her at the hospital was starting to take effect as the searing pain in her head reduced to a dull throbbing ache.

Macy devoured the breakfast she had ordered in record time. Now that her tummy was full, and appeased, she cleaned up from her night in the woods. She took a shower as best she could, trying to avoid wetting her head where the stitches were, even though she would have loved a shampoo. She dried off and wrapped a robe around her for comfort. She crawled onto the bed, and began to go over the previous night's events, hoping to make some sense of it all. She cursed herself for letting the killer get away. She remembered Max saying something about a white house just before she died, but without an address, it would be impossible to determine which house she was referring to. She also remembered stabbing her assailant's leg before he got away, and knew if she saw the hand with the missing finger, she would recognize it. But it would be like searching for a needle in a haystack, given the population of the Washington, DC area. Macy was beginning to get that sinking feeling again, similar to the day when she'd run out of clues. Either way, she knew she would have to let Senator Jordan know about Maxine before the press put two and two together and started questioning the sudden death of a woman the Senator had recently identified as a potential witness in the investigation into the death of her husband.

Macy phoned the Senator's office and asked her aide for an appointment with the Senator, telling her it was imperative she see her as soon as possible. Since the Senator was already expecting her call, the aide set the appointment for that afternoon at two. Macy hoped she would be able to clear the cobwebs from her head in time to carry on an intelligent conversation with Vanessa. After she hung up, she thought it best to give her brother a call.

"George Merit," answered George in his professional tone.

"Is this a bad time?" asked Macy.

"No. As a matter of fact, I'm eating lunch."

"Where are you?"

"I decided to come home for lunch today," he said. "I felt like getting out of the city."

"Good for you," said Macy. "So, what's up?"

Macy told him about her meeting with Senator Jordan, the press conference, her meeting with Max, and finally Max's death, saying all she had to go on was what Max said just before she died about a white house, and she was looking for a man with a limp and a missing finger.

"Sounds to me like you're well on your way," said George, rather cheerily.

"What do you mean?" asked Macy. "How am I going to find this guy?"

"Think about it, Mace. What did Maxine tell us the first time we spoke to her?"

"I don't follow."

"Remember? She said it went a lot higher than us, with an emphasis on 'a lot,'" he reminded her. "I think the white house she was referring to is *the* White House."

"You mean you think the killer is in the White House?" asked Macy, incredulously. "The same place where the President of the United States lives?"

"The one and the same."

"Well that certainly is a lot higher than us. Now all I have to do is to somehow get inside the White House and go from office to office until I find a man with only four fingers on his left hand. Piece of cake," she said, letting out a huge sigh.

"I didn't say it would be easy. Why don't you go over this with Senator Jordan and see if she has any suggestions on how to ferret out this person?" he advised.

"Great idea. I have a meeting with her this afternoon," said Macy. "Hopefully she can help me get into the White House and find this guy. Thanks, George. I don't know why I didn't think of that."

"Glad I could help," he said. "Besides, you're still suffering from the effects of the concussion, I think. Normally, you would've figured that out on your own."

She thanked him again and ended the call. She had to get ready for her meeting with Senator Jordan that afternoon.

Checking her clothing selections, she picked out a nice skirt and top, not planning on needing an outfit that provided ease of movement. Even if the Senator could get her into the White House, she'd prefer to wait at least until the next day to clear out the fog from her brain. She wanted to be as fresh as she could in case she had another run-in with the killer, or anything else that might pop up to take her by surprise.

Although the pain pills had kicked in, her head was still aching from last night's collision with that rock. But she shrugged it off, not allowing a little pain to deter her from her purpose. Macy placed the finishing touches on her makeup and left the hotel, heading toward the Capitol building.

Chapter 33

Washington, DC

Macy arrived at Senator Jordan's office just before two o'clock. She was eager to report her findings to Vanessa, and hoped she could provide a viable solution as to how to get into the White House and locate the killer. Senator Jordan met her in the outer office and led her into her private office, closing the door behind them.

"Thank you for seeing me on such short notice, Senator," said Macy.

"Call me Vanessa, please Macy," she said. "I hope by your urgent call you made a breakthrough on the case. I assume you heard the press conference."

"Actually, no I didn't," said Macy. "I was outside Maxine West's apartment so I could keep tabs on her, in case your press conference made her the next target of the killer."

"And did it work?" asked Vanessa.

"Yes and no," Macy hesitated. "I followed Maxine to a local park where she was obviously waiting to meet someone. A man approached from the woods, and before I could react, he stabbed her and fled. I ran to Maxine, but all she said before she died was *white house*. I chased after the man until I caught up with him in the woods, but after a brief struggle, I fell backward, hit my head on a rock and was knocked out. Oh, he also cut me," said Macy, holding up her bandaged arm.

"Oh my, are you okay?" Vanessa asked in concern.

"Other than a slight concussion, I'm fine. My ego's bruised, though."

"So Maxine West, who was our last chance, was murdered. I assume this means we are at a dead end?"

"Not necessarily," said Macy. "Before I fell, I was able to wrestle the knife from the killer and stab him in the left leg. I watched him limp away before I passed out and he had one finger missing from his left hand. When Maxine said *white house*, I'm certain she was referring to the White House itself, especially since she once mentioned this operation went a lot higher than me."

"So you believe the killer could be someone inside the White House?" asked Vanessa, an unmistaken look of shock and disbelief spreading across her face.

"Yes, and that's why I'm here. "I was hoping you might know a way we could get into the White House and look around. All I need to do is find the man with the missing finger on his left hand and I believe I can flush him out."

"It may be possible for us to get inside the White House. But after that, I'm not sure how you'd be able to go about searching for this man."

"All I need is to get inside," she assured the Senator. "I can figure out the rest."

Senator Jordan agreed to see what she could do about getting them in while Macy returned to her hotel to wait for her call. Macy had just opened the door to her hotel room when her cell phone rang. Senator Jordan had arranged a meeting with the President for eight o'clock tomorrow morning. She asked Macy to meet her at her office at seven-thirty and they would go together.

Macy thanked her for her help, and assured Vanessa she'd be at her office on time. She felt her stomach begin to tighten as Vanessa's words resonated in her head. She was actually going to meet the President of the United States. She knew she would have to be on her best behavior, but how was she going to conduct an investigation with the President there? she wondered. Just thinking about it caused her to break out in a cold sweat as she imagined trying to explain what she knew so far, only to watch as the President burst out in laughter from what he considered to be the craziest thing he had heard to date. She realized to anyone not directly involved, her story would sound suspicious. But she knew the truth, and now that she had involved Senator Jordan, she had to see this through.

Macy was able to eat very little for dinner, her stomach constantly churned nervously from the prospect of tomorrow's big meeting. After she finished picking over her meal, she returned to her room, tried to relax and formulate a plan of action. First, the initial meeting would take place, greetings and niceties would be exchanged, then she'd explain what she knew about the case so far, and the deaths surrounding it. Stressing the death of Senator Jordan's husband was extremely vital, since he was one of the more important players to die so far. If she could convince the President the two deaths were connected, she believed she could garner his support. The main problem, though, was how to track down the killer among all of the people within the White House without causing a panic, alerting the media, or worse yet, tipping their hand to the killer allowing him to escape.

A long night was in store, as she tossed and turned from worry over tomorrow's meeting. This was undoubtedly the most important encounter she had ever experienced and she wanted to make sure she didn't blow it.

She was staring at the hotel phone when it rang to announce her wake up call for six o'clock. Wearily, she dragged her body to the shower, but by the time she finished, her nerves had taken over, giving her that much-needed jolt and she was very much awake. Dressing in a business suit, she wanted to look as professional as she could to meet the *Leader of the Free World*. She grabbed a bagel and some coffee from the café downstairs before making her way to the rental car.

She arrived at the Capitol building twenty minutes early, finished her bagel and sipped her coffee, hoping she would be able to keep from vomiting once she got inside the White House. She realized she was more nervous with the prospect of meeting the President than she had ever been before an operation, even though she had met with people who were much more dangerous.

She closed her eyes and reminded herself this was no different than any other mission and she had to think of it that way. She was simply meeting with a contact on the inside to gain access to the building. She ordered herself not to think of him as the President, but rather as an informant. Macy took a few deep breaths, and finally felt a strange calm wash over her. She was ready.

Macy walked to Senator Jordan's office, and as she entered, she found Vanessa waiting for her. They made small talk as they walked to the Senator's car. Once inside Macy asked, "So, how were you able to manage this meeting?"

"The President and I are friends," Vanessa simply told her.

They remained silent for the rest of the short drive, each focused on rehearsing what they would say. Before long, they were at the front gate, Vanessa announcing to the guard who she was to see. He checked his list, and after verifying her identification, waved them through. As they entered the White House, they were greeted by the President's personal secretary. They were led to the Roosevelt room to wait while the President was finishing an important overseas call. After about thirty minutes, he entered the room. Both Macy and Vanessa stood as he approached, Vanessa being the first to extend her hand when he drew near.

"Senator Jordan, always good to see you," he greeted. "Thank you for seeing us, Mr. President," Vanessa replied, turning to introduce Macy, who politely shook his hand and also thanked him for allowing them to meet with him.

President Crawford motioned for them to follow him as he left the room and walked down the hall. He informed them he wanted to bring Robert Gorman, White House Chief of Staff, in on the meeting as well in case there was anything he could do to assist them. As they entered Bob's office, he stood up from behind the desk and politely smiled as President Crawford made the introductions. The first thing Macy noticed was how slow it seemed for him to stand, then noted he was missing a pinky finger. She managed not to ask about it as it might be considered rude if she did so now.

The President asked Vanessa how they could help. Immediately, she recapped the surroundings of her husband's death and how she refused the idea that he committed suicide. She let Macy explain about Agent Vrama and the lab experiments in San Antonio. President Crawford and the Chief of Staff listened without interrupting until both finished their story. The President turned his attention to Bob and asked what his take was on these allegations.

"Wasn't there something about some misappropriated funds?" asked Bob.

"That was in the so-called suicide note," Vanessa responded, "but it's not true.

"Perhaps he was using the money for these experiments," Bob suggested. Vanessa turned red and was just beginning to respond when Crawford interrupted.

"Now Bob, let's not jump to conclusions, or start pointing fingers," he cautioned, turning to Vanessa. "Now what can we do to help you?"

Macy straightened in her chair and gave her recommendations. "Well, for starters, I'd like for Mr. Gorman to show us his left calf."

Bob turned red as he began to get angry. "What exactly is going on here?" he demanded."

"May we see it?"

"No, you may not," said Bob.

"What's with the sudden fascination about Bob's leg?" asked President Crawford.

"Excuse me for one minute, Mr. President, then I'll explain everything," she said, stood up and briskly walked out of the room. A few seconds later, they heard a cell phone ringing. As it continued to ring, Macy walked back into the room.

"Aren't you going to answer that, Mr. Gorman?" she asked.

Bob grew an even darker shade of red as he reached into his jacket pocket and pulled out a cell phone, pressing the button to silence the call.

"What's going on here?" asked President Crawford.

"I believe you should ask Mr. Gorman that question," said Macy. "I first became suspicious when I noticed the missing finger on his left hand, along with your difficulty in standing, Mr. Gorman. Then when you questioned Senator Jordan about her husband, you appeared defensive. Of course, I still had no proof, that's when I decided to use this cell phone to call the last number that called it."

She held up Gordon's cell phone. "This cell phone belonged to Gordon McCain. He used to be in Naval Intelligence Special Operations, but after leaving the Navy, became a mercenary. He killed Senator Jordan's husband and Detective Josh Price of the Holden Beach police department. Mr. Gorman was the last person to call McCain's cell phone, trying to hire him to kill Maxine West, the team leader of the crew who ran the experiments in San Antonio. Apparently, Mr. Gorman saw Senator Jordan's press conference and was afraid Max was about to implicate him in all of this. How am I doing so far, Mr. Gorman?"

"Just who do you think you are coming in here and throwing around accusations?" shouted Bob, looking as if he might explode.

"President Crawford, Mr. Gorman is the person behind whatever experiments were going on in San Antonio, and is responsible for several deaths," said Macy confidently. "And if you'll take a look at his leg, I believe you'll find a deep knife wound." Macy turned and smiled wryly at Bob. "Isn't that right, Mr. Gorman?"

"Why you little...," Bob said, jumping to his feet. Crawford jumped in and pushed him back into his seat.

"What about it, Bob? What have you been up to?"

Bob adjusted his tie and sat straight in his chair. He reached into a drawer and pulled out a .45 caliber semi-automatic and pointed it at them.

"Very good, Ms. Merit," he commended snidely. "But how did you know so much about McCain?"

"We worked together in Naval Intelligence," she related. "Ah, so you're the woman responsible for his early departure from the Navy. I'm sure they miss your cognitive skills." He turned his attention to Crawford, a menacing look in his eyes. "I did this for you, Will," he said. "You were facing a tough re-election bid, and needed solutions for fuel prices, social security, and the economy. I had this brilliant idea. I was watching a news report about the avian influenza and it hit me. This was the answer to our prayers. All we had to do was develop a strain of bird flu that could be easily spread from human-to-human. Once we isolated this virus, we could develop a vaccine."

"But why bird flu?" interrupted Crawford.

"Don't you see?" Bob posed. "Who are the most susceptible to influenza? Children, people with compromised immune systems, and the elderly. By determining select communities that receive a larger percentage of social security and welfare revenue, we can substitute this new strain of bird flu in place of their annual flu shot. This would result in the deaths of a large proportion of people who currently draw money from the social security fund. We would then leak it into areas where unemployment is higher, to thin out some of the extra population and lower the number of idle workers. Of course, many would receive the vaccine to prevent uncontrollable infection. Lastly, we could leak the new virus into oil-producing countries, then come to their aid with a vaccine, which would require payment for the vaccine in the form of oil at greatly reduced prices. You see, Will, the public is so terrified of the possibility that bird flu will mutate into a strain which can be passed from human-to-human, this is the perfect scenario to control the very forces that endanger your term in office."

"But why?" asked Crawford. "Don't you realize once this gets out, my Presidency is over?"

"I would never do anything to harm your legacy, Will," he vowed. He reached once more into his desk and retrieved a file. "In this folder, you will find documentation which links the misappropriated CDC funds to Vice-President David Sims. That's right. Sims is the one behind this scheme. I found these documents after your husband's death, Senator Jordan. I regret they didn't surface until now. As you can see, Vice-President Sims procured the funds from the CDC and used them for top secret experiments of an undisclosed nature. There's no need at this point to unnecessarily alarm the public with all of the details."

"Where are the virus and the vaccine stored?" asked Macy.

"After Senator Jordan's press conference, I went to the lab here in Washington and destroyed all of the vials myself," he told them. "They're all gone."

"Are you sure?" asked Crawford.

"Yes, Will. I'm sure. Forgive me, Will, but I couldn't just idly sit by and watch what you worked so hard for go down the drain. Of course, you've still got a lot of hard work ahead to fix these problems the old fashioned way, but at least you're still in the fight."

"What am I going to do now?" asked Crawford, letting out a big sigh.

"Don't worry, Will. As usual, I've taken care of everything for you. Along with the proof against Sims, this file also contains my resignation letter, so to speak. I was only trying to help you. I love you, Will."

He raised the gun and placed the end of the barrel into his mouth. Before anyone could reach him, he pulled the trigger sending brain matter splattering against the wall behind him. President Crawford leaped up to go to the aid of his friend, but Senator Jordan grabbed his arm and eased him back into his chair just as the Secret Service agents came rushing in. They quickly made certain the President was not in danger before escorting the three of them back to the Oval Office where they began making preparations to secure the scene.

Visibly shaken, President Crawford sank down at his desk while Senator Jordan and Macy sat across from him. They sat in silence for a long time before anyone spoke. Finally Crawford broke the silence.

"With Bob's death, it appears all of the players in this caper are dead," he said.

"Yes, it seems that way," said Macy.

"Senator Jordan, we now have official proof Jack didn't commit suicide, nor did he take any funds from the CDC illegally."

"Where do we go from here?" asked Vanessa.

"First, I will ask for Sims's resignation," said Crawford. "Then, we issue a statement which will explain Sims's resignation along with Jack's innocence."

"Thank you, Mr. President," she said.

"Miss Merit, I would like to personally thank you for all you did to bring this matter to light. We need more people like you."

"Thank you, Mr. President," said Macy.

After a few other comments back and forth, Senator Jordan and Macy excused themselves and walked out of the Oval Office. They returned to the Senator's office, where she thanked Macy again for clearing her husband's name. She offered to pay her for her services, but Macy refused, simply asking she refer anyone she may come in contact with later who could use her services. Vanessa commended what she was doing, saying it was a very noble thing, but insisted on giving Macy a check for fifty thousand dollars as an expression of her gratitude. She reluctantly took the check, folded it in half, and stuck it in her pocket.

Macy left Senator Jordan's office and drove back to the hotel, immediately booked a flight back to Lexington, and then checked out. On the way to the airport, she stopped at a fast food restaurant and ordered a burger, fries, and a shake, as a small celebration the case was finally over.

Now that her meeting with the President was over, her appetite was back. She was surprised at how much she felt at ease talking with him, seeing he was such a personable man. She reminded herself never to let a person's position intimidate her again.

Macy boarded the plane and sat back with her eyes closed as she digested the quickly unfolding events of the morning. Before long, she fell asleep for a short nap before the plane touched down in Cincinnati. She nodded off again on the flight to Lexington, but sat up eagerly as the plane taxied toward the gate. She was looking forward to a few days' rest and relaxation, and was eager to start. She stepped off the plane with the other passengers and set off to gather her luggage. Shortly, she was driving back to George's, unable to contain the smile gracing her lips. She couldn't wait to tell George everything, but didn't want to do it over the phone. This was one time she wanted to tell him face to face when he got home this evening.

As soon as she got in and freshened up, Macy began cooking spaghetti for dinner, which was one of George's favorite meals. As she poured the noodles into the strainer, she heard his key in the door.

CHAPTER 34

LEXINGTON, KENTUCKY

Macy flashed a smile at George as he entered the kitchen.
He smiled back, but also had a look of confusion as he asked,
"When did you get back?"

"This afternoon," she replied. "Are you hungry?"

"Starved," he responded.

Macy decided to wait until after dinner to tell him about her day and
how she solved the case. As they were finishing dessert, she gave it up,
unable to wait any longer. She told George all about her meeting with
President Crawford, Bob Gorman's confession, and Senator Jordan finally
getting her husband's name cleared.

"Wow, that's some day you had," he commented.

"And to think I was so close to coming up empty-handed," she ventured
with a sigh.

"I knew you could do it. I had faith in you all along."

"Thanks, George, but if it hadn't been for a couple of lucky breaks, the
outcome might have been a lot different."

"What? Doesn't The Avenger believe truth and justice always triumphs
over evil?" he chuckled, unable to contain his laughter.

"What The Avenger believes and what actually happens is sometimes not the same thing," she replied.

"So, how does it feel to solve your first case?"

"It feels great. It's funny. I was looking forward to some free time to rest, but now I'm already starting to wish I had another case to work on."

"Don't worry," he assured her. "I'm sure as soon as word gets out about you and how quickly you solved the unsolvable, you'll have more than you wish for. As a matter of fact, I'm in the early stages of a case involving the father of an old college buddy that might need your expertise. I'll let you know if the Judge needs your assistance."

"You're probably right," she countered. "Maybe I should just enjoy what free time I have. Are you up for some cards tonight?"

"Sure," said George, helping to clear the table. They played cards and chatted late into the evening, both excited about Macy's success and what lie in store.

Washington, DC

Senator Jordan arrived at the White House at exactly seven-thirty in the evening. She was escorted to the Oval Office by the President's personal secretary, who excused herself for the evening after announcing the Senator's arrival. Senator Jordan took a seat across from President Crawford as he poured scotch into two glasses.

"Here's to the next and first female, Vice-President of the United States," he said, holding up his glass in a toast.

"Thank you, Mr. President," she replied, touching his glass with hers. He stood up and crossed over to her chair.

"Walk with me," he said, taking her hand as she rose from the chair. He escorted her from the Oval Office to the personal residence upstairs, where they ate dinner together. After they finished their meal, he excused the kitchen staff and they retired to the bedroom. Once inside with the door shut, Crawford grabbed her tightly and pulled her close to him. He pressed his lips full against hers, their kiss seeming to last forever.

"I've missed you," he confessed.

"I understand," she replied. "I've missed you too, but we had no choice but to lay low for a while with all of the attention focused here after Bob's death."

"You were great playing the part of the grieving widow trying to prove the innocence of her beloved husband," he said with a smile.

"I did love him... once," she offered. "Besides, if I were going to be able to make it to the White House some day myself, I couldn't afford any kind of scandal hanging over me or my family."

"I must admit, I hated having to share you with Jack," he said. "I thought about you a lot when you were with him in North Carolina on weekends."

"I know, darling, but you had me throughout the week."

"And after I leave office, I plan to have you all the time," he stated firmly. "We can finally get married once I'm no longer President."

"Are you sure that's what you want?" she asked.

"More than anything," he returned without a pause. "Besides, I don't think it will hurt your election bid should you decide to run for President after I leave office."

"I'd rather have you. That's several years away anyway, so let's cross that bridge when we get to it."

"I still can't believe Bob would try such a thing."

"Well, he did have a point about how it would solve your problems."

"I could never let my political ambitions drive me to kill innocent people," he said. "I would rather resign first."

"Don't worry, dear," she said. "You won't have to resign. Everyone's safe for now."

She reached up and stroked his graying temples, leaning in for another kiss. They hungrily explored each other's mouths as they tore at their clothing. He carried her to the bed where they made love for a long time, consumed in the fires of their passion. As they lay gently stroking each other while basking in the afterglow, their intimate time was cut short by the telephone. Crawford answered and spoke only a few words before hanging up.

"I've got to go, dear," he said. "It seems there's always some problem in some country somewhere we've got to get involved in."

"I understand," she said. "I'll sneak out after I clean up a little."

"I'll see you at your swearing in ceremony, Mrs. Vice-President," he said, smiling.

He rose and dressed, and left the room. As soon as he was gone, Vanessa grabbed her cell phone and punched in a number. After a couple of rings a man's voice came on the other end.

"Major Harris, where are we with the production of the necessary vials?" she asked.

"Right on schedule, ma'am," he confirmed.

"Excellent," said Vanessa. "Once they're ready, just keep them somewhere safe. Hopefully, we won't need them, but I want them ready just in case."

"Yes, ma'am," he said, as she hung up.

Vanessa rolled over in bed and grasped Will's pillow, breathing his scent into her nostrils, laid back and whispered, "Vice-President Jordan. President Jordan."

About the Author

Dale Crotts is the author of *The Reckoning*, the first in the Macy Merit/ Spencer Rawlings series. Dale grew up in a small community known as Glenola, located in Randolph County, North Carolina. He attended Randleman High School, and later graduated from High Point College with a Bachelors Degree in Business Administration. After working several years in banking, Dale earned his MBA from the University of North Carolina at Greensboro. His passion for writing began early, as he wrote plays for his drama class in middle school. A professional opportunity took Dale to Kentucky, where he lived for four years, and then moved to Michigan for one year, before returning to North Carolina. Many of the locations and characters in his writing come from his travels throughout the Midwest. When not working or writing, Dale enjoys traveling, reading, and golf. He is a huge fan of the television series *House*, and also enjoys watching college basketball, especially the High Point University Panthers, his alma mater. Dale currently resides in North Carolina.